havoc

A DEVIANTS NOVEL

ALSO BY JEFF SAMPSON

VESPER
A DEVIANTS NOVEL

havoc

A DEVIANTS NOVEL

JEFF SAMPSON

Balzer + Bray
An Imprint of HarperCollins*Publishers*

Balzer + Bray is an imprint of HarperCollins Publishers.

Havoc: A Deviants Novel
Copyright © 2012 by Jeff Sampson
All rights reserved. Printed in the United States of America.

Library of Congress Cataloging-in-Publication Data
Sampson, Jeff.
 Havoc : a Deviants novel / Jeff Sampson. — 1st ed.
  p. cm.
 Summary: After genetic engineering endows sixteen-year-old Emily and her friends with super-powers and changes them into werewolves, the teenagers set off on a dangerous mission to find the people who made them what they are, and to discover why.
 ISBN 978-0-06-199278-0
 [1. Werewolves—Fiction. 2. Friendship—Fiction. 3. Genetic engineering—Fiction. 4. Science fiction.] I. Title.
PZ7.S164Hav 2012   2011022898
[Fic]—dc23   CIP
                                                                        AC

Typography by Jennifer Rozbruch
11 12 13 14 15 LP/RRDH 10 9 8 7 6 5 4 3 2 1
❖
First Edition

Details of Video Footage Recorded Oct. 31, 2010,
Part 1

*Note: This video transcription follows the end
of the "Partial Transcript of the Interrogation
of Branch B's Vesper 1." Refer to the initial
transcript for details prior to the following.

20:22:03 PST—Interrogation Room C7

Two subjects in room identified as:

—Franklin Savage, Vesper Company employee
White male, 42 years old
—Emily Webb, Branch B's Vesper 1 (designated
"Deviant")
White female, 16 years old

Vesper 1(B) sits at a desk opposite Savage. She
leaps to her feet, breaking the chains that bind her
wrists. Savage flinches, cowering behind his hands
as the girl stares him down.

Behind Savage, the steel-reinforced door buckles

inward and then flies across the room to slam
against the opposite wall. A third subject enters
the room, identified by intel as:

—Amy Delgado, Branch A's Vesper 2.1 (designated
"Deviant")
Hispanic female, 16 years old

VESPER 2.1(A): Going somewhere?

The two Deviants discuss what to do with Savage
and choose to let him scurry out of the room ~~like
a coward~~. Limon, please refrain from inserting your personal
opinions into these transcripts.—MH

After more discussion, Vesper 1(B) chooses to leave
behind the tape recording of her conversation with
Savage and the document she wrote detailing the
events spanning Sept. 7, 2010, through Sept. 13, 2010,
in Skopamish, WA. The two Deviants exit the room.

20:33:17 PST—Hallway 3, Sector C

Several guards lie unconscious behind and ahead
of the two Deviants, the product of Vesper 2.1(A)'s
trek to break Vesper 1(B) out of the interrogation
room. One wonders if perhaps our guard staff was
not adequately trained to handle adversaries with
telekinesis, as was brought up in a meeting on the
evening of October 25, 2010. It has been noted several
times, Limon, no need to continue to do so. —MH

Stepping over the fallen guards, Vesper 1(B) reaches the door of office C12, twists its doorknob, and breaks the lock, allowing the Deviants to enter.

20:37:09 PST—Office C12, Temporary Office of Franklin Savage

Vesper 1(B) and Vesper 2.1(A) cross to Savage's desk. Vesper 1(B) rifles through loose papers until she has prepared a neat stack. The papers have since been identified as the second part of her account of the events prior to the Incident. Vesper 2.1(A) questions her motives for leaving the papers intact. Vesper 1(B) looks into the camera, speaking directly to it.

VESPER 1(B): Same reason I haven't been smashing cameras. They want to know what we can do? Then I say we let them watch us, and we let them read all about it.
VESPER 2.1(A): I continue to like your style, girl.
VESPER 1(B): Thanks. It's all here. Let's move.

Part 1 of Relevant Video Footage Concluded

WHAT ARE YOU?

I stood in front of my bathroom mirror and studied the bags under my eyes, which were half-hidden behind my crooked glasses. Looked at how limp and mousy my hair was, definitely not shampoo-commercial ready. I held a pair of sleeping pills, halfheartedly telling myself to pop 'em back. Go all sleazy starlet and abuse those prescription drugs like there's no tomorrow.

Don't do it, a voice whispered in the back of my head. An angry voice. One that kept popping into my thoughts more and more over the past few evenings. *Let me out. You know you want to.*

I ignored her.

It had been two nights since I'd helped kill a man after

transforming into a genetically engineered werewolf. Two nights since I'd let loose my wild sides to find the man who'd murdered Emily Cooke and tried to kill Dalton McKinney. Knowing the consequences of letting myself go like that . . . I couldn't do it again.

So, I was trying out a new nighttime routine.

First, an early dinner with Dad, my stepmom, Katherine, and my stepsister, Dawn.

Then, hastily banging through my homework during the hour I had left to do it, all the while staring forlornly at my book and DVD cases, remembering the good old days when I'd had entire evenings to indulge in a little escapism.

Finally, giving up on the homework halfway through because eight o'clock was rapidly approaching. Which meant sneaking into the bathroom and pouring a couple of my stepmother's prescription-strength sleeping pills into my palm, downing them, and passing out to avoid changing into Nighttime Emily, the wild, superpowered version of me. Herself a midway state between normal me and full-on wolf-girl.

This new routine was most definitely the product of some utterly strange circumstances.

It was Tuesday night. Exactly one week since the day that regular, geeky Emily Webb—me—first turned into wild-child Nighttime Emily, the same night Emily Cooke had been murdered by a man named Dr. Gunther Elliott. I hadn't known it at the time, but Emily Cooke was also a werewolf like me. She'd lost her life because of it.

I clenched my eyes closed and took in a deep breath. Blinking them open, I snatched up a plastic cup from the counter, filled it with tap water, then hastily retreated to my bedroom. I set the cup on my bedside table, then lay back against my pillow.

Drugging ourselves was what Spencer and I had agreed to do, at least until we figured out what the whole changing-into-mythical-beasts thing was all about. Drug away the changes, so we don't get into trouble. Do research during the day, when we're more ourselves.

But your daytime selves can't solve problems like I can. The voice again. Nighttime me, or at least what I imagined nighttime me would say. *Besides, there's no reason to hide in your stuffy room, girl. The bad guy is gone. We killed him. Let me out.*

A shiver ran through me. "Wrong thing to say," I whispered to myself.

The images of Sunday night came back to me in a rush, like they always did, just when I thought I was free of them for a few moments.

A man in a fedora. A gun.

Me and Spencer, both wolf-human hybrids, stalking the man.

A knife lashing out, cutting me, cutting the wolf-boy.

And we leap to rip the man apart, our vision red, our goal to kill.

I could still taste his rotting flesh no matter how much I brushed my teeth. Scope wasn't exactly clearing up this plaque. The stench of his unwashed body, of his fear, sometimes seemed to overwhelm my nostrils. And his eyes . . . his empty, blank eyes . . .

I guess this is what they call post-traumatic stress. Fun, huh? I now totally relate to the lone survivors of horror movies when they pop up in sequels. Laurie Strode in *Halloween H20*? I feel you, girl. You too, Sidney Prescott. Not so much the girl from *Friday the 13th*. She basically got a raw deal.

The only time I didn't think about what I'd done as a wolf-girl was when I was around Spencer and his wonderful, calming scent, or when I was rushing through the blur that had become school, half focusing on teachers while thinking about all that I still needed to know about the changes.

And, of course, when I was deep asleep I didn't have to worry. If I had dreams about that night, well, I didn't remember them once I woke up. One small mercy.

I popped the sleeping pills from my sweaty palm into my mouth, then downed the cup of lukewarm tap water. No, Nighttime Emily, I was not going to let you out, because letting you out would lead to the werewolf, which would lead . . . Who knows where.

I didn't want to think anymore. Or remember. The pills swirled in my stomach, and my lids grew heavy.

Do you think you can hide from this forever? Don't you think our stepmom is going to notice her disappearing pills sooner or later? Someday you're going to have to let yourself face the night. You know it's true.

I ignored the voice, even knowing that she made far too much sense.

And then sleep came and took everything away.

My eyes snapped open, pulling me from my dreamless sleep.

It was dark in my room save for the glow from my digital alarm clock and the faint tinge of streetlight that seeped through my curtains. I wasn't supposed to be awake before morning.

A chill draft touched my skin. Goose bumps bristled on my arms. My heart pounded fast, as though my body knew what my sleep-addled brain didn't want to know.

Someone was watching me.

I pulled the covers to my chin and cradled my stuffed

toy dog, Ein, as I scanned my room. Everything that wasn't veiled in black was in shades of gray. The room was still, silent. Outside I could hear a car alarm going off somewhere down the street. I half expected to see Dr. Gunther Elliot there, some undead version of him coming to take his revenge on me for killing him.

No one was there. It was PTSD, I rationalized. Just more residual fear from a night that seemed so very far away even at the same time it felt like it had just happened moments ago.

My self-assurances didn't stop my hands from shaking or my pulse from pumping.

For what felt like a long time, I lay in bed, my eyes darting around my room from the closet to the door to the window, my brain telling me to calm down, my body refusing to listen.

Then, out of the corner of my eye: movement.

My eyes shot toward the window and came to settle on a figure at the foot of my bed, the size and shape of a grown man. Only this man was a shroud of misty blackness that had congealed to form a featureless, three-dimensional shadow that stood perfectly still and silent.

My heart thudded faster, pounding out a dance-track beat that became all I could hear. I swallowed, trying to convince myself that I was not seeing what I thought I was seeing. Because I'd seen this thing before, or something like it. Before, it had appeared only when I was a wolf. I wasn't a wolf now.

Yet here it was.

I could see my DVD case and TV right through it, but it was more than a shadow, I knew it, I *felt* it. It wasn't the dead man. It was something worse. I whimpered as a primal fear I had only ever experienced as a wolf came over me.

The shadow's head tilted, slowly, methodically. It was studying me.

I squeezed my eyes closed, willing the thing to disappear, to leave me the hell alone. I lay there, sheets to my nose, for how long I couldn't tell you. Then, as my heart finally began to slow to a waltzlike crawl, I opened my eyes.

The shadowman was above me, its featureless face inches from my own. It raised a hand, reaching for my head with long, slender, translucent fingers.

I opened my mouth to scream. But all that came out was a squeak, like some pitiful horror-movie cliché. As I lay there, unable to move, the shadowman's cold fingers grazed my cheek. It wasn't solid, exactly; more like the wispy touch of wet fog against my bare skin.

Still, it was *touching me*. Now was not the time to get all paralyzed.

I rolled to my left, away from the shadowman. I knocked

Ein to the floor and grabbed a lamp from the bedside table, the squat one that my best friend, Megan, and I had long ago decorated with various shades of glittery nail polish.

Yanking the lamp, I managed to pull its cord free from the wall. In the same motion I turned back toward the shadowman and swung.

The lamp and my hand went right through it.

My fingers stiffened with cold, became numb and heavy. The nail-polish lamp slipped out of my useless hand and clattered to the floor.

I yanked my arm back, clutching my frozen wrist in my other hand. The shadowman stood at the side of my bed, watching me with a tilted head, like a dog trying to understand what its master is saying.

"What do you want?" I wheezed. "What are you?"

The shadowman's smoky black arm rose slowly, as if someone had dropped the speed on the Blu-ray player. It walked sluggishly forward—*through my bed*.

Yeah, *no*.

Rolling again to the side, I dropped off my bed opposite the shadowman. I landed on all fours, crouched and silent like a cat. Which was strange, since I was supposed to be me, regular old Emily Webb, not the death-defying version of me that could do that kind of thing. Regular me would have landed with an "Oof!"—limbs flying every which way like I was going for a pratfall on a bad sitcom. In my head I was me, at least, but the reflexes were all Nighttime.

I didn't have time to worry about it.

I leaped up to my feet and spun to face my bedroom door—and the shadowman was there, nose to nose with me. So close that the fine hairs rose on my arms as its chill seeped through my oversize T-shirt and into my skin.

I spun again, this time toward the window. The same second-story window I'd jumped out of several times already—but never as normal me.

Did I really have Nighttime's reflexes? What if it was just adrenaline? Could I really leap out a window and not break both my legs? How could I know?

Swallowing a trembling breath, I realized I had no choice. It was the only way out.

I darted forward and whipped open the curtains. My thawing fingers scrambled over the latches to unlock the thing and get myself free. Icy air brushed against my back, and I sensed the shadowman growing closer, way too close. I needed to get out, now, now, outside NOW, why wouldn't my hand work already and get the latches open?

A chill flowed down my neck, coating my shoulder blades and making me shiver. The shadowman was directly behind me.

My heart thudding, I gasped for air and spun around,

my back as close to the window as I could get without smashing through.

There was nothing, no one, there.

I stood there for a long moment, half sitting on the sill, taking in shallow, gulping breaths. The room was dark, and none of the shadows cast by the streetlight outside my window moved or were alive. Slowly, my heart began to pace itself back to normal. My breaths evened out, and the hand that had gone through the shadowman's incorporeal body once more flowed with warmth.

I turned back to the window, half expecting to find the shadowman floating outside. If this was a horror movie, the director totally would have done that as an easy jump scare. In fact, if I ever sell the movie rights to my life, I'm totally suggesting that the director do that.

But in reality, there was nothing there. Just a view of the clear, starry sky and the darkened streets.

Something caught my eye in the road. A large dog, maybe, lumbering down the center of the street.

Only it wasn't a dog, even if that's what was reported by the local newspaper my dad insists on getting instead of just reading the news online like normal people.

It was a werewolf.

Shaking my head, I closed the curtains. "You were supposed to take the sleeping pills, Spencer," I muttered.

I closed my curtains and, after a cursory glance around the room to be sure the shadowman was gone, climbed back beneath my covers. I pulled the comforter over my head, willing my breath to slow down, iiiiiin and ooooout, to calm myself down. Whatever that thing was, it was gone now.

But it had been so close. Much closer than any of the previous times I'd seen the shadowmen—which up until now had only been as werewolf me. I didn't know what that meant.

A clattering and buzzing sounded from my end table. I took in a sharp breath, then realized that, duh, it was just my phone.

Lowering the covers, I slapped the end table until I grabbed my phone. The glowy screen on the front read SPENCER.

I flipped it open to see I had a text message.

2:34 AM PST: Em Dub, u awake

I blinked at the message a few moments, because hold up, hadn't I just seen Spencer outside? As a wolf-boy?

Behind the times as I am, I slowly hunted down the keys to type back a message—and I mean the number-pad keys, folks, as in press 1 three times just to type a *c*. Megan used to be the only person who ever called me, and she hated texting, so I never really had to do it before. How I longed for a smartphone, especially since I can't *not* type in complete sentences. It's a thing.

The pads of my thumbs beginning to ache, I finished typing my response and hit send.

> 2:37 AM PST: Yeah, I'm awake. I thought I just saw you outside.
>
> 2:37 AM PST: not me. Im in my room, just saw shadowman. it came at me but then it dispprd.

My fingers trembled. I looked around the room again, expecting the shadowman to leap out at me, grab me with its icy fingers. Nothing was there.

But it had been. And it had coordinated a visit between me and Spencer. It had to mean something.

> 2:41 AM PST: That happened to me, too. Just a few minutes before you texted me. It chased me around the room, and then vanished.
>
> 2:41 AM PST: wird. we need to talk about this in the am. can I pick u up?
>
> 2:43 AM PST: Yeah. Also, Spencer? I saw a werewolf outside. If it wasn't one of us, it means it must be the girl. Or Dalton.
>
> 2:44 AM PST: r u srs? this nite is fd up.
>
> 2:45 AM PST: Yes, it is. Get some sleep, okay?
>
> 2:45 AM PST: k Em. c u tmrw.
>
> 2:46 AM PST: kk

Oh man. Did I really just type "kk"? Texting was going

to be the death of me. Or make me a normal teenager. Whatever.

I closed the phone and set it back on the table. I lay back for a moment, staring at the ceiling, then leaned over my bed, picked up the fallen lamp, and grabbed Ein from where he'd been unceremoniously kicked.

Cradling my stuffed dog, I closed my eyes and tried to go back to sleep. I expected visions of the shadowmen or worse to invade my thoughts and keep me awake, but my adrenaline was dying down, and whatever remnants of the sleeping pills that were still inside me let me drift off once more, back into dreams that I wouldn't remember.

YOU ARE SUCH A NERD

The following morning I sat on my front steps, knees to chest, waiting for Spencer to pick me up. I was bundled up in a hoodie, my glasses were firmly on my face, and my backpack sat beside me. It was three days since I'd last been Nighttime Emily or the werewolf. I was me again. More or less.

You're not all you. The voice again. *You know you miss being me, too.*

You'd think I'd find it strange to be hearing voices, right? Well, strange was the definition of my life these days. Weirdly, I found hearing her sort of a good thing. It helped to literally talk with myself while trying to figure things out.

And she was right. I did miss Nighttime's confidence.

Even though a little had bled into my daytime self, it wasn't nearly the same as Nighttime's unbridled fearlessness. But I couldn't risk changing. Right? Not when the consequences after the last time were so horrible. I'd helped kill someone, and I'd *liked* it. It had been in self-defense, sure, but that didn't keep me from feeling this nauseating guilt whenever I remembered what I'd done.

Consequences? Guilt? He got what he deserved. We did what we needed to do.

"I know," I said aloud. "Just . . . Yeah. I know."

I waited for a moment. The voice—my imagination running rampant, Nighttime herself, who knows—didn't say anything more.

My hands were shoved inside my pockets, and I rocked back and forth a little, staring up at the overcast September morning sky. My thoughts raced, same as they had the past few mornings. Things I thought couldn't possibly be real now were. Everything I thought was true about myself had been, at most, a partial truth.

And though I did my best to distract myself with schoolwork and TV and discussions with Spencer, whenever it was just me and my thoughts, I still kept seeing the man from BioZenith, Dr. Elliott, hunting me.

I closed my eyes. I needed a new distraction, someone to call, maybe. And that's when I remembered—Megan was on her way to pick me up. She'd *always* picked me up, at least until recently. And I hadn't let her know I had other plans.

I slipped my phone out of my pocket, clicked over to the contacts list, and selected REEDY—my nickname for her. The phone rang once, twice, then she picked up.

"Hey, I know I'm not late, so what's up?" she answered.

"And a good morning to you too," I said.

"Mm-hmm, yeah, good morning." A crunch as she bit into something on the other end. "I'm eating," she said with a full mouth, "and then I'm on my way."

My free fingers fidgeted with one of my backpack straps. "Um, actually, that's why I'm calling. I don't need a ride today."

Silence on the other end, save for more crunching as she finished chewing.

Clearing my throat, I said, "So, you know, take your time with breakfast. Yay, free time!"

"Are you walking?" she said at last. "Or are you getting a ride from someone?"

"I'm getting a ride. From Spencer."

I heard Megan snort. "Well, all right. Saves me the gas. I'll see you at school."

Before I could respond, the line went dead.

I was hoping we'd magically be past this, this jealousy

Megan had when it came to me and Spencer. But things had been weird between us since Monday morning, which I guessed was only normal. I mean, I couldn't really blame her. The weekend before, I'd drugged her, stole her car, and then basically made her hoof it up to Seattle to reclaim said car since I'd sorta abandoned it there. Well, Nighttime Emily did. But I'd already established with Spencer at this point that no matter how different she was, Nighttime Emily was still me. I couldn't put all the blame on the Hyde to my Jekyll.

And then the past couple of days at school I'd kept sneaking away during lunch and free periods to convene with Spencer, talk about everything that was happening to us. Megan knew I was keeping secrets from her, there was no way she couldn't know. We'd told each other everything since elementary school, and I wasn't exactly the world's greatest liar. I hated doing it. But whatever was going on with me had sent someone to *kill* me, and the last thing I wanted was to put her in danger.

I just hated the rift it was starting to put between us. As I put my phone back in my pocket, I vowed then and there to force myself to find some Emily-Megan bonding time. Just because I was sort of "blossoming" didn't mean I had to leave behind my oldest—*wait for it*—"bud."

Get it? Blossoming? Bud? Ha. Whew. Yeah, I'm corny.

I was pulled from my thoughts by the screeching of brakes. A tan minivan pulled up in front of my curb, and Spencer leaned over to wave out the passenger-side window. His messy brown hair had fallen into his face, and he was grinning in that endearingly goofy way of his.

I couldn't help but smile when seeing him, because with Spencer came the kind of distraction I needed to get out of my head. Grabbing my bag, I leaped up and raced across the lawn to his car. I opened the door, and his smell—his musk, his pheromones, whatever it was—washed over me.

The harried thoughts, the visions of dead Dr. Elliott, the stress about Megan—all of it whooshed away as I climbed inside, shut the car door, and found myself surrounded by the wonderful scent that always enveloped me in the presence of my mate.

Uh. Not that we'd *mated*. The terminology, it's a werewolf thing.

I dropped the bag between my feet, then leaned across the driveshaft to give him an awkward hug.

"Sweet, a morning hug," he said as I pulled back.

My cheeks burned. "Sorry. It's just nice to see you, especially after last night."

He grinned at me, then put the car in drive as I pulled on my seat belt. "Always good to see you, Em Dub."

It was strange. Spencer and I had always gone to school

together. Skopamish wasn't a very big city, and though we had new kids coming in and kids moving away every year, those of us who'd lived there our whole lives more or less knew of one another. But until a week before, I'd never really noticed Spencer as anything other than the short, funny kid who always hung around with Mikey Harris and Zach Nickerson and Dalton McKinney, cracking jokes and making wise. He wasn't exactly what I'd considered my "type," not that I'd had any real experience to tell me what my type was.

Then, when all this started—the nighttime changes, this urge to *sniff* out things—his personal scent gripped me in ways I'd never felt before. His smell identified him in that strange, werewolf part of my brain as my "mate."

I didn't tell him this, but sometimes when we were apart I wondered if maybe this was on purpose. We'd more or less figured out that we were "created" by scientists at BioZenith, one of whom knew full well he could get my attention by using chemical versions of male werewolf pheromones. I wondered if they *wanted* us to seek each other out and pair up.

But when I was actually side by side with Spencer, it didn't matter. I'd spent years alone in my room, watching movies and TV, wondering what it was like to be around a boy you felt a deep connection with. Now I knew—the flutteriness inside, the desire never to be apart. It wasn't exactly "I shall watch you sleep for an eternity, my immortal love," but I liked what it was. I didn't want to overthink it and make it go away.

Spencer pulled onto the street and began driving us to school. Checking his rearview mirror, he said, "Right, so you want to go first?"

Hot air blasted from his vents. I unzipped my hoodie. "Well, not much to say. I woke up and a shadowman was there. I thought it'd just go away like all the other times, but then it was right in front of me. I freaked out and swung a lamp through it, and it made my hand freeze solid."

He cast me a concerned look. "Are you okay?"

"I am, yeah," I said. "It disappeared after chasing me around the room for a minute. What about you?"

He didn't answer for a moment, and his eyes glazed over. I looked ahead to see if he was watching anything in particular—and found that we were about to barrel straight past a stop sign and into a busy intersection.

"Holy crap, Spencer!" I shouted, jumping back up in my seat, my fingers clutching the pleather beneath me.

Blinking back to attention, he slammed on his brakes. We jerked forward into our seat belts as the tires screeched to a stop a few feet past the stop sign. A car that had the right of way zoomed past, the driver leaning on his horn.

Spencer looked at me sheepishly, his hair fallen over his eyes. "Uh, sorry, I was trying to remember. I have trouble concentrating sometimes."

My eyes wide and heart pounding, I lowered myself back into my seat. "It's all right. Just, you know, if the choice is to pay attention to the road or remember something, I say avoid heading down memory lane."

"Sorry, Em Dub."

He leaned forward to look both ways, then turned us right. The pheromones swirled together with the hot air from the heater, and my limbs untensed.

"Okay," I said after a moment. "So, what did happen with you?"

Eyes on the road, Spencer furrowed his brow. "It was basically the same as you. The shadowman followed me around my room while I tripped over computer parts, then it disappeared."

Despite the warmth of the front seats, I shivered. "Those things are ridiculously freaky. I mean, are they ghosts? Aliens? Why are they following us around all the time?"

"Ooh, I wonder if they *are* aliens." Spencer perked up at the thought as he made a turn down a new street.

Shaking my head, I looked out my window and watched the trees rush by. "I'm just getting used to werewolves and killer scientists, Spence. I'm not sure I'm ready for aliens.

Unless Sharlto Copley is waiting in the wings to show us that they're secretly just misunderstood."

Spencer grinned at me. "Hey, you like *District 9* too? I loved that movie! It totally should have won best picture this year. I mean, who saw that locker movie anyway?"

I snorted. "You are such a nerd. And I liked *The Hurt Locker*!"

He held his hands up momentarily from the wheel, mock defensively. "Hey, I can't help it if the Oscar people are biased against fun movies! But I'm sure the locker movie was probably good. To the five people who saw it."

I laughed. "Megan said the same thing. You remind me of her sometimes."

Spencer looked at me side-eyed. "Uh . . . thanks?"

"No, I mean that in a good way," I said. "You're more like how Megan used to be when we were kids, before junior high. She was always super positive and making jokes, just like you. I, you know . . . I like it."

"So you like me, huh?" Eyes back on the road, Spencer grinned once more.

Heat rushed to my cheeks, and I sat back. "Maybe a little. Sometimes you're funny. But only sometimes." I cleared my throat. "Okay, back to last night. Were you, you know, *human* when you saw the shadowman?"

"Yeah. You?"

"Yeah." I bit my lip, remembering the first times we'd seen the shadowmen. "Before, we could only see them as wolves, right? And they didn't even try to do anything to us then. Now we can still be us when we see them, and they can go all foggy and, like, *touch* us. It doesn't make any sense."

"Not much of this does, Em Dub." Spencer cranked the wheel and took us down another street. "Shape-shifting within the span of a few minutes shouldn't be scientifically possible, but unless we're both crazy, we do it all the time."

"So basically we need to find more time to research all of this. Or find a deus ex machina-y adult to lay out the exposition."

Spencer scrunched his eyebrows at me. "A deus what?"

I waved my hand. "Nothing. Just wishful thinking. All this would be a lot easier if we didn't have to figure it out by ourselves."

"That's for sure."

The minivan's tires crunched over gravel as Spencer pulled into the auxiliary parking lot at Carver Senior High School. He waved at other students as he slowly made his way to a spot big enough for the car. With the minivan in park, he turned the key and the engine died with a grumble. Chill fall air seeped through the windows, and I zipped my hoodie back up.

"Well, here we are," he said, turning in his seat to face me.

His eyes were on mine. His lips parted into a pleasant smile. I felt mine do the same. With all that was going on, it seemed so silly to smile all goofy at a boy. But I couldn't help it.

"So, you got a plan for today?" he asked.

"Oh," I said, feeling myself blush again. "Yeah. Research. How about lunch hour we go to the library? Maybe there are books about shadowmen like there are about werewolves. Not that the werewolf books were all that helpful."

"Well, maybe shadowmen books will be." Reaching behind him into the backseat, he said, "Didn't your text say something about seeing another werewolf?"

"Yeah. It wasn't you, so it had to be either Dalton or the girl you sniffed out at the party last week." Spencer and I had established when we first talked that there was a fourth werewolf, a girl, though who it was we didn't know. "This is good. Maybe if we find them, they'll know more about all of this."

With backpack in hand, Spencer pulled himself back into the front seat. He tapped the side of his nose. "I'll keep my nostrils open, then."

I tapped my nose as well. "Me too. Though if it's Dalton, I guess my eyes will work just fine."

He laughed and shook his head. "You're hilarious, Em Dub."

I opened my mouth to respond, but someone banged rapidly on the window behind me, and I jumped. For a second I was certain it was another shadowman, or even Dr. Elliott in his fedora, with his gun aimed at me, ready to kill me—

But when I turned, I saw it was just Megan. An obviously annoyed Megan.

I undid my seat belt, then grabbed my bag, opened the door, and hopped out. Spencer did the same, then rounded the hood to wave and say, "Hey, Megan!"

Her eyes darted to him and then back to me. She offered him a brusque, "Hey."

"Allll righty, then," he said, his eyes absurdly wide. He backed away and said, "See you later, Em," then turned and hustled toward the school.

Megan leaned back against the minivan and crossed her arms. She was wearing all black, per usual—a knitted baggy sweater that hung limply from her tall, skinny frame, and jeans that would have been supertight on anyone who wasn't her. Her long, white-blond hair was pulled back in a ponytail.

With Spencer gone, all the pheromone-elation I'd been feeling drifted away, replaced with the horrible awkwardness that now seemed to wash over me whenever I was around Megan.

"Hey, you got here the same time as us, how about that," I said, trying to fill the silence.

She shrugged. "Yeah, I was hoping to catch up to you. I thought maybe we could hang out and then head to homeroom together."

I smiled. "Definitely."

I hiked my bag over my shoulder, and she did the same. We walked side by side across the baseball field that separated the auxiliary parking lot from the front of the school. The sky darkened, and misty rain began to drizzle down. Beyond the school, Mount Rainier was shrouded in gray fog.

"So—" she started to say.

"I—" I said at the same time. We giggled nervously, and I said, "Go ahead."

She kicked at the dirt. "I was just going to ask, is it, like, official now? Are you dating Spencer?"

I didn't answer right away.

She raised her hands before I could say anything. "It's cool if you are, Em, don't worry. I'm happy for you."

Her eyes told me she was lying. I asked, "You are?"

"Of course I am." Her voice was cold despite her efforts.

"You're my best friend, Emily, nothing's going to change that, right?"

"Right."

She slung her long, narrow arm over my shoulder. "So, as your best friend for life, of course I'm happy when you find love or whatever cheesy thing you want to call it."

I wanted to sigh, but I stopped myself. "Well, I'm not really sure what it is right now." *Except that we're both werewolves who are supposed to be mates, though whether that's in the British slang sense or the* Wild Kingdom *sense, I'm not entirely sure.* "But I triple promise you, it's not going to keep me from hanging out with you."

Megan shrugged and began to say something. She stopped walking instead, and I followed her gaze to see a crowd of kids forming at the front of the school. They were loud and laughing, some girls were hugging, I saw a couple guys high-fiving.

"Oh God, what pep rally hell is this?" Megan snarled.

I saw a head slightly above the crowd, one with red hair and chiseled features.

Dalton McKinney. Football player. Attempted murder victim who'd been shot in the head. Werewolf.

One of my pack. Another voice. Not Nighttime this time.

Just seeing Dalton up and walking, his eyes bright and alert, grinning as kids slapped him on the back—relief washed over me, and I couldn't help but smile, giddy.

"Dalton's back," I whispered.

Megan rolled her eyes. "Yay." Then, with a quick shake of her head, she added, "But wait. He was shot in the head, like, a week ago. Why would they let him out of the hospital and back to school? Did they just pretend his injury was worse than it was or what?"

"It must have been him," I said to myself, momentarily forgetting Megan was even there.

"What must have?" Megan asked.

I barely heard her. I was already racing forward, my bag slapping against my back, ready to meet the third member of our would-be pack and see if he had any answers.

DAL-TON

By the time I was underneath the covered walkway that led to the front entrance of the school, Dalton was absolutely mobbed by students. I reached the back of the crowd and jumped up and down, trying to get a look at him.

From what I could tell, he actually looked *good*. He was grinning, slapping friends on the back, chest-bumping football teammates. Color had returned to his flushed cheeks, and he was dressed in his pristinely pressed khakis, polo, and letterman jacket. The only sign that he'd been, y'know, *shot in the head* was a fresh square bandage on his temple and the peach fuzz of red hair growing over his emergency-room-shaved skull.

It was subtle, but a bit of the earthy, boyish musk I'd

come to associate with Spencer wafted off Dalton, swirling through the damp air before meeting my nose. As it did, a voice in the back of my head distantly commanded, *Gather your fellows.*

Dalton's friend Mikey Harris was next to him, holding a football high and leading the crowd in a chant of, "Dal-TON, Dal-TON, Dal-TON." His cheerleader girlfriend, Nikki, all porcelain-white complexion and burgundy hair, hugged his side possessively, unable to contain her glee at having him back alive. Behind her were her fellow cheerleaders, the triplets Delgado—Amy, Brittany, and Casey, with Amy smirking at the crowd.

"Excuse you, thank you." Someone shoved me aside, and I barely caught a glimpse of cocoa-brown skin and bobbing black curls before the speaker dug her way into the mass.

"Uh, yeah, excuse *you.*"

I turned to see Mai Sato beside me. She was one of the school's track stars, and also best friend of the recently deceased Emily Cooke. She took in the scene at the back of the crowd with a look between disgust and sadness, then wandered away. She left behind her a scent trail of some flowery perfume. Strange. I'd never pegged Mai as the perfume type.

The pushy girl was, of course, Tracie Townsend, our

class president. She wore a prim yellow blouse and skirt, with a matching headband holding back her curls—halfway to Stepford Wives territory, though somehow it worked for her. Despite being smaller than half the people who made up the inner circle of the crowd surrounding Dalton, she expertly shoved her way to stand directly before him.

Holding up her hands, Tracie smiled forcefully until the chants of "Dal-TON" finally died down.

"Wonderful, thank you!" she said, her voice loud, crisp, and curt. "We are all super glad that our very own Dalton McKinney has overcome such tragic circumstances to come back to Carver. Give him a hand, everyone!"

The crowd hollered and clapped, and I couldn't help but do the same, my hands slapping against each other as fast as a hummingbird's wings. I could barely see Dalton, but the glimpses I got made me feel one step closer to whole—one step closer to a pack. All these weird feelings were hardwired instincts, I knew that, just strange wolfy desires that were ingrained in my DNA by invasive scientists. That didn't stop the connection between me and Spencer, and me and Dalton, from feeling stronger than even that of my own family.

Tracie raised her hands once more, and the crowd died down. Gently shoving aside Mikey and Nikki, Tracie strung her arm through Dalton's and made him step forward. "I am going to go to Principal Alexander later today and ask that we prepare a special assembly to celebrate. But I think from the glares of the office staff—hellooo, yes, we see you! Ha-ha!—we should probably disperse and clear the walkway." She let go of Dalton and strode through the crowd toward the front entrance, shooing with her hands. "All right, let's go."

"Yo, Tracie!" a guy I couldn't see yelled. "Disperse *this*." People laughed at whatever gesture he'd made toward her, but Tracie ignored him, unfazed.

The crowd did disperse a little, or at least became less packed. I tried to push my way to Dalton, determined to catch him before the bell rang, but unlike Tracie, I wasn't able to dig my way through.

Then Spencer was beside me. I felt my nerves calm in a rush of relief.

"Hey, there you are," he said. "Dalton's back."

"Oh, I thought everyone was chanting about some other Dalton," I said, then dug into his side playfully. "We should—"

Spencer grabbed my shoulder, stopping me. "Whoa, hold on. I smell her. Do you smell that?"

I glanced around me to make sure no one was watching, then sniffed at the air. Aside from the musty, damp air and the body odor of everyone around me—including the absolutely atrocious stench coming off the pudgy guy near me, who I recognized as Terrance Sedgwick—all I smelled were Spencer's and Dalton's respective wolf scents.

"I don't smell anything. Was she here?" I asked, peering about the crowd. "Is she here now? She must be another student then!"

Spencer was nodding. "Yeah, yeah, she was somewhere here, or is here, I can't tell. Her scent is masked by some sort of perfume."

"Perfume?" I asked. "Is it sort of flowery? I smelled Mai wearing some perfume. She went down the walkway. Does it go that way?"

Nose scrunched, Spencer spun around, ignoring me.

"Spencer, does it lead to Mai?"

"Huh?" he said, whipping back to me. "Oh. No, I don't know. More than one girl is wearing it, and they all went different directions."

I grabbed Spencer's hand and led him through the thinning crowd toward Dalton. "Keep sniffing," I whispered. "But we need to add Mai to the list of possibilities. Maybe she even knew about Emily C."

"Okay," Spencer said as I dragged him.

Dalton's back was to me as we approached. He was laughing with Mikey and Nikki—then stopped suddenly as I grew near. He spun to face us, incredulous.

"You," he said, eyes locked on mine.

Amy Delgado, arms crossed and eyes set to death glare, stepped beside him. "*Her.* What do you want, Emily?"

Mikey and Nikki and the remaining two Delgado triplets grouped up behind Dalton. I could practically taste the disdain. Of course, their recent experiences with me included me getting drunk at Mikey's memorial for Emily Cooke, where I brazenly slobbered all over Dalton in front of Nikki. That was right before I shoved Mikey across his foyer—and right before Dalton was shot.

I wasn't exactly going to be invited to costar in their eventual rich kid reality show, is what I'm getting at.

Before all the craziness of the week before, I might have shied away. Slunk into the shadows to hide in shame. But that was before a man tried to kill me. Before I had to fight for my life. Before werewolves, and before shadowmen.

Bitchy teen girls can be scary as hell. But I'd seen scarier.

I met Amy's gaze and forced myself to smile. "I just wanted to welcome Dalton back."

"Yeah, me too," Spencer said. He jumped forward and punched Dalton in the arm. "Hey, man. Who knew someone could look so good with bullet wounds?"

Mikey and the girls groaned. Dalton didn't really react. He kept staring at me quizzically, a smile playing on his face.

"Too soon, bro, too soon," Mikey said, playfully putting Spencer in a chokehold and mussing his hair.

Spencer broke free. "Whoa, dude, not the hair. I spent a whole thirty seconds on it this morning."

Nikki wrapped her arm around Dalton's waist and raised her eyebrows at me and Spencer. "Well, thanks for the welcome back. Dalton appreciates it. We need to go to class now."

"Actually," Spencer said, "we were wondering if we could talk to Dalton for a second. Um, alone."

"What?" Amy scoffed. "Uh, no, he's not going anywhere with her *alone*."

Dalton raised a hand. "Nah, it's cool. I need to talk to them, too."

"You do?" Nikki asked. "Why?"

He ignored her and started walking toward the side of the school. I looked between Amy and Nikki, shrugged, and then followed, Spencer behind me.

"Dalton, where are you going?" Nikki said, raising her voice.

"It'll just be a second!" he called over his shoulder.

We rounded the corner of the building, quickening our pace as we stomped over wet grass. Misty rain dampened our hair and splattered the lenses of my glasses. I looked behind us, but no one followed. Yet.

Then Dalton stopped. He grabbed me gently by the sides of my face with his large hands, leaned in, and took in a long, loud whiff of my hair.

"Oh," I said. "Okay. This is happening."

Spencer put a hand on Dalton's shoulder, and the bigger boy let me go and stood back, a giant grin on his face.

"You're her," he said. "I smelled you all morning, but there was perfume. I—" He shook his head. "Are you like me?"

I swallowed and looked at Spencer, then back at Dalton. My pulse began to race, my hands shook. I was almost certain Dalton was another werewolf. He had to be. It all fit. But saying the words to him out loud would make it real. My cheeks hurt from how much I was smiling, and my hands were shaking again; from anticipation, this time, not fear.

"If by 'like me' you mean . . ." I paused, then leaned in and whispered, "A werewolf."

Dalton barked a laugh. He looked up at the gray sky and shook his head. "Oh yes. Yes!" His voice echoed through the schoolyard. Several crows darted off the scaffolding. "Sorry," he said, looking back at us. "It's just, I thought I've been going insane. I thought my brain wasn't healed right or something." His face twisted. "Unless I'm imagining this. Maybe I'm not even awake."

Spencer punched him in the bicep, hard, and Dalton rubbed his arm. "Ow, man."

Spencer shrugged. "See, not a dream."

36

Unhooking his backpack's straps, Dalton let it fall to the ground and began to pace back and forth, restless. "So, tell me everything. How is this possible? Were you bit or something? I wasn't. I don't think I was, anyway. Sometimes I don't remember so— Well, and there are these shadows—"

I'm going to break out a cliché here: My heart sank. I got it then, where that phrase came from, because it literally felt like all these hopes I'd had stored up in my chest were collapsing into my gut.

So Dalton didn't know anything about this, either. He was as much in the dark as we were. What exhilaration there was at finally having him as part of the pack was crushed by my frustration about not knowing why the hell any of this was happening to us.

The first bell rang, echoing across the school grounds. What stragglers there were outside began to stream toward the entrance, but the three of us stood there, Dalton still pacing, Spencer and I meeting each other's disappointed eyes.

I reached out and grabbed Dalton's arm, stopping him midstride. "We don't really know much. Yet. All we know is that this isn't magic. We were created by scientists, we think. By a company called BioZenith."

Dalton stiffened, then looked down at both of us. "But that's where my father works. They just do stuff with food."

Spencer shook his head. "It has to be a cover story. The

guy who shot you was from there. He knew all about us."

"It doesn't make any sense, though." Dalton raised a trembling hand to touch his bandaged temple.

Out of the corner of my eye I saw two figures round the side of the school. Nikki and Amy. The two cheerleaders stood there, arms crossed, eyes narrowed.

And behind them was Megan, leaning against a tree and watching me. She was only there a moment before a boy I recognized as Patrick Kelly came up, said something to her, and picked up her backpack. Since when were they friends? Last week Patrick was just a new kid from London, all broody good looks and quiet demeanor. I'd thought for a while he might be a werewolf, or even the killer after us, but I'd been wrong on both counts.

But I didn't have time to worry about it just then. I leaned in close to Dalton and Spencer, lowering my voice. "We need to get to class. We should meet up later and talk through all this, though, okay?"

Dalton nodded, staring forward without seeming to focus on anything. "Yeah, all right. Yeah. You two should come by my house later. If you're right about BioZenith, maybe . . ." He trailed off, his eyes finally focusing on mine. "I can't believe it was you all this time."

I could sense Nikki watching us intently. And though I wasn't really afraid of her, that didn't mean I wanted her to think I was after her boyfriend, either. Well, not any more than she already did.

"Yup, it was me! But I think you should go walk your girlfriend to class before she murders all of us."

Dalton's head darted up, and he caught sight of Nikki, now waiting alone. He raised a hand to her, then reached down and grabbed his backpack.

"Later," he whispered, then ran past us to Nikki.

I watched him try to wrap an arm around her shoulder as he reached her, but she brushed it off. She flounced off toward the front doors, Dalton at her heels.

"I lost the girl's scent," Spencer said beside me, deflated.

"Oh well," I said. "I'm sure you'll find it again. But can we not talk about it any more right now? I'm suddenly feeling a little overwhelmed."

Spencer shrugged. "All righty, then. May I walk you to class, Em Dub?"

I smiled at him. "You may."

We followed in Dalton and Nikki's footsteps, just as the final bell rang. All sorts of thoughts and worries swirled within my head, threatening to keep me from focusing all day.

So I let Spencer's pheromones wash over me, placate me. And the worries drifted away.

Details of Video Footage Recorded Oct. 31, 2010,
Part 2

20:57:57 PST—Hallway 1, Sector D

Vesper 1(B) and Vesper 2.1(A) enter the hallway
unmolested. Many Vesper Company employees, including
several who are not now nor ever were prepared for
violent contact, lie unconscious against the walls.
Important paperwork that will now be quite difficult
to file litters the floors.

VESPER 1(B): Wow, Amy, you were busy.
VESPER 2.1(A): Well, it took a while to find where
they were holding you. I was looking for the control
room when one of these guys told me where to go.
[She points at a Vesper Company employee lying just
out of camera view; investigations into who helped
aid the Deviant are ongoing.] That guy. I was gentle
with him.
VESPER 1(B): Do you know where the control room is?
That's where we can find where the others are, right?

VESPER 2.1(A): Right. And no, I don't know where. I went to get you first.

The two Deviants brazenly continue down the hall. Vesper 1(B) notices the plates on the wall indicating directions to locations that perhaps should not have been out in view just in case of incidents like this occurring. Live and learn, I suppose. Again, please stick to the facts.—MH

21:00:12 PST: Hallway 20, Sector D

The Deviants move cautiously as they enter this new hallway. There is no one visible in the hall save for the two Deviants. They continue to follow the plaques on the walls until they are in front of the door to the control center for this sector.

Vesper 1(B) stands to the side as Vesper 2.1(A) moves in front of the door. She closes her eyes and raises both hands, palms facing the door. Slowed-down footage shows the steel door buckling from its center, directly opposite Vesper 2.1(A)'s hands, before being pushed off its hinges and breaking the locks. The door bursts inward.

21:01:04 PST: Control Room D1

The door lands in the center of the spacious control room. The usual personnel have already been evacuated, and the Deviants come face-to-face with ten armed guards dressed in full body gear. Nine

stand around the perimeter of the room, while the
tenth rushes to stand in the doorway. All ten guards
point their weapons at the girls.

GUARD CAPTAIN COLLINS: Don't move! We don't want to
shoot you!

The Deviants look at each other, unmoving.

VESPER 1(B): You ready to do this?
VESPER 2.1(A): Oh yeah.

The camera glitches. The screen goes black.
Transcript will continue with footage from backup
data center.

Part 2 of Relevant Video Footage Concluded

LONELY AND GETTING
ALL HYPERBOLIC

I used to be good at being alone. In fact, I'd sort of preferred it.

I was never very good at playing with a team. I'd taken ballet when I was little, but I was always out of sync, so I mostly ended up pirouetting into other girls, so much so that I had to be assigned my own special corner for practice. Same when I was in tae kwon do—I don't think the boy next to me appreciated my enthusiastic would-be roundhouse kicks as much as I did.

Then came the body changes, the strange stares and inappropriate touches from some truly assholish boys, and I was no longer interested in being around groups of any size. Say hello to my dad's humongous DVD collection and a bunch of old, nerdy sci-fi shows and terrible horror movies. Hello also to a fully stocked personal library. I could spend as much time alone as I wanted, watching and reading about fictional girls doing exciting fictional things, and I was straight-up content.

That was, of course, before the day I found myself transformed into a whole new girl, ready to leap from a window and take on the night. And before the day Dalton came back to school and I began to form my pack.

I was alone that afternoon, back in my bedroom, waiting for Spencer to text to let me know it was time to head to Dalton's house. I'd made a trip to the library after school to check out some books on anything resembling the topic of shadowmen, then opted to avoid the welcome-home rally for Dalton. I assumed Nikki and friends wouldn't miss me.

My dad and stepmom were both out. My stepsister, Dawn, was home, but she had some sort of paper to work on, so she might as well have been in the wilds of the Amazon for how easy it was to get in touch with her.

I was surrounded by all my creature comforts—my personal collections of DVDs and books, all organized in the particular way I like them; the geeky posters on my walls; Ein, the stuffed corgi.

But I was far from feeling comfortable.

All I could think about was the shadowman from the

night before. I kept staring at the foot of my bed where I'd seen it. All my lights were on, blazingly bright yellow, but I knew that wouldn't stop it if it felt like materializing to watch me.

And when I wasn't thinking about the shadowman, I was remembering Dr. Gunther Elliott. I remembered the night at the club when he lured me outside, then fired a gun at me. I remembered the night he'd found me outside Patrick's and Spencer's respective houses and tried to kill me.

That was the night Spencer and I became wolves together. Leaped at Dr. Elliott. Tore into his neck and chest with our terrible, monstrous teeth. Hot, oily blood leaked from horrific wounds, filling my mouth, coating my tongue. And the shadowmen were there, watching us do it.

Applauding us.

I was a killer. I was a freak. A . . .

I gasped a sob on my bed, where I lay thinking these thoughts. I was made this way and I didn't know why, and it seemed like no one else knew, either.

But I was also strong now, right? I could be fearless, if I let myself. I had a connection to others, my pack, that reminded me of being a little kid, when I last felt like I was really close to my family. It was the feeling of Christmases with the grandparents over, everyone in sweaters, a fire in the fireplace, me tossing wrapping paper into the air while they laughed and videotaped the present-opening carnage. It was cuddling next to my dad, an old knitted afghan over us as we watched *Alias*, me wondering aloud why sometimes Sydney Bristow wore only her underwear when doing spy stuff. And it was Megan and me running around with blankets slung over our shoulders as royal robes, screaming at the top of our lungs while we pretended we were being chased by carnivorous unicorns.

I mean, it's not like my family wasn't still close. We were just all . . . doing our own thing now, I guess. And in the span of a week Megan and I had drifted apart. But when Spencer was there, and now Dalton, those old, fuzzy feelings all came back somehow. That feeling of me needing them, and them needing me, and together we could just be relentlessly *happy*.

Only my pack wasn't there just then. One, Emily Cooke, would never be there. I was alone with all this craziness, and all I wanted was to find Spencer and let our biochemistry mingle and keep me in a dopey, goofy haze.

Sick, right? It was funny, but at first I'd thought I could handle all of this alone. I'd thought I'd sort of reconciled all the sides of myself and I was an independent woman, strutting like Beyoncé and getting all single ladies up in here. Except I was preventing myself from turning into Nighttime and Wolftime, the stronger versions of Emily. And the only time the past few days I'd felt all wanton and worry free was when I was with a boy.

It doesn't have to be that way, girl. Nighttime. *Stop being so damn afraid. You know you're better than that. You proved it. Believe it, already!*

"I know, I know," I muttered. "You're so awesome, I'm so lame, blah, blah and, oh look over here, in the back of the closet behind an old pair of bright red galoshes: another *blah*."

I pulled my glasses off my face, squeezed my eyes closed, and massaged the bridge of my nose. Considering all the sleep I was getting, I shouldn't have felt so tired. But being consumed all the time by sci-fi craziness on top of, y'know, school and angry best friends can be a bit of a drain.

Oh. Angry best friend. Maybe of all my problems, that was one I could actually fix without too much hassle.

I glanced at my clock—it was a little after four p.m. I still had some time to kill. I probably should have done homework. But I wasn't really in the mood to parse mathematical equations. Instead, I had an idea about how to bond with Megan.

I grabbed my phone and went downstairs. The house was eerily quiet—when Dawn disappears into her room to study, she *really* disappears. Hugging myself to warm up my bare arms, I walked across the hardwood to the couch, plopped down, and wrapped myself in the afghan draped over the cushions. Snatching up the remote from the coffee table, I flipped on the TV and scrolled to the movie channel listings.

Perfect timing. A bad old horror movie was about to start. I selected the channel and cranked the volume up, letting the surround sound fill the front room and chase away the freaky silence.

I flipped open my phone and dialed REEDY. Megan picked up right away.

"Hello?"

"Hi!" I sounded way too chipper. I coughed and attempted to tone it down. "Hey, are you near a TV?"

"Uh, yeah," Megan replied from the other end. "Why?"

"Well, we haven't watched a movie by phone in forever, so I thought, if you're not busy, we could now."

Silence. I bit my lip, waiting.

"Let's do it," Megan finally said. "I was just reading the internet anyway."

I let out a shaky breath and smiled to myself. Okay. So far so good. Megan didn't sound annoyed or anything, at least. In fact, I could almost hear the grin in her voice.

The other end crackled, and I heard shuffling as Megan moved through her house to get to the TV. I switched the phone to my other ear.

"Okay, what are we watching?" Megan asked.

"Look for *Urban Legend*," I told her. "It's like bad *Scream* fan fic, so prepare to mock mercilessly."

Megan laughed. "Anyone famous in it, or is this one of those movies where this is the only thing on the actors' IMDb pages?"

"Actually, Joshua Jackson from *Fringe* is in this," I said. "And the lead singer from Thirty Seconds to Mars. Sometime in the past decade they decided to trade hairstyles, too."

"So weird." Megan laughed.

We watched the opening sequence, squealing in glee when we recognized Horror Movie Icon Brad Dourif as a stuttering gas station attendant, and then openly wondering how smart the killer must be to decapitate someone who is currently driving a car that he is also in. Then came much mocking of some truly cracktastic acting.

It really felt, for that half an hour, like we were back to normal. We'd watched movies like this tons of times—not always by phone, sometimes it was by IM, but when we couldn't hang out and watch something together, it was the next best thing. There was nothing I found more fun than finding a movie Megan had never heard of and getting to hear her unbridled first impression. And she was truly on her game that afternoon.

"Wow, this lead girl is a total downer," she said from the phone. "She's, like, sapping my will to live. I want the guy in the fur coat to come hang me from a tree right now."

I laughed. "I know, right? I'd much rather her roommate, Sort of Horror Movie Icon Danielle Harris, be the lead. No one expects the angry goth girl to survive."

"Oh wait, I know this one," Megan said. "Danielle Harris is . . . uh . . ."

I curled my legs up under me and smiled, even though Megan couldn't see it. "You know this, come on."

"Oh! Was she the little girl in the later Halloween movies?"

I laughed again. "I'm proud. Truly the student is becoming the master."

Megan giggled—actually giggled!—at my cliché and then, for a few moments, we both went silent. From my TV and through my cell phone I could hear more bad acting, and Megan's soft breathing.

"You know, Em, I missed this," Megan said quietly after a moment. "I was beginning to think . . ."

"I know," I said. "I've missed it too. I've been way too busy lately to just . . . like, hang out."

"Well, you know how to reach me when you want to. This is a lot more productive than reading fan-boy rants on message boards all afternoon, at least for me. Maybe that's a good time for you, I don't know."

Grinning, I pulled the afghan tighter around me. "Yeah, no, I'm good on avoiding rants. Oh, wait, okay, I think someone is about to die."

We went back to the movie then. Megan was mid-riff on the dubious talent of Tara Reid when my phone buzzed against the side of my face. Startled, I let the phone fall to my lap—where I saw a text on the screen, from Spencer.

4:32 PM PST: yo Em. Dalton is on his way home,
u ready

My pulse pumped with excitement—this was it, finally we could talk to Dalton in private—and immediately guilt rushed over me. Megan and I were actually talking normally for the first time in a week. Actually having fun, like we used to. And now I was going to have to ruin it.

I put the phone to my ear. Megan was giggling to herself about whatever joke I'd just missed. I swallowed, opened my mouth to speak, then couldn't say anything. After another moment of quiet, I closed my eyes and decided to just rip off the Band-Aid.

"Hey, Megan? Um, I really hate to do this, but I have to go."

Again I was met with silence. All I could hear were the

echoing dialogue and sound effects from our TVs.

"What's up?" she finally asked.

I swallowed again. "I have an important project that I'm supposed to do. Uh, with Spencer. I thought I'd have time to watch the whole movie. I'm really—"

"Fine."

"Megan, I'm really, really sorry," I said. "I wouldn't ditch you if this wasn't important."

A sigh on the other end. "I said it's fine, Emily. This movie isn't that much fun, anyway."

"We can find another one," I said. "Only in person next time, okay?"

"Yeah. But don't let me keep you. Go do your project. I've got plenty of butthurt people on the internet to read about."

Before I could respond, the phone clicked dead. I stared at it for a moment. I'd screwed up. Again.

Closing my eyes, I shook my head. I couldn't worry about it now. Megan and I would talk tomorrow. I hoped. With her no longer on the phone, the TV just felt like meaningless noise and color. I flicked off the TV, and those same worries that I'd momentarily shoved away started to come back. The house suddenly felt even more cavernous and empty.

My fingers darted over the number keys of my cell as I

finally texted Spencer back.

> 4:37 PM PST: For the love of all things good in the world come save me.

> 4:37 PM PST: lol? u ok?

I grinned at the phone. Apparently faux histrionics don't translate well via text.

> 4:39 PM PST: I'm fine, just lonely and getting all hyperbolic. I'll meet you outside.

YEAH, HE'S SUPER FRIENDLY

Spencer and I pulled up in front of Dalton's house at five on the dot. Dalton lived on the richer side of town, and predictably his house was of the lavish multistory type that seemed straight out of one of those Real Housewives shows. They had a broad, beautifully tended yard and garden. Even though it was beginning to rain, an older, tanned man who clearly wasn't Dalton's father was mowing the lawn as Spencer pulled the minivan to park behind Dalton's parents' Lexus. Or one of their Lexuses, anyway. Lexii?

"I guess BioZenith pays its employees pretty well," I said as I climbed out of the car, grabbing my backpack full of shadowmen-related books as I did.

"It probably takes a particular skill set to genetically

engineer people," Spencer shouted over the din of the lawn mower as he rounded the car and came to my side.

"Guess so."

We nodded politely to the old gardener, then stood on Dalton's porch and rang the doorbell. There was a wicker-and-faux-fall-leaf wreath on the door and stacks of browning gourds at our feet. *Très* Martha Stewart.

A minute later a small woman with short, blond-streaked hair opened the door. She was dressed like Martha too—all *Better Homes & Gardens* in a sensible blouse and slacks, with a pair of handcrafted pumpkin earrings. "Hello?" she asked, offering us a timid smile.

"Hi," I said. "We—"

Loud, sharp barks burst from the foyer behind the woman, and a large yellow Lab leaped around her, nearly knocking her over. I jumped back, unsure if I was about to meet the family guard dog. But the gold-furred Lab just bounced from foot to foot, looking up at us both, tongue lolling out, its tail an excited blur.

"Bad dog," the woman said wearily. She grabbed it by its collar and tried to pull the dog back inside. Unable to get the dog to do more than move a tiny bit to the left, she looked back up at us and sighed. "May I help you?"

"We're here to see Dalton?" I said, sounding less confident than I'd intended.

"Oh, I'm not sure he's up for any more visitors after the busy day he's had, dear, he really should be resting and—"

"No, Mom, it's cool, I invited them."

Dalton appeared behind his mother, dressed down in sweatpants and a muscle shirt. His skin glistened with sweat, and he was breathing heavily. The Lab turned all its attention to Dalton now, leaping up at his midsection. Dalton crouched down, rubbing his dog's fur.

"Good boy, Max," he said in a goofy voice. "Who's a good boy?" He looked up at Spencer and me, still roughly petting Max. His face broke into a huge smile at the sight of us.

"Are you sure?" Dalton's mother asked, almost stuttering over her words. "The doctors said you're doing far better than they ever could have hoped, but you really shouldn't be straining yourself."

He stood up and gave her a sweaty half hug around the shoulders. "Don't worry so much, Mom. I'm fine. You heard what they said, I'm a miracle." He pulled her in tighter and kissed her hair, and a smile appeared on the woman's weary face. She clasped his hand.

"How about I help you with dinner later?" Dalton asked her.

His mom shook her head. "No, don't worry about it, dear," she said. "Invite your friends in, it's chilly out."

No longer interested in Dalton, his dog stepped forward and started sniffing around my pelvis. I'd never played with dogs much. I patted him softly on the head. He continued snorting my lady bits.

Dalton let go of his mom and waved us forward. "Come on in, guys. Spence, you know Max. Emily, don't mind him, he's just friendly."

Spencer laughed. "Yeah, he's *super* friendly!"

"Max, come!" Dalton commanded. He slapped his thighs and the dog thumped back inside, then disappeared into a hallway. Dalton motioned for me and Spencer to follow.

I nodded politely at Mrs. McKinney as we passed. She offered me a smile, but it wasn't genuine, not like with Dalton—she was clearly not pleased with the intrusion.

Dalton had us take off our shoes and leave them by the front door, then led us out of the spacious foyer. We went up a flight of stairs, the carpet soft beneath my socked feet, to an impeccable professionally decorated hall. And I mean impeccable—there wasn't a bit of animal fur on the carpet, not a smudge of dirt on the walls. The pictures were aligned perfectly straight, arranged symmetrically with various potted plants.

Dalton opened a door and ushered us into his bedroom. It was twice as big as mine, with half designated for his sleeping area—including a king-size bed covered with tangled sheets and a dresser with most of the drawers pulled out, socks and shirts hanging over the edge—and half for a messy desk, a recliner, and a workout bench.

Snagging a dirty towel off a barbell, he halfheartedly swabbed down the bench and sat down. Spencer plopped into the recliner familiarly, and I pulled out the desk chair. There were a couple of workout magazines on it, so I set those on the desk and sat down.

Not that I was going to say anything to Dalton, but I could no longer smell his and Spencer's musky scents. The room stank overwhelmingly of *boy*.

Dalton leaned onto his knees, grinning at both of us. "I'm so glad you guys actually came. I was worried I imagined it all."

I bit my lip. "It was real, I promise. And . . . are you really okay, Dalton? I mean, you were shot in the head, but you look like you just got a scratch. I'm surprised they even let you out of the hospital."

Spencer seemed to be ignoring us both, intently focused as he was on getting the recliner to spin him 360 degrees just with a shove off from the tip of his sock-covered toes.

Dalton's grin faded. "Yeah, I think I'm all right. I think so." His hand rose to absentmindedly touch his bandaged temple. "The doctors said that I'm lucky to be alive, let alone walking and talking normally so soon. They couldn't believe how fast I healed up. They didn't even want to release me, but my father insisted very angrily until they let me out. I'm guessing I'm only better because of what we are, huh?"

"I guess it must be," I said. "I mean, Spencer and I both got stabbed when . . . well, when we fought the BioZenith guy. By morning there weren't even scars."

"BioZenith guy?" Dalton asked. "You mean my father?" He laughed to himself before I could correct him. "No, that's dumb. You mean the man with the hat. The one who shot me."

Flashes of Dr. Elliott's face hit my head. The stubbly jowls. The defeated, defiant eyes. The contortions of fear that his features were stuck in after he was dead.

"Yeah. Dr. Gunther Elliott. Do you remember much of what happened that night?"

Dalton shook his head. "I dunno, I was just feeling real antsy, real angry. That happens sometimes, but usually it's not as bad as that night. I tried to drown it with beer, even though Coach says to avoid the stuff, and then you were there, and Nik was mad at me, and then . . . that's it. Next thing I remember I was in a hospital bed, then home."

"What about last night?" I asked. "I saw a wolf outside. Was that you?"

Nodding rapidly, Dalton said, "Yeah, that was me.

They brought me home and I got all antsy again, just like that night. I snuck out for a walk—my mom doesn't like me going out by myself anymore—and then . . . I was just turning into this *thing*. It hurt, man, but when I was running around . . . it felt like I was finally me again. My brain didn't lose track. I didn't have any worries. Just me and the woods and the streets."

There came a *pop* and a *bang*, and I jumped. I turned to find Spencer staring at us sheepishly, having just accidentally popped out the footrest on the recliner. I couldn't help but laugh at his expression. He was embarrassed, and it was *adorable*.

"Sorry," he said. "But man, first night back and you already got out more than I ever did. Emily was out at clubs and stuff, and I always just stayed home programming."

Dalton looked at me with that vague smile again. It felt a little weird, like he was seeing something that wasn't there.

"You went clubbing?" he asked. "You don't seem like that's your thing. But you looked different at the party."

I shrugged. "Yeah, well, nighttime me is a bit more, uh, carefree than I usually am."

He leaned forward again, a fire behind his eyes. "They told me that they found the shooter behind Spencer's house," he said in a low voice. "Dead. Dogs did it, but that isn't right, is it? It was you guys."

Spencer and I both fell silent. Embarrassed heat rushed over my skin—embarrassed, of all things. I know, right? Whoops, tore out a man's throat, how untoward of me! So not toward.

Eventually I nodded, confirming.

Dalton's eyes darted between us. "What was it like?" he asked.

A chill ran up my arms. I didn't know how to answer. I didn't *want* to answer. It wasn't something I had expected anyone to ask, let alone Dalton "helps old ladies cross the street" McKinney.

As though sensing my discomfort, Spencer piped up. "Um, it's not really a good memory, man," he said. "Maybe we'll talk about it some other time. We should start doing some research or something before it gets too late."

Dalton lay back against the workout bench, his arms behind his head. "It's fine, we have all night. My mom and father won't make me get rid of my friends. They're tiptoeing around me."

"Actually, we don't have all night," I said. "Spencer and I . . . well, we've sort of been taking sleeping pills to keep us from changing."

Dalton furrowed his brow. "Why?"

I crossed my arms. "So, uh, we don't get into trouble. Or any more trouble anyway. Last time we went nighttime, we . . . that was when Dr. Elliott found us."

Crunching his stomach, Dalton rose back up to sit. "Man, it sounds like I missed out on all the excitement."

Spencer kicked down the footrest and swiveled the recliner once more. "Totally, man. Next time try not to get shot."

Dalton laughed, a little too loudly, then shook his head. "Okay. Research. Yeah, just love research. What do you guys know about all this?"

We went back and forth, Spencer and I, relaying the relevant info: our respective nighttime changes (how I became all uninhibited, how he became super focused), how Dr. Elliott had targeted us, how we kept seeing shadowy beings when we were wolves, and how two of the shadowmen had sort of attacked us in our beds the night before. I mentioned how aside from Emily Cooke and Dalton, we only knew for sure that there was one more of us—a female who we were still trying to sniff out. Or Spencer was, anyway. My only guess so far was Mai Sato, though granted that was on some flimsy circumstantial evidence.

I also told him how we'd looked up connections between ourselves and BioZenith, and though both Dalton and Emily Cooke had a parent who worked there, as far as Spencer and I knew, neither of us did.

At that last part, Dalton got up and walked to the

desk. He leaned over me, smelling overwhelmingly like a locker room, then waved his mouse to clear the screen saver and began clicking on his monitor. He seemed completely unaware that his armpit was inches from my face. Eyes wide, I leaned back—hello, privacy invasion.

When he finally pulled back, I surreptitiously took in a deeeeep breath of comparatively fresh air and took a look at what he'd brought up on-screen. It was some sort of spreadsheet listing times and dates.

"What's that?" I asked.

"It's the schedule," Dalton said simply. It seemed completely unintelligible to me, but he scanned it with his eyes, then nodded.

"He'll be home any second now."

And downstairs I heard the front door slam heavily and a man's voice echo up through the floorboards.

Dalton looked between me and Spencer. "Let's see if we can get anything out of my father."

6

WE WANT TO KNOW
ABOUT BIOZENITH

I tiptoed down the plush steps behind Dalton and Spencer, one hand clinging to the railing as we descended to the first floor. I could hear Dalton's dad clearly now. He wasn't shouting, exactly, but he talked as if he was speaking to an auditorium, and his deep voice reverberated through the halls.

"I know he just got back from the hospital, Darla, but he knows that his friends only park on the street. He knows that."

I heard Dalton's mom respond, but she was so quiet I couldn't make out the words.

Dalton's dad sighed. "Fine. For today, fine."

Dalton walked confidently through the foyer, leading us

into a den (where Max now lay snoozing on a plush baby-blue love seat), then through a large dining room, and finally into the kitchen, where we saw his parents both standing by the sink. Mrs. McKinney was quietly putting dishes in the dishwasher while behind her, on the stove, something simmered in a pot. Mr. McKinney had his back to us and was drinking from a mug as he leafed through mail that had been set on the counter.

Mr. McKinney was almost the spitting image of what I imagined Dalton would look like in thirty years: tall, graying at the temples, still well built but a little soft around the middle from no longer being as active. He turned as he heard the three of us pad into the kitchen, and I saw that he shared Dalton's green eyes, though they were wrinkled at the edges.

Mr. McKinney gave me a strange look. "Uh, hello, Spencer, and . . . friend." To Dalton, he said, "I'll let it slide today, D, but tomorrow I don't want to come home to find my driveway taken up by other vehicles."

Dalton's eyes darted back and forth, studying his dad's face. His expression was unreadable, though I sensed a vague smirk. "No," Dalton said. "No, I think when it's raining, it's fine for my friends not to have to hike across the yard to get inside."

Mr. McKinney's lips pressed into a tight line, and he set

his mug down on the counter, hard. He looked as if he was about to say something—until Dalton absently raised his hand once more and rubbed at the bandage that covered his healing wound.

Uh, wow, manipulative. I didn't know Dalton had it in him. I wondered if he'd even known he'd made the gesture—if so, maybe he wasn't exactly the nice guy I'd assumed he was.

Dalton's father breathed out through his nose. "We'll talk about it later. How about you kids clear out of the kitchen so your mother can finish our dinner. She feels crowded."

Mrs. McKinney said nothing, just kept up the pattern of rinsing a dish, then placing it into the dishwasher with little clinks.

"Actually, Father, we wanted to ask you some questions," Dalton said.

Mr. McKinney raised an eyebrow. "Oh? About what?"

"About your job. We're supposed to do a project on an exceptional person's exceptional work. We chose you."

Tossing down the mail, Mr. McKinney smiled. "Ah, a school project." His eyes darting to me, he said, "That explains it."

Yeah. Thanks. Even aside from being part of the whole evil-bioengineering-firm thing, I wasn't exactly growing very fond of Dalton's dad.

"Well, come on then, I have a couple of free minutes. Let's go back to my office."

Mr. McKinney left the kitchen, and Dalton gestured for us to follow. I gave Spencer a wide-eyed look, and he whispered to me, "You get used to him."

We went down another hallway, this one slick hardwood. My socked feet slid and I almost fell, my arms pinwheeling wildly until Dalton caught me firmly by the arm and helped me regain my balance. Both he and Spencer held back their laughter as an oblivious Mr. McKinney opened up a door to reveal a large study.

Oh, daytime me. The epitome of grace and poise, am I right?

Unlike the rest of the house, which was all homey and looked like it was probably updated to reflect each holiday, the study was sleek, clinical. The wood floor continued in here, but was mostly covered by a sleet-gray rug. Steel-and-glass shelves lined the walls, and a similarly styled desk sat front and center, with an expensive-looking computer on it. Behind the desk hung a large abstract painting.

Mr. McKinney sat back in a leather chair behind the desk and motioned for the three of us to sit on some chairs. Chairs that were designed like one of Lady Gaga's shoes, in that at first glance, they seemed impossible to hold one's weight. Yet deceptively, they did just that.

"So, what sort of questions are you supposed to ask?" Mr. McKinney asked us.

Gripping the sides of my seat, still not sure how the chair even worked, I started to say, "Well, Mr. McKinney, we—"

"Your name?"

I blinked. "Sorry?"

Mr. McKinney leaned forward onto the glass top of his desk. I couldn't help but notice there wasn't a streak or a spot of dust on it. "What is your name?" he asked slowly. "We haven't met."

"Oh," I said, feeling a blush spread annoyingly over my cheeks. "Sorry. Yeah, hi, I'm Emily. Emily Webb."

I swear, for just a moment I thought I saw a flash of worried recognition cross the man's face. If it was ever there, he hid it quickly with a satisfied expression as he leaned back and crossed his arms. "Hello, Emily Webb. I take it you were assigned to this group, then? I know Dalton has lots of girls trying to team up with him on projects like this."

"Excuse me?" I sputtered.

Beside me, Spencer shuffled uncomfortably in his seat.

"Actually, Father, she's my friend," Dalton said, his voice as steely as the room around us. "I want her to ask the questions."

Mr. McKinney looked between his son, Spencer, and me, then waved a hand. "Go ahead, then, Emily Webb."

My fingers clenched into the side of my chair, and my blush was fully gone now. Yeah, no, I definitely did *not* like this man.

I let out a slow breath of air through my teeth. "All right, Mr. McKinney. We want to know about BioZenith."

Mr. McKinney crossed his legs, his eyes boring into my own. "BioZenith is a bioengineering firm that was formed in 1978. Its goal is to improve the science of horticulture, most specifically in the fields of mass farming. We're the reason you can get seedless grapes and tomatoes year-round. We are considered number one when it comes to these sciences—hence the company name. We are the zenith, the first and the best."

I nodded, but did not tear my gaze away from his. I could sense he was purposely doing the same, and I could feel the wolf part of me in the back of my head absolutely refusing to look away. He slowly rocked in his chair, back and forth, back and forth, thinking he was the alpha here. It was really pissing werewolf me off—and regular me, too, for that matter.

"Interesting," I said. "So BioZenith has always been just about fruits and veggies? You never, ever experimented with, say, livestock or other animals?"

Mr. McKinney stopped rocking, uncrossed his legs. "Not to my knowledge, Emily Webb, no. I joined BioZenith in 1990, well after the company was first founded. If there was ever any experimentation with livestock or"—his mouth twitched—"other animals, it would have been in the early years, long before I was even in college."

Our staring contest remained unfinished. Again I could feel Spencer shifting uncomfortably beside me.

"All right, on to more modern stuff then," I said. My lips were tight. My fingers clenched into the seat even tighter. "So do you have any theories on why a scientist from your veggie lab tried to kill your son six days ago?"

"Whoa, Em Dub," Spencer whispered beside me.

Dalton laughed involuntarily, then caught himself.

Mr. McKinney's whole face twitched, and finally, his gaze faltered.

"Dalton, what is this?" he said, his voice low but firm.

"Just questions, Father," Dalton said softly, his tone icy.

"These aren't questions I'm going to answer," the man said, refusing to look at me anymore. "In fact, considering that what happened to you is part of an ongoing police investigation, I *can't* answer questions like this from your classmates." He stood up, shoving his chair back. "I think you should show your friends out now, D. I'm sure your mother has dinner almost ready. And I have work to get to."

"Sure thing," Dalton said, getting up from his own weird chair and gesturing for Spencer and me to do the

70

same. "We'll finish our research later, guys."

I forced myself to contain my shaking as Spencer and I followed Dalton out into the hall. Mr. McKinney followed us as we headed back into the kitchen. I could almost feel him glaring into the back of my skull, and I hated the feeling. It reminded me of what it felt like to sense the shadowmen watching. Or Dr. Elliott.

The kitchen was empty when we came back into it. But there were voices coming from the dining room. Several voices.

The three of us and Dalton's father exited the kitchen— and found Mrs. McKinney sitting at the table, laughing amicably with a pair of girls I recognized immediately.

Dalton's gorgeous girlfriend, Nikki, with her perfect pale skin and long, deep red hair.

And beautiful, tanned Amy Delgado, with her mane of purposely untamed black hair and the telltale mole next to her nose that made it easy to tell her apart from her sisters.

At the sight of me, both girls stopped laughing. To their credit, they did their best to hide any sneers they wanted to shoot my way.

Well, I was certainly feeling loved in the McKinney household that day, let me tell you what.

"Heeey, Nik," Dalton drawled. He came up behind her, draped his arms over her shoulders, and kissed the top of her head for several seconds. She clasped his hands and closed her eyes as he did, a contented smile on her face.

"Nikki!" Dalton's father boomed as he caught sight of her himself. As Dalton moved away, his father placed a hand on Nikki's shoulder. "How are you holding up? School go well today?"

"Yeah, it went fine," Nikki said with a shrug.

Amy laughed, and I swear it was the first time I'd ever seen her express anything other than revulsion when she was around me. "Oh girl, please, it was epic. Mr. McKinney, not only did everyone absolutely mob your son, they demanded we have an impromptu, after-school gathering. Like, most of the school came, and us girls did a cheer for him. The class president got us cake and pizza. It was great."

"All for our little superhero, huh?" Mr. McKinney said. Smiling proudly, he slapped Dalton on the back. Dalton just shrugged.

"It *was* pretty sweet, Em, you shoulda come," Spencer said.

Nikki turned in her seat, as though noticing us for the first time. "Oh, hey, Spencer. Emily."

I offered a tight smile and a quick wave. Amy rolled her eyes.

Mr. McKinney took a seat at the head of the table. "So what brought you girls by?"

"They want to have a party here, dear," Mrs. McKinney said.

Dalton's father gave his wife a sidelong glance. "Honey, you know I wasn't talking to you. It's been a long time since you were a girl." He boomed another laugh. Everyone except Dalton and me offered a chuckle.

"Well, the celebration after school was fine," Nikki said, taking up where Mrs. McKinney left off. "But we figure it wasn't as much fun as it could be not on school grounds."

Again Mr. McKinney laughed. "Well, of course."

"So," Nikki went on, "we were hoping we could hold a private party here Friday night. A welcome home for Dalton."

Mr. McKinney stood from his chair, all smiles and good cheer. "Of course you can. But I'm going to let you girls talk it out, as I need to work. Once Dalton walks his guests out, he can help you. Right, D?"

Dalton blinked slowly. He looked around the table, then shrugged. "I can't right now. I promised to drive Emily home."

"You what?" Spencer said.

Dalton elbowed him.

Mr. McKinney grunted. "Fine. Take her home, then straight back here. You may be a superhero, but you still need to rest after what happened. You've only been home for a day."

"Fine," Dalton said.

Mr. McKinney met my eyes again. He was still smiling, but his eyes were cold.

"It was interesting meeting you, Emily Webb."

I swallowed, then nodded. "You too, Mr. McKinney."

Dalton's father left by way of the kitchen, and again Dalton turned to usher Spencer and me forward. As I turned, I saw Amy flick her fingers at me dismissively. The skin on the back of my skull prickled at the gesture, like needles were poking me. God, that girl bugged me.

"I'll see you later, Dalton," Nikki said softly.

"'Kay, Nik."

And then, we were mercifully away from Dalton's father and the cheerleaders who hated me, and back in the foyer.

I let out a long, deep breath. My hands were shaking. Had I really just asked a man if he knew why a coworker tried to kill his son? Had I been wrong in sensing he knew something? If I wasn't, did that mean he knew who and what I was? What if he wanted to pick up where Dr. Elliott left off?

Distantly I heard Spencer ask, "You really want to drive Emily home?"

"Yeah," Dalton responded, his voice just as far away. "If it's cool. I just don't want to plan a party all night."

Arms wrapped around me in a hug. Spencer. His musky,

sweet scent washed over me like it always did when we were this close. My hands stopped shaking. My mind stopped racing.

He pulled away, much too soon. "See you tomorrow, Em Dub."

"Yeah," I said. "Actually, we should meet up for sure. That party they're planning might be a good time to get back into Mr. McKinney's office."

Dalton nodded. "Could be. He won't be home."

"Sounds good to me," Spencer said. To Dalton, he said, "Okay, she's all yours. Don't try to take advantage of her or anything."

Dalton looked between Spencer and me. "She your girl now, man?"

"No," I answered quickly.

Spencer looked at me, eyes hurt, but he shrugged it off with a goofy grin. "Just friends, man. But you saw Emily with your dad. She's sort of a badass."

I ducked my head. "Yeah, not quite."

Dalton shook his head, not quite looking at me. "Nah, Emily," he said. "You kinda are."

Spencer left first to get his minivan out of the way. I slipped on my shoes and stood on the now-dark porch, listening to the rain patter against the roof as I waited for Dalton to gather my bag with the still-unread shadowmen books.

Spencer's scent had calmed me down, like it always did, but with him gone I could feel the fears and worries inching back. But hey, soon I'd be home, and I could pilfer a couple more of my stepmom's sleeping pills, and then—merciful escape.

Oh wow, how druggie does that sound? Sleeping pills and a boy's smell to erase my problems—a slippery slope to hard-core escapist drug abuse? Soon it would be crack cocaine! Black tar heroin! Crystal meth!

Or not.

Dalton finally came outside with my bag, still in his workout clothes but now wearing a jacket with the hood up. I put my hood over my head as well, and we ran to the Lexus in the driveway. Soon we were on our way back to my house, the radio blaring some song in full digital surround sound. Dalton sang along at the top of his lungs. Or tried to, anyway. He kept forgetting the words and sort of mumbled nonsense to the melody, laughing to himself but not saying much to me.

Finally we pulled up in front of my house, which seemed incredibly dinky and low rent after being in Dalton's pristine and magazine-style home. And not a moment too soon. I'm not sure how the time had flown by so fast, but it was already getting close to eight p.m.

Dalton watched me silently as I gathered my bag and checked my pockets to make sure they still contained everything I'd brought with me—my keys, my ID.

"Well, thanks for the ride," I said. "And for the talk. It's nice to find another one of us, even if we don't know why we are what we are."

He said nothing, just smiled at me.

I bit my lip. "And, uh, sorry about the weirdness with your dad. He kind of made me a little mad. I swear I'm not usually like that. I never talk back to anyone, ever." I thought of the recent nights when I'd gotten into fights, tossed boys around, and punched a killer in the face. "Well, mostly not. Okay, yeah. I'll see you tomorrow."

As I grabbed the door handle, his hand shot out and caught my wrist.

"Hey," he said, leaning in close.

I leaned away. He was getting way too close again, just like in his room. Like he was invading my space but didn't quite realize it wasn't normal.

"H-hey?" I said, my voice quiet. "Do you want me to grab some sleeping pills for you? Oh, maybe I should."

He closed his eyes and took in a long, deep breath through his nose. He exhaled, an elated look on his face.

"Wow," he said, then opened his eyes once more. "Do you know how you smell?"

"Uh . . ."

He shook his head. "Not bad, Emily. It isn't bad. It makes me feel calm. I don't ever feel calm." He leaned in closer and smelled me again.

And I realized: Pheromones. Was this what I was like when I was around Spencer? All clingy and sniffy? How immensely embarrassing. Suddenly I longed to retroactively erase every encounter I'd had with Spencer since Sunday.

But wait, the only reason I reacted to Spencer that way was because he is, I guess, my "mate." Right? I could smell Dalton's own personal wolf scent, but it didn't do much except remind me of what was missing. And that was Spencer. So why would Dalton find *me* so alluring? I mean, the guy was cute and all, but despite nighttime me's face-licking the week before, I wasn't exactly pining for the dude. Surely I was only meant to have the one mate, and he me.

Unless it was just that he hadn't found *his* so-called mate. Maybe that was the other girl, the one we hadn't found yet. When I was in my searching phase, I definitely hadn't been picky. I lusted after a vial of liquid pheromones, even. Talk about desperate.

Gently, I shoved Dalton back. "I know this is all new to you, but this is normal, I think. It's just pheromones. It's the wolf brain talking, okay? I'm not doing anything or wearing any perfume."

He let go of my wrist and nodded. Then he said, "No."

"No?"

"I don't want sleeping pills. You asked before."

I nodded slowly. "Oh. Okay. But Dalton, if you don't take them . . ."

"I know," he said, running his hand over his stubbly red hair. "But I don't care, Emily. And I don't know why you do either. From the stories you told me, you sound like you get hard-core. When you change, I mean."

I thought of the last time I'd changed. The terrifying images of the killer scientist. The smell of death, the taste of blood.

But it was true, by night, when I was her, or that side of me, or whatever it is—when I was Nighttime, none of that bothered me. I was fearless. I owned the night.

A night where now shadowmen could find me when I was asleep, unprepared, unchanged, just normal me. Like last night.

Dalton was close to me again, whispering in my ear excitedly. "Don't go to sleep, Emily," he said. "Change with me. Show me how to do it right. I don't want to just sleep when I know I can be so much more than I usually am."

I swallowed, then looked out the window to my dark bedroom window. I could almost swear I saw a shadowy figure moving behind the curtains. Any normal person could rationalize that away as nerves, post-traumatic stress, whatever. But I was living in my own insane TV show now. It felt like anything and everything someone could conjure up in their demented brain could and probably would happen.

The pills, Spencer, they placated me. But only for so long. All the fears were there, just beneath the surface, no matter what I did.

It sucked.

Besides, I didn't want a newly changed Dalton roaming the streets alone, getting into trouble.

Maybe for one night, just one night, I could let go again. Let myself be fearless and crazy and worry free. I wouldn't let it go too far. Nighttime Emily and I had made sort of an agreement about that, hadn't we? The night I went after Emily Cooke's killer?

Yes, we did. The voice in my head. *Listen to yourself. Listen to* me. *Together we can be awesome again. You know we can.*

I looked into Dalton's excited, waiting eyes. And I told him, "All right. Let's do it."

I'M RIDING SHOTGUN

I left Dalton in his car and ran inside my house. I paused to hug my dad playing his MMO at his desk, assured him I'd eaten at Dalton's even though I hadn't, told my stepmom my school day went well when she asked, then speed walked as nonchalantly as I could up to my room.

And I sat rigidly straight at the foot of my bed, then changed into the same black sweatpants and turtleneck that I'd worn the night Spencer and I faced Dr. Elliott in a dark backyard. I picked at my amateur stitching attempt on the pant leg, where a few nights earlier I'd been stabbed with a serrated hunting knife. Aside from that scar of black thread, and the turtleneck being stretched out in strange places because I had worn it when I changed into wolf-girl, there wasn't any sign that it had been worn during the battle. My blood and the blades of grass had all been washed away.

I didn't want to be wearing those clothes, but I figured if I was going to let myself change, I should probably be productive and get all stealthy. Maybe scope out BioZenith again. It'd be easier in all black.

I breathed in slowly, eyes closed, shutting away the blurry, bright room. Waiting. My alarm clock had said 8:11 when I set my glasses next to it after getting dressed.

"Okay, Nighttime," I whispered, my eyes still shut. "We worked together well last time. I know we can do it again. So . . . just don't get into trouble or anything. Please."

Nighttime didn't say anything back.

I breathed out. Breathed in once more—and the breath caught in my throat.

My eyes snapped open. My vision was crystal clear.

I was back. After two nights of being forced into unconsciousness, I was finally, mercifully, wide awake.

"Hell yeah," I said, my lips splitting into a grin. "Don't worry, Daytime. I got your back."

The routine was quick by now: Pillows artfully stuffed beneath Daytime Emily's covers to more or less resemble the shape of a nonbreathing and feather-stuffed person. Lights out. Window open. Feet on the sill—and a leap to the dark, wet grass below.

I landed in a crouch, my sneakers squelching in the damp ground. The rain had petered out now and the air was crisp, clear. I breathed in the earthy smells around me, the air scrubbed clean of exhaust. It was so good to be outside again, to stretch my muscles and let them move in the ways I'd longed to for the past few nights, trapped as I was behind a haze of stupid pills.

Even if I was dressed all cat burglar again instead of as fabulously hot as I knew I could be. Whatever. I'd play nice for Daytime Emily. I mean, for me. The both of us.

Across the street came a steady, thudding, muffled beat. Dalton. Still in the car, waiting for me. Only now he had his fancy sound system on full blast. I saw him through the window, banging his head, waving his hands around to pound on invisible drums.

I grinned and stalked toward the car. I rounded to the passenger side and opened the door, freeing the music. It was louder than I'd expected, so much that I couldn't even recognize what was actually playing. I cringed, but quickly leaped into the passenger seat and slammed the car door shut. Last thing I needed was a neighbor or my parents stepping outside and catching me sneaking off with a guy. That would certainly dampen the evening, and I was so not down with damp.

Dalton didn't notice I'd come back. His eyes were closed,

and he was singing in an off-key, high-pitched voice, his head bopping up and down, his fists lunging back and forth. I rolled my eyes, then reached forward and turned down the volume until it wasn't at a decibel level that would destroy small children's eardrums.

Dalton snapped his head toward me, a dark look on his face. But it lasted only a moment—he breathed in, inhaling all of me, and his face softened.

Awesome.

"You trying to see if you can literally make your speakers explode?" I asked. "Or did you get shot in the part of your brain that processes sound?"

Dalton boomed a laugh, sounding a lot like his ass of a father. He pounded his palms against the steering wheel and jumped up and down in his seat. "It's music, man!" he said. "I love it loud. I love it pounding inside me till my heart wants to explode. Love it!" He slammed his hands so hard against the steering wheel that it knocked itself into a new position.

"Whoa there, Sparky, I get it, you like music." I pressed down on his shoulder until he stopped bouncing. "You miss your dose of Ritalin?"

He looked at me, shaking with barely contained energy. "Nah, you don't get it, Emily," he said. "It always has to be quiet at my house. I put my earbuds in when I'm lifting, but it's not the same as having it all around you. It makes me want to—" He stopped, shook his head. "This is awesome. I feel strong as hell right now. Feel this."

He unzipped his jacket, flung it off, then flexed his right bicep. It bulged like there was a boulder beneath his skin. His veins pulsed across it.

"Come on, feel it," he urged.

I shrugged. "All right." I poked the muscle with my finger. And it didn't just look like a rock—it felt like one. His skin was smooth and warm. I let my hand linger, caressing his arm, enjoying the feel of a strong boy showing off to try and impress me.

A memory of Spencer popped into my head. Short, slender, muscle-less Spencer grinning at me, his messy brown hair falling into his eyes. A pang of guilt flashed through me, and I yanked my hand away, scowling.

Dalton nodded at me, grinning wide. "Right? Right? I could punch through a steel wall right now!"

"Well, don't," I said. "Was your whole goal of getting me down here to make me feel your muscles? Because, hate to break it to you, but I'm not into you like that."

It was true, even though I despised admitting it. I was Nighttime. Boys were there to entertain me, not make me get all fluttery like Daytime whenever Spencer popped up. Still, Spencer was my *mate*. Dalton most certainly wasn't. It was supposed to just be me and Spencer, Spencer and me, and—

What was this romantic nonsense? Was boring Emily seeping into my Nighttime fabulousness? Or was it Wolftime, getting all hormonal?

Screw that.

Dalton lowered his arm, his face dark again.

"Look, your muscles are great, Dalton," I said. "But I have better things to do than sit here all night and play doctor."

"What's the plan?" Dalton said, jittering in his seat. "Where are we going? A club?"

"I was thinking we could go scope out BioZenith. Find out more about who did this to us. You know, like . . ." I waved my hand. "Intel."

Dalton tilted his head back. "Boooring!" he boomed.

I scrunched my eyebrows and looked at him side-eyed. "Uh, excuse me?"

He shook his head at me. "*Man*, that sounds boring. I don't want to go look at some empty building all night. My dad works there, I've been there. It's just cubicles."

Well. When he put it that way, it did sound pretty dull. And I did not want dull, not when I was finally *free*. I was wide awake now; energy coursed through me. I needed to do something to ramp up the adrenaline—and digging through paperwork in offices wasn't going to cut it.

Licking my lips, I nodded. "Yeah, you're right," I said, grinning now, imagining the strobes and beats of a club. The feel of all that energy and tension, all eyes on me. Only this time, there'd be no killer to worry about and ruin my night. "We should—" I began to say.

"Got it!" Dalton shouted. He was already putting the car into drive and pulling out into the street as he spoke. "I know what we're doing."

Crossing my legs, I leaned back into the leather seat. "And what's that?"

Dalton grinned dangerously at me. "Street race."

I raised an eyebrow. "Like *The Fast and the Furious* drag racing or something?"

"You got it. Scott Schwartz does 'em. I know there's one tonight. I never go, but *man* I want to. I could outdrive all their asses!"

I looked out at the dark, slick street of the quiet suburban neighborhood. It would be dangerous. Possibly deadly. And completely over the top.

It sounded perfect.

"All right, Paul Walker," I said. "Let's do it."

I rolled down the window as Dalton drove, sticking my head outside and letting the wind tousle my hair. I closed my eyes and inhaled deeply. The air after the rain was still crisp, and the cool wind was refreshing as it washed over me. I'd almost forgotten this part of being nighttime me, the way my senses were heightened, the way the world felt so vibrant that being Daytime felt numb in comparison.

Not that she'd—I'd—noticed the difference during the day, what with being so stupidly worried all the time about *everything*.

Dalton turned his music back up, not as loud this time, and I heard him slamming his palm against the steering wheel to the beat as he steered the car to wherever he was taking me. I opened an eye and peered at him to see him driving with his eyes half-closed, head banging like he was front row at a concert. I thought I'd had a lot of energy, but Nighttime Dalton seemed like he'd snorted freeze-dried Red Bull or something.

I smiled and went back to letting my head loll out the open window.

Headlights flashed through my eyelids, and I heard the grumbling of cars, the sounds of voices. The car slowed, and I looked up to find that we had turned down some road lined with empty, industrial-looking buildings with real estate signs stuck to the blank windows. Probably companies that caved with the economy so bad. I recognized the area as part of the business district in north Skopamish—the same area where BioZenith was based.

Go check it out, a distant voice whispered in my head. *You're here anyway.*

I snapped up and sat straight. Daytime Emily, talking to me? Not a chance. Right? She—I—never had before. Though on the night I kicked Gunther Elliott's ass, I distinctly remember feeling as though she and I had become one and the same, for at least a little while. But that didn't mean I wanted her around all the time.

Of course, the past few days I'd been talking to Daytime. Or at least she thought I had been. I wasn't sure anymore who said or thought what.

Check it out, Daytime's voice insisted.

"Chill out," I muttered to myself. "We're going to have some fun tonight. You need it, and you know it."

The voice, if it was ever there, didn't respond.

Good.

The car stopped, and Dalton held down a button to lower his window. He turned off the radio, then leaned out and waved over some guys led by a tall kid I didn't know. He was all broad shoulders and bodybuilder mass up top, with disproportionately skinny legs. He had a military haircut and smoked a cigarette.

"Yo, Dalton!" The guy flicked away his cigarette and slapped Dalton's hand as he came to the window.

Dalton tilted his chin up in greeting. His left leg shook anxiously.

"What up, Scott," he said.

"Just the usual, bro. Getting ready to race. You here to watch?"

Dalton laughed. "Hell no, man, I'm here to race!"

One of the guys behind bodybuilder Scott laughed. "In an old-man Lexus? Are you joking?"

Scott looked over Dalton's lap and shouted back, "It's even an automatic." It was then that the guy noticed me. I raised an eyebrow and smirked as he checked me out. "Hello there."

"Hello there back," I said. "I'm Emily."

"Well, you definitely ain't Nikki," Scott said. He grinned and shook his head at Dalton. "Man, if you're trying to hit on a new girl, do you really want to embarrass yourself by racing me?"

Dalton nodded. "I'm not the one who's gonna be embarrassed."

Scott pulled out a pack of cigarettes, slapped it against his palm, then placed one between his lips. His lighter cast his face in flickering orange as he lit the tip. Inhaling, his eyes flicked from Dalton, to me, and to the car. Then he snorted out two streams of smoke.

"Fine," he said. "You'll get the first race with me.

Nothing fancy, just side by side to the end of the road, around the roundabout, then back here."

Dalton raised his hand and slapped the hood of the car. "Easy! Give me a challenge, man!"

Taking another drag, Scott shook his head. "Trust me, I'm a challenge." He peered back at me over Dalton. "You can watch with the other girls. They're in the parking lot over there." He gestured behind him.

I rolled my eyes. "Are you serious? I'm not a sideline kind of girl. I'm riding shotgun."

"You ever been in a car going over eighty miles per hour on a residential road?" he asked me.

"Can't say that I have. But I've survived worse."

Scott smirked at me. "If you say so." He patted the side of the car and told Dalton where to go, then took off with his buddies.

Dalton inched the car forward and stopped at the arbitrary start line that Scott had indicated. We both rolled up our windows. Lining the road on either side were sports cars and muscle cars with guys and some girls on the hoods, drinking from cans and waving around cash while they laid down bets. Just as Scott had said, a group of six or so girls huddled together under a blanket in the bed of a truck, watching from a parking lot.

An engine revved as Scott's car pulled up beside ours.

It was small and sleek, straight out of the movies, with an orange paint job and white racing stripes. Scott sat focused inside, eyes straight ahead. Beside me, Dalton bounced in his seat, his shoulders going up and down and back and forth along to some manic beat only he could hear.

I gripped the sides of my seat, unable to contain my grin. Ahead of us, the road was dark and glistened wet under the streetlights. There was no one around except for the group of us kids and our cars. The road, the night, was ours to have fun with, danger be damned.

I'd let Dalton have this race. But I was definitely going to take the wheel for the rematch.

Dalton revved the engine, his right hand on the driveshaft. "Tell me about when you killed him," he said, not looking at me, just staring straight ahead and waiting for the signal to go.

An odd time for questions. "Uh, what? Why?"

"Just tell me," he said, his voice barely above a whisper. "He tried to kill me. I want to know."

I shrugged. Whatever. I'm not going to lie—I'd enjoyed beating Dr. Elliott's face in, after all he'd done to me. *To my pack*, werewolf me added distantly. Dalton deserved to know all the gritty details.

"Fine," I said, remembering the rush of rage that had come over me when I first saw the killer. "It was just me and

Dr. Elliott at first. He tried to shoot me, but I slapped the gun away. He tried to stab me, too, but I pounced on the guy and knocked him to the ground."

"Yeah," Dalton said, grinning dangerously. "I could have done that if I hadn't been drunk and if Nikki hadn't been screaming at me. Just lunge at the guy and tackle him."

I opened my mouth to continue, but a guy leaned into the street and waved a fluorescent orange flag.

And Dalton's hand flew, putting the car into drive. His foot slammed down and we burst forward, the momentum slamming me back into my seat.

It was like being in a spaceship bursting into warp speed, a roller coaster rounding the top of the track. It was *awesome*.

I whooped almost involuntarily, then laughed at myself. Out my window was Scott, still focused, neck and neck with us. The buildings and streetlamps beside us turned into unrecognizable streaks, and the engine whirred louder and louder. Scott began to pull ahead.

"Keep going!" Dalton shouted, his expression still manic. "Tell me more!"

"I punched him," I said, one hand up to grab the handhold above the door now, my shoulders taut, my back straight as I watched us burst down the slick street. "I smacked him again and again until he talked."

"Punched him till his face was all bloody and bruised, hell yeah!" Dalton yanked the wheel to the right, swerving across the street, narrowly missing Scott's bumper as the other boy pulled in front of us. "Dammit!" He turned to me, scowling, and shouted, "What next?"

I took in a shaky, exhilarated breath. "Spencer was there, but he was a wolf. And Elliott went after him while I changed." Ahead, the roundabout was growing closer, bigger. We'd be there in seconds. "We clawed his face. I bit his arm. He tried to get away, but we leaped at him."

Scott's car swerved right at the last second, entering the roundabout. It looked almost as if his car was riding only its two right wheels, and the back end threatened to fishtail, but he expertly swerved around the circle.

Dalton yanked the wheel right, spinning us in a dizzying turn. The world swirled lazily around us, almost in slow motion. When we screeched to a stop, we blocked the exit from the roundabout, facing back the way we'd come. The harsh scent of melted rubber burned my nose.

"You cut him off," Dalton finished for me. "You ripped that asshole's throat out!" He laughed wildly as we heard Scott's car scream to a stop. I looked out the window to see Scott frantically yanking his wheel to avoid ramming right into us. His car spun in a full circle and he ended up half on the sidewalk and half on the road.

Scott pulled his door open and leaped out, shouting obscenities. Dalton ignored him and pressed down on the gas, rushing us back down the road. I pressed the button to roll down my window and leaned out, waving back at the diminishing figure that was a fuming Scott.

I leaned back in, grinning. Dalton's expression matched my own, though his gaze was distant as he drove.

"That must have been incredible," Dalton said as we neared the cluster of cars at the other end of the road. "Taking out a guy like that. I wish I'd been there to just *hit* that guy. Just over and over again."

I sighed, exasperated. "Well, Dalton, I killed him for you, so no need to keep going on about it. You should grovel to Scott for forgiveness and let me race next."

He didn't seem to hear me. "I'd yank that bastard's arms behind him and put him in a chokehold and squeeze until his face turned red and was about to explode."

He drove past the angry crowd of racers, turned down a side street, kept going.

I looked back behind us. "Whoa, what's the deal? That was just the first round."

"I'd kick him in the nuts and in the ribs and stomp on his neck." Dalton was muttering now.

My stomach roiled, nauseous, as though the vehicular acrobatics were finally catching up to me. Suddenly I wasn't feeling quite so nonchalant. Everything looked gray. Suppressing a gag, I turned back to look at the road in front of us.

A dozen shadowmen were in the middle of the street, standing still in a staggered, random formation. They tilted their heads to the side, watching us barrel toward them.

Though I was still Nighttime, Daytime was suddenly there too, and the wolf as well. How, I didn't know; all I knew was that the panic from the night before—the pounding heart, the trembling limbs—was back. My head throbbed with a headachy fear as I watched those *things* standing there, waiting for us to pass by so they could grab us, poke at us, do—

"No!" I screamed. Not thinking, I grabbed the wheel from Dalton and yanked it to the right. He blinked back to attention and slammed on the brakes. The car skidded to a stop parallel to the staggered group of man-shaped shadows.

I turned away from them, hands fumbling over the passenger door as I struggled to find the lock, find the handle, the button to lower the window—some way to escape. But as I looked through my window, I saw more of them were on my side of the car too. They surrounded us, standing perfectly still, watching. I froze.

"What the hell!" Dalton roared. He grabbed me by my

arm and yanked me toward him.

All semblance of nighttime fearlessness was sapped from me. I trembled as I looked up at Dalton, his features all black and white in the scant light. Almost as if I had Wolftime vision.

"Don't you see them?" I asked.

"See what?"

"The shadowmen!" I shouted. I gestured beyond his window, to where I'd first seen them.

They were gone.

Dalton scowled. "I don't see anything."

I was shaking. This wasn't right. Dalton was talking crazy about beating up a dead guy, and there were shadowmen here, too. I shouldn't have gone out. I was Nighttime, I was Daytime, I was the wolf—somehow. But we all agreed on this right then.

"Take me home," I whispered. "Please, take me home."

"I'm not ready yet," Dalton said.

I placed a hand on his arm, gentle. Looked into his eyes. Saw him inhale my scent, sensed him calming down.

"Please," I said.

He nodded, then put his foot on the gas and continued down the street.

YOU RECOVER
FROM THE BIG NIGHT?

As soon as Dalton dropped me off, I ran to the front door, then remembered—I was supposed to be asleep.

I had no idea what was happening to me. My arms and my legs tensed with raw strength, but my brain wasn't Nighttime, it was me, normal Emily. Mostly. Partially. And my vision was that of the wolf, constantly darting, scanning the grass, the trees, the skies.

My brain told me to move to the window, quietly, while my body wanted to stomp over confidently, and my eyes kept wanting to look anywhere but where I wanted to go, so focused on making sure no one and nothing was about.

It was like all three parts of me had been pulverized in

a blender, poured into a casserole dish, and popped into the oven until underbaked.

Clenching my teeth, I struggled to pull myself together. I couldn't stand outside all night, and I couldn't try and get past my dad and stepmom, not after they had already grounded me for the first time in my life when I disappeared all night after Mikey Harris's party the week before.

Concentrating hard, I managed to get myself beneath my still-open bedroom window. No one was watching, wolf me was quite certain of that, so I leaped, flying up with the ease of a cat hopping on top of a counter. I slammed against the siding, my hands clinging to the sill, the metal edges biting into my palms and making me hiss in pain. My sneakers slipped against the damp siding as I flexed my arms and pulled myself into my room, landing silently on all fours as I brushed past my curtains.

How's that for upper-body strength? I grinned despite myself. I didn't exactly have Dalton biceps, but I could hold my own.

This was the first time daytime me was truly all there when I was this strong. It was disconcerting and thrilling, but it was hard to focus on anything clearly, not then, not in this weird everything-and-nothing state. I didn't know why, exactly, I was in this muddled form. My best guess was that my slow-to-rev transformations were going faster, and maybe this meant that I was about to become a wolf. And I couldn't become a wolf, couldn't be that out of control, couldn't risk being caught.

I peeked out my bedroom door. It was after ten and the hall was dark. My stepmom and Dawn were probably sleeping. I saw the blue glow of a computer screen lighting up the stairs at the end of the hall—my dad, downstairs in the foyer/computer room, playing his game.

Quickly, I snuck into the bathroom and downed a couple of sleeping pills. Then it was back to my room, under the covers, Ein clutched in my arms. I hadn't eaten for hours, and the pills quickly dissolved in my stomach.

And mercifully, I fell asleep.

The next morning was a blur.

I remember opening my eyes just before my alarm, my lashes crusted together, my body sore, my head bursting with a tense, painful headache. I blinked and stared blearily at the ceiling of my room, taking in shallow, shaky breaths, trying to get my bearings.

Letting myself change hadn't exactly solved all my problems. If anything, I felt worse than I had in days.

I lay there until my alarm blared its irritating screech, then rushed to get ready. As far as I could tell, aside from feeling like I had a hangover, I was back to full daytime me. The day went as normal—a quick breakfast to fill the gnawing in my gut, a ride to school from Spencer along with his mood-boosting pheromones, homeroom with Megan barely talking to me—though not for a lack of trying. I felt horrible about ditching her the way I had, but her only response to my apologies was a grunt before she darted out of the room to her first period.

Great.

After that, classes and lunch were a haze of talking people and squeaking chairs and blazing bright fluorescent lights everywhere I went. After my attempt to smooth things over with Megan, I was sucked right back into my head.

I'd thought I'd be used to all of this by now. I had adapted pretty quickly to the whole Nighttime and werewolf thing when Dr. Elliott was busy trying to kill people, and by the time he was dead, I'd thought I'd sort of managed to find an understanding of how all this worked. I'd had my origin story, and now it was time to rise up and face the various hilariously inept and over-the-top supervillains that were to become my rogues' gallery, taking them out with ease.

But the rules kept changing on me. The way I transformed was no longer strictly black and white. Before, there'd been an easy line between me and Nighttime Emily and Werewolf Emily. I hit some threshold, and *bam*, new personality.

What, then, was this new development? Some weird hybrid self? Was that the endgame, all three of us in one body, with Nighttime losing her edge because I was there to get all fearful, and just in general always seeing the world in literal shades of gray like I do when I'm a wolf? I like seeing in color. Color is awesome. So if I had to give up color to become all-powerful, that was gonna be a deal breaker.

Letting myself turn into Nighttime Emily had sent me into a tailspin. If I couldn't escape worry at night, by sleeping or transforming, when could I? If I couldn't anticipate when I'd get all simpering at the sight of a bunch of scary shadowy beings, how could I get anything accomplished?

I probably don't need to say, but I wasn't exactly super concentrated on school that day. I drifted through my classes, pretending to take notes, avoiding Spencer and Dalton and Megan, waging an endless battle in my head between racing thoughts and trying to tell my brain to *just. Shut. Up. Let me exist for a few waking hours without being consumed by the whole werewolf thing. Please.*

I gave up on that at the end of the day. Spencer had caught me between my last two periods and told me he and Dalton wanted to hunker down in the library after school and actually take the time to do some research. Which, yes, we needed to do. It was my plan, after all. I had to focus.

Gotta tell you, having superpowers turns out to be a lot of work.

Spencer leaped up and waved excitedly as I entered the library. I blushed, offered him a hand in return, and rushed through the room to the table where he had a bunch of books laid out. He held a chair out for me, gentleman-like, and I took it.

I had planned to resist, but after the awful, brain-busy day I'd had, I really, really wanted to just calm down. I scooted my chair in close to Spencer, enough so that irresistible musk washed over me. Immediately my brain slowed down, going from a race to a crawl. I closed my eyes and let it soak into me, let it flood out the worries and fears. I knew this feeling was only temporary, and that I needed to stop relying on it to handle my business. But, for just that afternoon, it would help.

"Mmm," I moaned.

"Uh, you falling asleep?" Spencer asked.

I shot straight up, my eyes snapped open. "Sorry," I said. "It's just I've been running around all day, and it's nice to sit in a quiet place."

He grinned at me. "I'm glad you enjoy my company."

If he only knew.

"Hey."

Dalton appeared then, and I felt myself stiffen. He sat down in the chair next to me, offered me a smile, and nodded at Spencer. And it was then that I remembered how he'd acted the night before. I'd been so consumed with worries about yet more bodily changes, about those damn shadowmen, that I'd let it slide.

But he'd asked me what it was like to kill a man. He'd kept going on in graphic detail about what he would have done. As though he'd have woken up the next morning, seen the dead body, and *enjoyed* it.

I looked at his face. It was chiseled but still had a hint of boyishness. There was a light brush of freckles on his cheeks, a lighthearted glint to his eyes. He was the same Dalton I'd always seen around school. The friendly jock everyone loved. It had to have just been his nighttime personality. I mean, I hadn't exactly been remorseful when I was Nighttime, either.

"You guys ready for a bunch of reading?" Spencer asked.

"Yeah, reading," Dalton said, thumbing at the cover of one of the books in front of us. "Can't wait."

I leaned down and dug through my backpack, producing the books I'd already found. While I did so, Spencer leaned back in his chair to address Dalton.

"So, man, you find her yet?"

Dalton shook his head. "Nah, but I've been sniffing, I

promise. I think I can sort of smell her, but she's not like Emily. Not as strong."

"And she's wearing some annoyingly common perfume or something," Spencer said. "I keep smelling *that*, but never her. Whoever she is, she must bathe in the stuff."

I looked between the two of them. "You guys have been looking for the other one of us?"

"Of course," Spencer said. "I was going to talk to you about it, but you seemed zoned out today."

I leaned closer to him, let his aroma waft into my nostrils. I smiled. "Sorry. I'm better now."

"You recover from the big night?" Dalton asked me.

Spencer reacted first. "Huh? Big night?"

"Uh, he means the whole weird confrontation with his dad," I answered quickly.

Dalton started to speak again, but I kicked him under the table. He clamped his lips shut.

"Oh," Spencer said, looking between the two of us. "Yeah, he was kind of harsh."

A pen tapped against the table, and all three of us looked up to find the librarian glaring at us. She was skinny and frail, her wire-frame glasses askew on her nose and her hair a white pouf. But her stare was all business.

"If you want to socialize," she said, her voice firm, "then I suggest the mall—" She stopped speaking, recognizing

Dalton. "Oh! Dalton! Sorry, dear, I didn't see it was you. It's been so lonely around here without you to help me shelve."

Dalton grinned up at her. "I missed you too, Ms. Levine. Maybe tomorrow I can come help out. That way you can get an early start on the weekend."

A blush came to Ms. Levine's cheeks, and she put her hand to her throat. "That would be lovely, Dalton, just—" Catching me giving her a strange look, the librarian cleared her throat. "Anyway, I know you are excited to be back at school, but please try to keep it down."

Dalton nodded at her, still grinning. "Of course, Ms. Levine."

The librarian left, and Spencer snorted, trying to hold in his laughter. "Dude, half the teachers here totally want to do you."

Dalton slouched over the table. "Shut up, man, no they don't."

I smiled. "Okay, how about we get to work? Maybe? Unless you guys want to keep talking about which teachers you'd do."

Neither did. We each grabbed a book.

There's a surprising amount of information on shadowmen—or, at least, the folklore of them. They're called lots of things—shadow folk, shadow beings, shadow ghosts. The paranormal-focused books say that maybe they're ghosts or demons, summoned to haunt you out of the corner of your eye, making you see someone in the periphery, freak out—and turn to find no one there.

One of these books had an artist's interpretation of a shadow being. It was an ink drawing, all intricate hashes and solid lines, indicating a figure standing in the corner of a bedroom. Doing nothing threatening. Just standing there. Waiting.

I turned from that page fast.

Then there were the scientific explanations, which I figured I should pay the most attention to. My own transformation turned out to be a science thing, not a paranormal thing. And ghosts are pretty much the definition of paranormal.

But the scientific explanations proved to be wholly inadequate. They went on about brain conditions causing you to perceive shadows in your peripheral vision as familiar shapes; about people who have sleep paralysis and are still dreaming even while partially awake, so that their subconscious summons up creepy images around them.

That last one sounded particularly terrifying, but it was easily explained as "not real." And my shadowmen were very real. I saw them out of the corner of my eye, and then they would full-on lunge at me. I mean, maybe I could reason that this was all just part of my brain playing tricks, if it wasn't for the fact that Spencer had seen them as well. Not to mention I'd touched one.

So, much like the werewolf books, these proved absolutely useless. I was back to knowing nothing. Again.

I shut the book I'd been reading and shoved it away. Beside me, Spencer had four books open, but he wasn't looking at any of them. Instead he leaned on his elbows and stared into space. Dalton read his own book, brow furrowed in concentration.

"So we sure they're not ghosts?" he asked.

"I have no idea," I muttered.

"One of my books talks about alien abduction," Spencer whispered, snapping to attention. "So that could still be it."

"I guess," I said.

He leaned close to me, concerned. "You don't seem thrilled."

"I'm not." Slouching in my chair, I crossed my arms. "On TV, it's always easy to find some book in, like, the dungeon area of a library that has all the detailed answers. Just find yourself a middle-aged British man with a head for ancient lore and, bam, problem solved. But all of these are just collections of myths. That doesn't help at all."

"Does our library?" Dalton asked.

"Huh?"

"Does it have a dungeon?"

I suppressed a laugh. "I'm pretty sure those type of libraries only exist in, like, small New England towns or something. Unless Ms. Levine has some sort of secret lair."

"Oh." He nodded knowingly. "Gotcha." He glanced up at Ms. Levine, back at her desk. She offered a smile and a wave, and he quickly turned away.

A shadow hovered over the table. I snorted in a breath and shoved myself back from the table, ready to toss back my chair and run for it, Ms. Levine be damned. If the shadowmen were here—

But darting my head to look up, I saw that this shadow was thankfully the normal type. Megan stood there with tall, brooding Patrick beside her. He of the black hair and the English accent and the mysterious stare. I remembered the awkward conversation we'd had in a convenience store when I thought he might be the werewolf that turned out to be Spencer. And watching him half-undressed through his bedroom window when I thought he was the killer instead. Turned out he was neither.

Heat rushed to my cheeks. I hoped he wouldn't remember me.

"Hey Emily," Megan said casually. "And friends."

Spencer grinned at her. "Hey!"

"Hi," I said, slamming my books shut. "What are you up to?"

She shrugged. "Patrick and I are doing some research for some homework assignment Mr. Philbrick gave us."

"Yeah," Patrick said.

I nodded slowly. "Oh. Neat."

It was at once way too casual and much too awkward. My two worlds, colliding. I wanted to recede into my hoodie until I disappeared.

Megan crossed her arms and gestured at the books with her chin. "So what are you three doing? Secret projects?"

"Just research," Dalton said. "Though I think we were supposed to talk about the party tomorrow, too. You're Megan, right?" He held out a hand.

Megan looked Dalton up and down, then held out her own hand, limp. Dalton shook it anyway.

"A party, huh?" Megan said. "How fun."

"Do you want to come?" Spencer asked.

I sat up straight. What were these two doing? Did they not understand stealth? We were supposed to be scoping out Dalton's dad's office; we weren't *really* going to be partying.

"No," I said. "Megan hates parties. Too much of a crowd for—"

"I'd love to come." Megan strung her arm through Patrick's. He looked down at her, his expression bored. "And Patrick, too. Actually, you know what, I'll do you one better: I'll get you a band."

Dalton perked up at that. "A band? Cool. Anyone I know?"

"Not yet!" Alarmingly perky, Megan jumped forward, snatched a piece of paper from one of our notebooks, produced a pen, and scribbled down a name and number. She slid it across the table to Dalton. "Give these guys a call. I'll let them know to expect it."

"Awesome." Dalton held the note up to his nose. "'Bubonic Teutonics.' Cool name. What's a 'Teutonic'?"

"Okay, well, we have to go do science class stuff," Megan said, ignoring the question and dragging Patrick away. "See you at the party."

"Hey, Megan," I said. "I'll call you later."

She didn't, but I could tell she wanted to roll her eyes. "I'll be waiting by the phone on pins and needles. Really sharp ones."

"She seems nice," Dalton said as Megan and Patrick disappeared into the stacks.

"Yeah," I said softly. "She's the best."

Dalton left shortly after the run-in with Megan. Being the guy he is, he apparently had other responsibilities after school. Plus, I was pretty sure if he stayed too long with me and Spencer, Nikki would get on his case.

Spencer and I spent another hour or so looking through

books—well, I did anyway; he mostly kept wandering off. I was about ready to give up on finding anything useful, when I looked up to find that someone else had entered the library: Mai Sato.

She sat at a table a little bit away from me, her jet-black hair in a loose, messy ponytail. She hunched over her books, holding her head up with one hand against her cheek, barely seeming to pay attention to what she was reading.

"Spencer," I hissed, turning to find him.

But he was gone. Again. Off in the stacks somewhere.

I turned back to Mai to see her closing up her books and putting them in her bag. She was about to leave. And it hit me then—I couldn't let her. For whatever reason, I couldn't smell the female werewolf, not like Spencer and Dalton could. But maybe being near her would give me that same gooey familial feeling I got with the boys.

The afternoon of shadowman research had turned out to be useless. But maybe if I could find another member of my pack, it would make all the time spent in the library worth it.

OKAY, YOU'RE NOT
STALKING ME, ARE YOU?

Hands in my pockets, I sauntered over to Mai's table as casually as I could. I did my best to look at anything *but* her, and then slid into a chair opposite her, pretending I spotted an interesting tome someone had happened to leave there. I flipped it open to see a cross section of a uterus, and my eyes went wide.

Mai side-eyed me as she continued to put her books in her bags. She was almost packed up, and then I was sure she'd leave. I darted my eyes over to my table to see if Spencer was back yet so I could get him over to smell the girl and confirm whether she was, in fact, who we were looking for.

Nope. He was still off on his blissful ADD trek somewhere.

Leaning forward onto the table, I breathed in slowly. That same heavy, flowery perfume I'd smelled the morning when Dalton first came back to school invaded my nostrils. But there was nothing else. No wolf scent that I'd come to associate with the two boys.

"Can I help you?" Mai asked, staring at me like I'd just shown up with my hair dyed the same color as hers and wearing her clothes.

Blinking, I looked up at her. "Oh. Hi, Mai. We have homeroom together."

I have no idea why that was the first thing that popped into my head to say. Internally I was smacking my forehead.

Not taking her eyes off me, she bent down slowly to pick up her bag, then set it on the table to zip fully closed.

"Yeah, I know," she said. "Did you need something?"

"Oh," I said. "Uh, I just smelled that perfume. It's pretty. You don't really seem like the perfume type, though. But it's nice."

Closing her eyes, she stopped moving for a moment, her hands hovering over the zipper to her bag. "Emily gave it to me," she said quietly. "She used to wear it. It reminds me of her." Clearing her throat, she added, "Plus, if I don't have time for a shower after PE, I can just douse myself in it."

I smiled awkwardly. I'd almost forgotten it had been

only a little more than a week since Mai's best friend had been murdered. I should have left her alone. But I had to know.

My eyes darted once more to my table. Spencer *still* wasn't there. I had to find a way to keep Mai from leaving.

"I'm so sorry about Emily," I said. "I didn't really know her, but I saw her art and stories after she . . ." I swallowed. "She seemed really talented. And like a really good person."

Mai sat down, letting her backpack droop in front of her. Her lip trembled and her eyes glistened, became watery. But she didn't cry.

"She really was," Mai finally said. Shaking her head, she looked up at the ceiling. "I don't even want to be here. I hate being here when she can't be, you know? I still expect to go to lunch and see her there, but she never is, and then I can't eat anything. Because she can't eat anything either, ever again."

I didn't know what to say. The last thing I'd wanted to do when I came over here was to dredge up Mai's memories like this.

Brushing a tear from her cheek, roughly as though mad at herself for letting it fall, Mai stood and pulled her backpack on. "Sorry, I don't mean to whine to someone I barely know. I'll let you get back to your book."

She started to walk off then. I jumped to my feet and

said, as loudly as I thought I could get away with, "Mai, wait."

Turning, she stared at me questioningly.

"Um," I said. Straightening my shoulders back, I went for it. "Look, I'm here for you if you need to talk about anything. Any . . . changes you might be going through since last week."

She blinked. "Changes?"

I nodded at her knowingly. "You know . . . *personal* changes. I've been going through it too."

Her eyes darted down to the book I'd sat in front of. And to its brightly drawn diagram of the female reproductive system splayed on the page. Her lips twitched up into a smile.

"Thanks for the offer," she said. "But I think I already know all about those changes." Shaking her head, amused despite her grief only moments earlier, she headed out of the library.

I looked around, desperate for some way to get the answers I needed. And I spotted Spencer leaning against the librarian's desk, casually trying to chat with an annoyed-looking Ms. Levine. Catching his eye, I waved frantically for him to come over.

"What is it?" he whispered as he came over to me. "Did you find anything useful about the shadowmen?"

"No," I whispered back. "Mai Sato was here. She just left."

Spencer looked between me and the exit to the library. "You want me to run after her?"

"Uh, no. I don't want to freak her out any more than I already have. Just . . . smell the air here. What do you smell?"

Placing both hands on the table, Spencer leaned forward and inhaled. "It's that perfume again," he said. "But I don't smell any wolf-girl, so— Hey, why are you reading about lady parts?"

I slammed the book shut. "You know me, always curious about the cycle of life," I said. "So that's it, then? If you don't smell the other werewolf . . ."

Spencer grinned at me and put his arm around my shoulder. His personal scent floated around me, mingling with Mai's lingering perfume.

"Maybe it just faded," he said. "Don't worry, Em Dub. If it's Mai or someone else, we'll find her."

I looked into his kind brown eyes. "Promise?" I asked.

He squeezed me closer. "I promise."

Spencer dropped me off at home. We hugged again, and I took in one last whiff of his scent to carry me through the evening. It wasn't even the musky smells so much anymore, really. I was starting to picture him idly in my thoughts, and even that was enough to give me a brief respite from the rest of my crazy-town thoughts.

I left the minivan just as Dawn pulled up in her car. She raised her eyebrows at me as we both reached the front door.

"New friend?" she asked as she pulled out a jangling bunch of keys and stuck one in the door.

Heat rushed to my cheeks. "Yeah. His name's Spencer."

Dawn couldn't help but grin. "Go, you! I'm glad to see that you haven't let last week's escapades keep you from losing that shell."

She pushed open the door, and I followed her in. "Well, what can I say, you're an inspiration."

Laughing, she dropped her bag and wrap on the dining room table. "Oh, by the way, Em, I've been meaning to ask—you keep leaving your window open. It's letting in a draft and, I'm sorry, but I'm not a girl who does cold well."

"Oh," I said, setting my own backpack by the front door. "Sorry."

She shrugged. "It's not a huge deal. I just remembered because I noticed it was open again when I pulled up."

I scrunched my forehead. "It is?" I coughed. "I mean, yeah, it is."

Thing was—I knew I hadn't left it open when I went to school.

Leaving Dawn behind, I swallowed and crept up the stairs. They creaked beneath me as I took them one at a time, slowly, eyes on my bedroom door. It was slightly ajar, and daylight seeped into the hallway.

Reaching the door, I held my breath. Poked at it so that it opened a little. Then, I kicked it all the way open and jumped into my room.

And nearly screamed at the sight of the dark figure at the edge of my bed.

"Whoa!" Dalton said, jumping to his feet, arms raised. "Don't yell. It's just me."

I smacked his chest, and he fell back down onto the bed. "What are you *doing*? Why are you in my room?" I reeled back. "Okay, you're not stalking me, are you? I told you last night, it's just pheromones."

He barked a laugh. "No. Not stalking. I just . . . I wanted to see you. Because I think you didn't get what you wanted done today."

I peered out my doorway to make sure no one noticed, then shut my door. I sat on the bed opposite Dalton—and noticed my open window.

"Did you jump in my window?" I asked, incredulous. "But it's not even night yet! Someone could have seen you!"

He shrugged. "No, I snuck in your back door. Someone left it open. I just got hot while I was waiting."

"Oh."

He turned on the bed to face me. "We should go out again tonight, Emily," he said, his voice hushed. "We were having so much fun. It was cut short. I don't want it cut short."

I sighed. "No, Dalton, we can't. Something happened to me last night that I can't explain, and there are those shadowmen out there."

"Aren't those shadows in here, too? It's not like hiding in your room is safe." He scooted close to me, his eyes wide and focused on mine. He clutched my arm with two strong, large hands. "We don't have to drag race or anything. We can do what you wanted last night. We can go to BioZenith. We can find out what you wanted to know about shadowmen that wasn't in those dumb books."

Biting my lip, I looked around my room. Saw the pile of books I hadn't yet returned still sitting on my desk. Useless tomes all about ghost folklore and sleep, nothing about what I truly wanted to know.

But I couldn't shake the unsettling feeling about being that weird hybrid . . . thing. It hadn't happened before, not that I knew of. Who knew when it would happen again? Maybe it was even caused by the shadowmen, meant to debilitate me. It was when they showed up that Nighttime disappeared.

Well, we won't let them make me disappear, will we?

"Come on, Emily," Dalton begged. "Please. I need to go out again. I want you with me. Please."

I squeezed my eyes closed. Spencer's scent had long since gone away. I couldn't deny it—I missed the strength, the confidence. And I *was* pretty annoyed by the lack of details about, well, everything.

Before I could second-guess myself, I said, "Fine. Let's do it. But tonight, we're going to BioZenith."

10

BUSTING INTO
THE ENEMY FORTRESS

I made Dalton hide in my room while I went through the motions of family time downstairs. He occupied himself with my computer, browsing forums about bodybuilding and other boring stuff. Meanwhile I ate dinner with Dad and Katherine and Dawn, forcing myself to laugh at bad jokes, making up stories about my day, swallowing homemade lasagna that was super delicious, but that my knotted stomach made hard to keep down.

Then, finally, I was able to head back upstairs under the guise of doing homework. Dalton and I sat on my bed, watching each other as the clock clicked past eight. Waiting.

And then, we shifted. Nighttime was back.

Dalton and I left my room by way of the bedroom

window, per usual. Not that I minded jumping outside, but it just wasn't nearly as thrilling as it had been at first. Front door would have been quicker.

Dalton was back to his jittery, verging-on-nuclear-explosion self, same as he'd been the night before. He hummed to himself constantly and randomly pounded his fist into his palm as we stalked down the street.

"I want to race," he announced as we reached the end of the street.

I grinned. "What's with you and races?"

"I don't know." He looked at me. "We could arm wrestle. Want to arm wrestle?"

I laughed. Running forward, I spun around and walked backward, facing him. "No, I'm good with racing. You know where we're going, right?"

He nodded rapidly. "Yeah, I've been there."

"Then try and catch up."

Before he could protest, I turned on my heel and burst down the sidewalk. I was in sneakers again, but I was getting used to the advantage it gave me over a pair of Dawn's date-night Jimmy Choos. Even if I did love those shoes.

Behind me, Dalton grunted, and before I knew it he was next to me. Chest thrust forward, veins bulging on his neck, he pumped his arms in a blur as his powerful legs thrust him forward. Our feet slapped against concrete, the sound echoing through the neighborhood.

But no matter how fast he ran, I kept stride easily.

Neither of us said a word, just continued to force ourselves to move faster, faster, so fast that we were like a pair of fighter jets whooshing through the air. My feet barely touched the ground anymore. The night's cool, wet air carried my hair back in streamers. I hollered a laugh, loving the surge of blood through my veins, the freedom from being so averagely *human* during the day.

The streets rushed by; a car honked at us as we zoomed in front of its fading headlights. Past the wooded hiking trails, past the smaller houses into the richer neighborhoods, into the industrial streets. We pounded through the dark, abandoned road where a night before a bunch of teenagers had raced their souped-up automobiles.

And then, the fenced-in compound that was BioZenith was straight ahead: a pair of boxy, white, two-story buildings protected by barbed wire.

Dalton and I were still neck and neck. But I'd been reserving an extra boost for the final stretch.

Let him win.

Daytime Emily.

I groaned. "What? Why?" I muttered between gulps of air. "Screw that, I'm faster."

Let him win, she said again. *Give him a little ego boost.*

124

He'll be easier to handle.

I arched an eyebrow. How devious, Daytime! I liked it.

I let myself falter ever so slightly as we neared BioZenith. Dalton zoomed ahead and ran into the fence hands first, followed by his body. The clang echoed through the empty parking lot beyond.

"Hell yeah!" he shouted, pumping his fists. "First!"

I slowed to a jog, came up beside him, and slapped the panting boy on the back. "Bully for you!" I said. "But we have to keep it down. We're on a mission, remember?"

He glowered at me. "I thought you were supposed to be a party girl at night."

I patted his cheek and smirked up at him. "Not tonight, sweet cheeks. The race is as much as I'm gonna give you. The shadowmen are pissing me off, and I need them gone."

I strode past him, looking through the fence at the buildings beyond the large and currently empty parking lot. They were innocuous enough: plain, two-story square buildings made of white brick, with a glass walkway connecting the two. They blended in with all the other modern-style business buildings up and down the street, with the exception, of course, of the fifteen-foot-tall fence topped with barbed wire.

Headlights glared from down the street. I grabbed Dalton by his arm and yanked him to get him to follow me, and the two of us dove behind a stone sign in front of the fence that read 304. We crouched behind the sign, and the car passed, hopefully without noticing the two suspicious-looking teenagers skulking about.

I looked back to the BioZenith buildings. They were dark save for a low blue glow from some of the upper windows. Just like the morning Spencer had taken daytime me to scope out the place, there seemed to be no one around. Despite the heavy-duty fence, the front gate was unguarded. Though it did have a pesky surveillance camera watching.

"How are we getting in?" Dalton whispered to me. His fingers tapped out a drumbeat on his knee as he looked up at the razor-sharp barbed wire.

My eyes went from the gate to the fence. It was high enough that I couldn't jump over it without landing directly in the midst of those razors. And the last thing I needed was to scar up my face.

I turned to Dalton, grinning. "I think you were wrong about this being boring," I said. "You up for some acrobatics?"

His brow furrowed. "How?"

I peeked over the sign. The coast was clear. I grabbed Dalton by the arm and led him around the fence—we'd need to take the next step out of view of the street.

"We aren't just strong at night," I said as we walked.

"We're also pretty nimble."

We rounded the corner of the fence and made our way into the shadows near the side of the building.

"Okay," I whispered. "Crouch down and face the fence. Follow my lead."

He did so. "Ready for you," he said.

I took a few steps back from him, then ran forward, jumped up, and landed on his shoulders, straddling his head. Unprepared, he almost tumbled forward and dropped me. I grabbed onto his stubbly head and held myself steady.

"What the hell?" he said. "I thought you were gonna use me like a jump-off point."

"No, we're going full cheerleader," I said. "Stand up. And you'd better not drop me."

Dalton wrapped his arms around my legs and his chest, then easily rose to stand at his full height. I held on to his head and looked up, judging the distance between me and the row of curled wire.

"All right," I said. "We're going to put your giant guns to work. I want you to grab me by the underside of my feet, then when I say go, shove me upward. Got it?"

"Yes, ma'am!"

I raised my arms and leaned forward in a sort of crouched position, carefully keeping my balance while Dalton took hold of my feet and began to lift me up. His biceps and shoulders tensed, tightening beneath his shirt.

"Ready, on three," I said.

"Three!" Dalton shouted. And he threw me upward.

The sudden shove off startled me, but I reacted instinctively. Pushing off with my feet right before he let go of my sneakers, I flew up in the air. I pulled my knees up to my chest as I passed over the barbed wire—and then braced myself to land neatly, quietly, on the asphalt on the other side.

I was in.

"So," Dalton said behind me. "How do I get in?"

Snap. I hadn't thought that far ahead. Not that I was going to admit that to Dalton.

"Here, follow me," I said.

I ran along the fence, Dalton on the other side, my finger grazing the metal wire and looking for a weakness. We reached the back of the fence, but as far as I could see: nothing.

"Hey," Dalton grunted. "Wait. Let me try something."

I stood back and crossed my arms. In the pale glow from a nearby floodlight, Dalton went up to the fence, gripped it with both hands, and began to pull it apart. His biceps threatened to burst from his shirt, and his neck was so tight I was certain that his head might pop off. Clenching his teeth, he yanked as hard as he could—and the wire fencing snapped apart in a line down the middle, like someone unzipping a zipper.

Dalton ducked through, smirking at me. "Told you I was strong." He flexed forward in a parody of a bodybuilder—at least, I hoped it was a parody. I patted him on his stubbly head.

"Good boy. Now let's keep moving."

We stalked up to the back of the building, then began to follow it, searching for some sort of rear access door. I didn't want to bust a window and set off an alarm, or kick open a door and do the same. I thought back to the movies I always watched as Daytime, and they told me: the roof.

"Look for a way to the roof," I whispered to Dalton.

He nodded, then pointed. "There," he said. "There's an access ladder."

I followed his finger and made it out in the shadows, just above us. This one was easy: It was no higher than the sill of my bedroom window, and I jumped into that all the time. I leaped up, gripped the bottom rung, then dug the soles of my sneakers into the craggy brick wall to climb up. Once I was high enough up, Dalton did the same.

I hefted myself up and onto the roof, then settled into a crouch to scan the area. It was straight out of any action-movie roof you've seen, with boxy metal structures and vents for the air-conditioning and circulation system.

I crouch-walked forward, the gravelly rooftop crunching beneath my sneakers, and peered over the edge of one of the vents.

In the center of the roof was an access door. It was sturdier-looking than I'd expected—no rusted hinges or easily busted chains here. A fluorescent light was attached to the wall above the door, lighting it up, and just as with the front gates, a security camera kept a watchful eye. Next to the door handle was an access panel, what looked to be a glass screen embedded in a steel frame. A blue light blinked above it.

Dalton crouched beside me, bouncing from foot to foot. "This is awesome," he whispered. "Busting into the enemy fortress."

"Not so boring, after all," I said. "Looks like the door to get in is pretty heavily protected."

Dalton snorted. "I can bust that camera off and smash that panel in. Who's gonna stop us?"

I tilted my head, considered. It was as good a plan as I had.

The door beeped, the sound echoing across the roof. I held up a finger, hushing Dalton. The door squealed and creaked as someone shoved it open from the inside.

A man appeared from the dark depths behind the door. He was dressed in a navy blue uniform that was halfway between police issue and military standard. A bulletproof vest covered his chest, and a rifle hung from his shoulder.

An identically dressed, similarly built man followed him out. They nodded to each other, and one placed his palm on the panel. The light blinked green, the panel beeped once more, and the door slammed shut. The two men—guards, apparently—began to walk around the perimeter of the roof.

"Armed guards at an innocuous bioengineering firm in the middle of Skopamish," I whispered. "Yeah, nothing secret being kept here."

"My father is full of crap," Dalton growled.

"Apparently."

Dalton didn't seem to hear me, slowly shaking his head back and forth. "I say we take them down, you go left and I go right. We knock 'em out and drag them to the door and use their hand to get us in."

I watched the man who'd gone to my left. He looked out over the parking lot, his shoulder slouched, his expression bored.

I grinned at Dalton. "Sounds like a plan. Let's go."

He nodded, then crawled on all fours to our right, toward the back end of the building where the other guy was wandering. I snuck to the left, crouched behind the convenient air vents, carefully taking each step so that I made no noise. I breathed in calmly, evenly, focused on my prey.

Prey? Ha. I could sense her, then, in the back of my head, speaking to me—Werewolf Emily. But her thoughts didn't speak to me in words, like Daytime had the night before. Werewolf's thoughts were flashes of images of her—me—skulking through underbrush. They were memories of smells, to differentiate between the scent of fear and the scent of wariness. They were ingrained memories of how to position myself depending on which way the wind was blowing.

They were also incredibly useful.

Sick.

I made it to the last vent duct between me and the guard. He hadn't moved from his spot, though now he was looking up at the stars. He wasn't a big guy, but his vest, his gear, made him appear bulky. My ears picked up the sound of his breathing, slow and steady, with a slight whistle every now and again through one of his nostrils.

He sensed nothing.

I placed the tips of my fingers on the ground, putting myself in a position like an Olympic runner at the start of a track. I tensed, about to race forward.

And behind me, Dalton roared. The other guard shouted in surprise. There was a clatter as his gun fell to the roof.

Then a thud as Dalton tackled him to the ground.

My guard jerked to attention, fumbled for his gun. He spun around and saw the commotion. "Holy hell, what the—"

He raised his rifle and began to hoof it toward his coworker.

So much for stealth.

I shoved myself off and raced forward, a dashing shadow. My guard saw me a split second before I was in front of him, but it was too late for him to react. I leaped up, grabbing his arms and shoving the gun to face the night sky. He struggled to fire, but his finger slipped off the trigger. And I was too strong for him to wrench the gun free.

Behind me I heard sick, wet thuds as fists hit flesh. I ignored it, focused on my guy. His eyes were wide, his breathing rapid. Hot breath washed over me. He looked like a scared child.

With a shout, I yanked his arms to the side. The gun fell from his hands and landed at our feet. Not wasting a moment, I placed a hand on his shoulder and propelled myself so that I was spinning around him, piggybacking him with my legs around his chest, my right arm grasping him around his neck. I tensed my arm against his throat, squeezing as hard as I could, cutting off his air. His gloved fingers clawed uselessly at the sleeve of my turtleneck as he stumbled back and forth, whipping and jerking his body to try and fling me off.

"Don't worry," I whispered in his ear. "Just go to sleep for a bit. That's a good boy."

After a few moments of this, he fell to his knees, his jerks becoming slow and sluggish. Finally, he went slack in my arms, and I let go of his throat, plopped my feet firm on the ground, and grabbed his shoulders to guide him to lie gently on his back. I crouched next to his prone form and held my hand over his lips and nose. Hot air seeped out, and he sucked cool air in. He was still alive.

I felt exhilarated. Of course I'd known I could take down a man solo; I'd done it before. But this was all so stealthy and hard-core. All those years watching action movies had paid off.

"Thanks, Daytime," I muttered as I stood back up.

And realized that the fleshy thuds of fists against skin were still echoing across the rooftop. I snapped to attention and saw Dalton straddling his guard's chest. He raised a fist and pounded down against the man's face. Then hefted his arm back to do it again.

Blood glistened from his knuckles. His eyes were wide and laser focused. His smile was unfaltering, tight-jawed, crazed.

I ran across the roof, pumping my arms and racing as

fast as I could. I leaped over a duct and skidded to a stop as I neared Dalton and his fallen guard.

"What are you doing?" I hissed. "He's down!"

The guard's face was unrecognizable. His cheeks and eyes were swelling, turning purple. Blood leaked from cuts on his forehead and his lips, seeped from a nose that looked as though it had been caved in. The man was clearly unconscious, his breaths strained and ragged.

Dalton ignored me and raised his fist back to smash the man's face in even more. I jumped forward and grabbed his arm, strength fighting strength as he attempted to slam down. "Stop!" I shouted.

"Get off!" Dalton's head snapped to the side, and he snarled up at me.

His features were moving, shifting.

The irises of his eyes faded from hazel to an unearthly yellow. His teeth were sharpening to points. His nose, his cheeks, were elongating, muscle and bone moving beneath flesh with sickening crunches and slurps. Flesh that was now sprouting a coat of brown-and-black fur.

I'd never seen someone else change into a werewolf before. It was impossible to look away from. The reality of it was so absurd that it felt instinctively like I should be telling myself, "Oh, Emily, it's just special effects. Yay, movie magic!" But this was real. Cells multiplying and mutating, transforming a person into a monster right in front of me.

My arm went slack, and Dalton took the opportunity to yank free from me. He leaped up to stand over the guard, his hands grasping at his shifting cheeks with fingers that were stretching longer and longer. His fingernails blackened like glass held over a flame as they became sharp, shredding claws.

He growled, and before I could make a move, he darted past me and raced to the back edge of the roof. He was at its edge for only a moment before he disappeared down the side of the building.

Great. He'd not only gone all madman, but now he was going to be on his own as a wolf, doing who knows what.

I spun to face the roof. I could see my guard stirring back awake. He'd find Dalton's guard, probably call an ambulance and the police.

Exploring BioZenith was out for the night, then. Instead, I turned and ran to the edge of the roof myself. I saw Dalton disappearing into the woods beyond the fence behind the BioZenith facility.

Looked like I had a wolf to catch.

The Vesper Company
"Envisioning the brightest stars, to lead our way."
- Internal Document, Do Not Reproduce -

Details of Video Footage Recorded Oct. 31, 2010,
Part 3

21:03:44 PST—Control Room D1

Aux. footage picks up after a blackout of 1 minute
and 22 seconds. Seven of the guards are down,
confirmed to have been found unconscious from cutoff
air supply and various head traumas.

Vesper 1(B) darts around one of the junior officers.
She kicks the man in the back of the knee and
forces him down. Then she picks up one of the fallen
men's assault rifles by the barrel and swings it
like a club, colliding with the back of the officer's
head. He falls slack.

A note: Perhaps we should have protocol in place
where the guards have ready access to tranquilizing
ammunition in case they are ambushed before reaching
our armory, as happened here.

While Vesper 1(B) takes down one guard, Vesper 2.1(A) lifts her fists and with them raises up another officer. She flings him across the room via telekinesis, where he smacks against a wall before tumbling to land slack atop another, similarly tossed guard.

From my count, only nine guards remained in the room. The tenth disappeared sometime during the camera blackout, which also affected the camera in Hallway 20, Sector D. We are investigating other footage to discover the identity of the man who ran. I recommend the coward be handled harshly. **Recommendation noted, but as before: facts only, please. —MH**

Their work done, the two Deviants run to look at the various security feeds. Vesper 2.1(A) is visibly frustrated.

VESPER 2.1(A): I don't see him on any of these. He's not here.
VESPER 1(B): I know there's at least one more of us being kept here. Wait, look.

Vesper 1(B) points to a screen showing a feed of Detention Cell 7, Sublevel Sector D, the holding cell for Branch B's Vesper 4. The image does not show her, but the walls of the room are clearly visible. Printer paper has been taped in neat rows and columns all over the wall, on which someone— presumably Vesper 4—has drawn a window with flowered

curtains, a door, potted plants, a bookshelf, and a
desk, all in crayon. The figure of someone—again,
presumably Vesper 4—appears briefly in frame from
Vesper 1(B) and Vesper 2.1(A)'s respective points of
view.

VESPER 1(B): Found her.

Part 3 of Relevant Video Footage Concluded

ALPHA

I leaped down from the roof, then shoved through the hole in the fence. Ahead of me Dalton wove through the trees, a shadow in front of shadows, his body mutating and shifting. As he ran, he tore off his clothes. I bounded past his T-shirt and jeans, clawed to shreds and hanging like garland from the low branches of the evergreen trees.

He was almost fully wolf-boy, and he went down on all fours, using his long arms to propel himself forward faster than I was able to run even as Nighttime.

"Come on," I muttered as I ducked beneath branches and leaped over fallen logs. "Change. Change!"

But the werewolf refused to come. I could feel her in my brain still. She was shooting messages to me constantly—*duck, move to the side, leap, run, run, run.* The woods were a blur around me, and I dodged trees at hyper-fast speed. I felt like I was in the speeder chase scene from *Return of the Jedi.*

Oh, hi, Daytime, I thought when the reference popped into my head. *Welcome to the party.*

Dalton had disappeared completely. But I could smell him, the familiar werewolf musk mingling with the oh-so-rancid *boy* smell that had permeated his nasty-ass room. I focused on the scent, the musk, and it was almost as if I could visualize a vapor trail snaking through the woods. It wasn't exactly ideal, but it would have to do. I followed the trail, sensing I was heading south, back toward the residential neighborhoods where I lived and played as daytime me.

I burst through a patch of hovering pheromones and put my foot out to stop myself. Dirt kicked up from my sneakers.

Dalton had stopped here, only for a moment, long enough for his scent to billow. I sniffed, spun around, and found his trail again. For some reason, he'd taken a sharp left turn to head east. He wasn't going home. He was going somewhere else.

Of course he was.

"What are you up to, crazy boy?" I muttered. I sighed, exasperated by his impulsiveness, then followed him.

And then, as I shoved between a pair of trees, I reached a street.

I halted and crouched just at the tree line. I wasn't familiar with the area, but I knew it had to be within the Skopamish city limits. It seemed more rural, with houses spaced farther apart and separated by trees. I looked left and right, and saw a street sign: East Knowe.

I scanned the house in front of me. It was a single-level ranch-style home, like one you'd see in California on, y'know, a ranch. Dalton's trail swirled over the road and curled behind the house. Either he'd run to the woods behind it, or this was where he'd been headed.

With a look both ways to make sure no cars were coming, I dashed across the road and crouched at the side of the house. No lights were on, and there wasn't a car in the driveway. I made my way toward the back of the house— and heard the sound of Dalton, sniffing and scratching at a window, his nails screeching on the glass.

I rounded the back of the house and saw him, standing full height and pawing with one hand at a bedroom window through which faint yellow light glowed. He was bigger than Spencer or I had been when we'd transformed, which I suppose was because he was bigger than us as a human. I scowled. How annoying. The guy was okay by day but was becoming more of an oaf by the second at night. If he wanted to be part of my entourage, he'd have to learn to frickin' chill.

It was the first time I'd really gotten a look at one of us as wolf people—Spencer and I had been so busy fighting Dr. Elliott that I hadn't really taken the time. We looked straight out of *An American Werewolf in London*, standing like tall humans with elongated heels like a dog. Dalton's chest was broad, his stomach flat and tight with muscles. His long arms were basically human, except for the claws at the ends of his fingers.

And of course there was the tail jutting from the base of his back. The long snout and pointed ears of a wolf. The sleek brown-and-black fur that covered him head to foot.

As I stood there, something shifted inside me, same as the night before. I was still Nighttime, in that I had her strength. But my vision went wolf gray. And Daytime's brain reemerged, mingling with the other two as much as it could.

In that state, the weird transitional, hybrid form that was all *and* nothing, I looked at Dalton, at what he'd become— what *I'd* become.

I gasped involuntarily, emotion flooding my chest.

He was magnificent.

I knew if I was just Daytime, if I was still me before any of this had happened, I'd find the image of a wolf/human hybrid monstrous and terrifying. But something inside my brain clicked and told me, *This is you. These are your fellows. Find them. Gather them.* And I couldn't help but love my pack, what we were, the incredible beings only a handful of us could become.

Now I wonder, as I always do, if this emotion, this elation, was programmed into me. Hard-coded right into my personal circuitry. But in that moment, the connection between all of us, the reality of our unique selves finally unleashed . . .

It was beautiful.

Fully hybrid—Daytime in the brain, Nighttime in the body, wolf in vision and instincts, but with all three of us mingling just beneath the surface—I approached Dalton. I laid a gentle hand on the small of his back, feeling his smooth fur beneath my fingers. His head snapped to look down at me and his wolfish lips pulled back in a snarl, revealing his sharp teeth. I smiled up at him, and his expression calmed. He nodded at me, then looked back through the window. He scratched again, then once more. His nails left trails down the glass.

I followed his gaze, and started as I saw what was inside.

The room itself was neat, the walls painted yellow. There were potted plants in the corner. But of course Dalton was not taking in the decor. His eyes, and mine, were on the werewolf lying on a bed directly opposite the window.

"It's her," I whispered. "We found her."

Dalton whined deep in his throat, confirming: He'd been sidetracked by the scent of the female werewolf.

She lay on her back, her legs awkwardly out straight and her arms behind her head. I was confused as to how she could possibly stand to be in such a position as a wolf, with her tail crushed beneath her body, but then I saw the chains. Before she'd turned, the girl must have locked herself down, because chains circled her wrists and ankles, connecting her to the posts of her bed. She squirmed and thrashed, her jaw snapping open and closed as she yelped in frustration.

She had been all alone the past week and a half, I'd realized. Changing just like me and Spencer, but without the luck to meet any of us and find support for what was happening to her. I didn't know what to do, no part of me did, and I stood there gaping, silent.

Until I saw the shadowman.

It was by the girl's bedroom door, hovering in a corner, watching her thrash. Its body shifted, rotated, so that it was looking directly at me and Dalton.

My pulse began to race. The shadowman was scary enough to daytime me, and simply annoying to Nighttime, but the werewolf part of me was frightened on a deeper, primal level. I couldn't contain its fear. Trembling, I backed away.

Dalton howled. He scratched with both hands on the glass now, scrabbling like a dog begging to be let in. A growl burst from deep within his throat, and he bared his teeth. Like on the roof of BioZenith when he'd been human, his now yellow eyes were wide and manic.

"We have to go, Dalton," I said to him. "The shadowman won't hurt her. You can't do anything to it. Let's go!"

Wolf-Dalton ignored me. And I realized: His eyes weren't on the shadowman, if he'd even noticed the creature at all. They were focused on the girl wolf tied helpless to her bed. He howled again, a frustrated shout into the night sky. Then he lowered his head and head-butted the window with his forehead. Glass crunched and cracks snaked over the window.

I deeply did not like where this was going. I shoved down the wolf brain and its fear and jumped forward. I grabbed Dalton around his bicep and yanked back with Nighttime's strength. He spun to face me, snapping his teeth. He lashed out with his other arm, and I leaped back, his sharp claws narrowly missing my chest.

"Are you serious?" I barked.

He tried to turn away from me and resume busting the glass of the girl werewolf's window, to get in there and do things I couldn't imagine. I lunged forward and shoved Dalton square in his muscled, fur-covered chest, sending him reeling back a few steps.

"You are not doing this," I commanded. "You're still in there, Dalton. You can't pretend you're not. Take control."

His claws clenched and his eyes narrowed on me. He leaned forward and opened his jaws, letting loose a roar that echoed through the trees. Spittle flew from his mouth, hitting my face, making me flinch.

And he leaped at me.

He landed on top of me, his claws clutching my shoulders, his body slamming into mine. I fell to the grass on my back, the wind knocked out of me. Dalton stood over me on all fours, his snout inches from my face, growling.

I expected him to calm down smelling my scent, since he went all crazy over my pheromones during the day. But he didn't. In fact, it was almost the opposite—it seemed like being near me made him angry. His eyes were narrowed, boring into my own, commanding me to stand down.

Commanding *me*?

Yeah, *no*.

I don't know if I made it happen, or if the transformation to werewolf happened on some timetable I couldn't predict. But my moments of being the muddled three-in-one Emily were done for the night. Daytime Emily and Nighttime Emily both faded into the back of my conscious mind. The wolf took control. And as Dalton hovered over me, eclipsing all I could see, I began to shift.

It happened quickly, painlessly. My body was used to this by now, these abnormal, impossible changes to the very structure of my skeleton, my musculature, my brain. Whoever had designed us to be these wolves had the good sense to dull whatever pain there might be, so that while the shifting flesh, the sprouting of fur, the twisting of bones could all be felt, the process didn't hurt.

In the span of several seconds, my torso contorted, tightened beneath the turtleneck. My nose and mouth merged together, splitting apart and lengthening into a snout. My teeth sharpened to points, my tongue grew fatter, longer. My ears climbed up the sides of my flattening skull, and my limbs lengthened. Claws appeared on my hands, my feet. My shoes were ruined. But the sweatpants and turtleneck stretched with the changes of my body.

And I was the wolf. A wolf being held down by another of my kind. One that was inferior. One that should not have dared to try and defy me.

I snarled right back at Dalton, not tearing my eyes away from his. I had beaten his dad in a staring contest. I would do the same with him.

But he didn't look away. He didn't move. In fact,

he lowered himself so that the space between us was minuscule. His ears were flat back against his head. His eyes challenged me.

Challenge accepted.

With a snarl, I curled my legs up beneath Dalton's stomach. I shot my clawed feet up, jackhammering into his gut. He flew off me, snorting for air. One of my claws had punctured his hide. Blood dripped from the wound.

I didn't wait for him to recover. I kicked up and arched my back, jumping to stand at my full height. As I did, my tail slipped through the hole cut in the back of my pants, helping me maintain my balance.

I lowered my head and barreled forward, like a linebacker. My shoulder met his chest, and I shoved forward with such force that he stumbled back, deeper into the girl werewolf's backyard. Dalton tripped over his feet, smashed to the ground on his back.

Jumping, I landed hard on his chest. I straddled him and shot my hands out to grab his wrists and hold his arms down on the lawn. Momentarily, memories of Nighttime in the same position with Dr. Elliott flooded my brain. But werewolf me brushed those memories aside. She out of all of us was not concerned with the silly dead man.

It was my turn to snarl down at Dalton. I leaned over

him, snout to snout, once more looking into his eyes. He struggled to escape, but even though he was the larger werewolf, I was the stronger of the two. I nipped at his nose, again and again, and he yowled each time in frustration. Until, finally, he got the hint and fell silent. Glaring up at me still, but silent, resigned.

He knew as well as I did that he was not in charge here. Because I was his alpha.

Alpha.

Most kids who learn about animals in elementary school know about the alpha of the pack. The leader. I always thought wolf alphas could only be male.

I also used to think werewolves and shadowy ghostly figures weren't real.

Apparently, the rules of genetically engineered werewolves were different from the rules for real wolves. I didn't know what made me the alpha. I didn't care. All I knew was that, in that moment of full-on werewolfness, I was in charge. I was the leader.

And Dalton, so out of control at night and as a wolf, realized it too.

His yellow eyes softened. He stopped thrashing, and his limbs went slack. His growls and yelps turned into plaintive, apologetic whines.

I let him go and rose to my full height. I watched him

warily as he rose as well. His tail was low, almost tucked between his legs.

I flicked a claw toward the window he'd smashed, then shook my head, growling. *No.* Dalton lowered his head and made no move to resume his relentless assault against the glass.

I looked back toward the window myself. From what I could see, the girl werewolf no longer thrashed. She lay still, her chest rising and falling so slowly that it seemed as if she'd fallen asleep. From the distance and angle I was at, I could not see the shadowman.

And though men with guns and crazed boy werewolves did not frighten me, those shadows did. I had no desire to get closer to see if the creature was still in the room.

I turned back to Dalton and gestured toward the woods. We got down on all fours, our claws digging into the earth. And I led us home.

12

WHY CAN'T YOU JUST TELL ME?

I woke the next morning slowly, and well before my alarm rang. Somehow I was lying upside down on my bed, with my feet on my pillows and my head dangling over the foot of the bed. Through bleary, blurry eyes, I saw my rows of DVDs, my TV, my bookshelf. Misty, gray daylight spilled into my room.

Yawning, I rolled over and stretched my arms. I scrambled across my bedspread to my end table and put on my glasses. My alarm clock came into focus: a little after seven a.m. I had an hour before I had to head to school.

I fluffed my pillows, then leaned back against them and looked up at the ceiling. Okay. Last night. What all had happened last night?

And it came back to me, in flashes. The race to BioZenith. Fighting the guards on the roof. Dalton punching the man until his face was destroyed. Dalton turning into a wolf, then me chasing him. Me going all hybrid again. The girl werewolf chained to her bed. The shadowman watching her. Me dominating Dalton. Because I was his alpha.

Alpha.

Okay, so all of that was a lot to take in first thing in the morning, fresh off fading dreams of a world where I *wasn't* some sort of paranormal monster. I latched on to the one that was easiest to process: the realization that, apparently, I was the leader.

I'd never thought of myself as a leader, ever. When it was just me and Megan hanging out all those years, I mostly just let her make decisions for the both of us. It was easier that way. Leading was lots and lots and lots of pressure, and pressure was what I did not want.

Or thought I didn't want. Because as I lay there, staring at the stubbly patterns on my bedroom ceiling, I actually liked the idea. Here I was, at the moment the only girl surrounded by two boy werewolves, and *I* was in charge. They could be bigger, they could be meaner, but at the end of the day they'd have to listen to *me*.

And I realized, ever since I first met Spencer as a wolf, we'd been in that sort of pattern. I comforted and protected him when he was hurt. He and Dalton both looked to my lead when dealing with research, when deciding how to handle all this craziness. The past few nights Dalton had tried to lead me, but I'd made him go to BioZenith. I'd towered over him when he started to get out of control.

This new development maybe should have freaked me out. But I liked it. It made me feel, for the first time in days, like I had some semblance of control. Even the strange, mingling hybrid version of myself—Nighttime, Daytime, and werewolf all aware at once—didn't feel so horribly strange. I was guessing it was some new transitional state, maybe, between human and wolf. All I knew was, when I first saw Dalton as a fully transformed wolf, being all three parts of me at once felt *right*. The emotion of Daytime. The strength of Nighttime. The instincts of the wolf.

Though I still wasn't down with the no-color thing.

This was all programming. Right? I wasn't a leader. I'd never been one.

But I hated that idea. That I was only strong because someone made me that way. So screw it—for that morning, I chose to believe I was the alpha because I *made* myself the alpha.

The thought kept me on a high that stayed with me through breakfast with the family, where I actually ate and chatted without my brain seeing strawberry preserves and automatically leaping to thoughts of dead Dr. Elliott.

The high didn't last for long, though, because when I went outside to meet Spencer, he wasn't alone.

He was parked at my curb, leaning against the passenger door. And in front of his car was Megan's white, rusty hatchback. She too leaned against her vehicle, arms crossed, eyes on me as I shut the front door.

I started to walk slowly across my lawn, wanting to delay the inevitable awkwardness as long as possible.

That is no way for an alpha to react, girl.

Of course not. I sucked it up, held my chin high, and strode to face my two friends.

"Hey, guys," I said as I drew close.

"Hey, Em Dub," Spencer said. He spread his arms for a hug, but I hung back. Dejected, he lowered his arms.

Megan sauntered over to stand next to us. "I haven't been able to get ahold of you for a few days," she said, glaring. "I figured just showing up would help."

I swallowed. "Yeah. Sorry. You know what, I'm glad you did. I've been so caught up in stuff that I keep forgetting to call."

"Mm-hmm."

Smiling at her, I pulled Spencer aside. Whispering, I said, "Sorry about the awkwardness."

He shrugged. "It's cool."

"I need a favor. Can you go to East Knowe? That's where the girl werewolf lives. Maybe you can find her."

"How do you know she's there?" he asked.

Behind us, Megan cleared her throat.

I glanced back at her, then back to Spencer. "I'll tell you later. Just let me know what you find."

We separated, and Spencer climbed into the minivan. As he pulled away, I said to Megan, "We're all good. Let's head out!"

She didn't say anything, just went to the driver's side of her car. I assumed that was as much of an invitation as I was going to get.

The door to Megan's car groaned in protest as I pulled with both arms on the handle. It slammed shut loudly, and I cringed. Only a few days in Spencer's and Dalton's respective cars and I'd already forgotten how temperamental Megan's was.

Megan got in on her side of the car and turned on the ignition. "Careful with the door."

"Sorry," I said as I buckled my seat belt. "But I don't think Little Rusty was hurt any."

She rolled her eyes. "Please don't call my car that. Not everyone can get a fancy car from their parents for their birthday or whatever."

"Actually, I think Spencer just drives his mom's . . ." I

trailed off as she gave me a look. "Yeah, all right. The Little Rusty name is now retired."

We pulled out onto the street and headed toward school in silence. The car grumbled and shuddered beneath me, and the smell of rusty carpet and cracked leather overwhelmed my nose. I cranked open a window and let a breeze rush in.

Finally, Megan said, "So, when are you going to tell me what's going on with you?"

"Hm?"

She tucked her long hair behind an ear and looked into her rearview mirror, then cast me a glance. "Look, I thought for a few days it was just that you had a thing with Spencer but didn't want to admit it to me or whatever." She cranked the wheel hard to turn down a side street. Little Rusty didn't exactly handle turns like a dream. "But now you're hanging out with Dalton McKinney of all people, too. A side of beef with the intellect to match. I mean, I heard you even went over to hang out at his house, and you never even spoke to him before a week ago."

"Oh," I said. My mind fumbled for a lie, and I felt a twinge of guilt. Was I really about to lie to Megan?

Why not? I had to lie to everyone who wasn't Spencer and Dalton, didn't I? My dad? The police? How do you tell the people in your life you've become something out of a horror movie?

Megan waited for me to continue, but when I didn't, she said, "Monday morning you promised me that you would tell me what you were up to. You also said that you never wanted us to drift apart and that you weren't leaving me for new friends." She stared straight ahead, her expression steely. "But for the whole week you've been blowing me off. You don't want to drive to school with me anymore. You ignore my phone calls. In the library yesterday, you obviously didn't want me to be invited to Dalton's stupid party tonight. Did I do something?"

"No," I said.

"Did I make you mad?" Her eyes glistened with impending tears, but she brushed them away, defiant. She never wanted to cry in front of anyone. "Did you decide I'm not cool enough for you? Was the whole leaving-my-car-in-Seattle thing some prank they had you pull to join their bitchy little group?"

"No!" I shouted.

Megan slammed on the brakes, and we both jerked forward. She'd gotten so worked up she'd almost run a stop sign. A car that had the right of way on the cross street also jerked to a stop momentarily, then honked at us as they drove away.

We sat at the stop sign, the only car around, the engine gurgling and sputtering as it waited to move.

"What then?" Megan asked softly.

I took in a long, deep breath. I was trembling, and I could feel myself start to tear up. I swallowed, trying to keep the emotion from bursting over.

"I . . . I can't tell you," I said.

Megan slammed her palm against the dashboard, and I jumped. She whipped her head to face me. "Why? Why can't you just tell me? What is such a big frickin' deal that you can't tell *me*?"

It would have been so easy to just say the words. *I'm a werewolf.* But I knew she'd think I was just trying to be a smart-ass, making fun of her when she was clearly emotional.

And I couldn't tell her, could I? Not yet. Not when I didn't have all the answers as to why I was the way I was, why someone wanted to kill me, why shadows followed me around at night. She'd try to help me, of course she would. Megan was many things, above all loyal. She was the one who'd forced me to see a nurse when all this had started, of course, had insisted on watching over me.

But she couldn't help. This new world I was involved in had guns and fangs. If she got hurt . . .

I swallowed again and ran a hand through my hair. "All I can say is that I can't tell you yet. I need to wait just a little bit longer."

Megan snorted, pushed down on the gas pedal, and drove us forward.

"But soon," I said, placing a hand on her arm. "I just need to figure some things out and then I'll tell you absolutely everything."

She didn't answer. I pulled my hand back and looked down into my lap.

We drove the last few minutes in silence. She pulled into the auxiliary parking lot at school, spinning into a spot so fast that she sent a sheet of dirt and gravel flying into the air, then she unbuckled her seat belt and pulled her keys from the ignition at the same time, grabbed her backpack, and jumped out her door.

She placed a hand on the roof and leaned into the car through the open door. "See you at the party," she said.

Then she slammed the door and stormed off toward the school.

I sat on one of the stone benches on the walkway leading to the front entrance of the school, waiting for Spencer to meet me. Kids walked past, laughing and chatting and bum-rushing one another. No one paid any attention to me. For the moment, at least, I was back to being invisible Emily. After the confrontation with Megan in her car, I'd suddenly felt like all the progress I thought I'd made in coming out of my shell was nothing but the world's biggest sham.

Someone plopped down to sit next to me. I didn't even have to look to see who it was, the smell was pretty familiar by now: Dalton.

He leaned into me and bumped me with his shoulder, offering me a smile. "Hey, Emily," he said.

I met his eyes but didn't return the smile. "Hey," I said. "Uh, where's Nikki?"

He laughed. "Don't worry, they won't attack you this morning. Their coach wanted them to practice. Before classes. The cheerleaders, I mean."

"Oh. Well, that's good."

Peering around conspiratorially, Dalton leaned in close—way too close—and whispered into my ear. His words came rapid-fire. "Emily, I'm so sorry about last night," he said. "I don't know what— I went nuts, man, and it felt good last night, but I woke up this morning, and all I could see was that man's face, all hamburger and blood, and the way I jumped on you, and I felt sick, I felt like the world's biggest asshole." He raised a fist and pounded it against the uninjured side of his head as he leaned back from me and shouted, "Asshole!"

Some kids walking by stopped to stare at Dalton's outburst, then laughed and walked away.

I placed a hand on his shoulder. "Shh, it's okay," I said.

"I think that guard will be okay. And you did something really good, Dalton. You found the girl werewolf."

He shook his head back and forth. "That's good, I guess," he muttered. "I can't believe the way I—I did such bad things."

"Maybe it's . . . normal? For people like us, I mean."

Our eyes met. "Did you go that crazy?" he asked me. "When you first started changing?"

I thought back to my first nights as Nighttime Emily. All the wild, uninhibited things I'd done. I had learned to get it under control, more or less.

But I'd never gone as far as I'd seen Dalton go. If I hadn't been there to stop him from pounding that man's face in . . .

"I did get a little wild, yeah," I said. "You remember me at Mikey Harris's party, right? I mean, I don't go crazy in the same ways you do, but we're all different. Spencer doesn't even go wild at all."

Brow furrowed, Dalton asked me, "Why?"

I shrugged. "We're still trying to find all this stuff out, remember? But . . . I guess Spencer and I think it's more like when we go Nighttime, a part of us deep inside comes out since we have no inhibitions." He gaped at me, and I quickly added, "Not that I think deep down you're violent or whatever. It may not even be that at all. We don't really know yet. Hence all the research."

"Yeah," he said. "Hence."

Again, he slowly shook his head. He looked away from me, across the baseball field at the overcast sky.

"Everyone thinks they know me," he said softly. "The guys on the team, they make fun of me sometimes 'cause I don't party hard. I don't like it when they pick on people. I don't get in fights." Looking back at me, he continued. "But I get real angry sometimes. Real angry. I can usually make it go away with lifting weights, working out till I'm 'bout to pass out. I need to make it go away. I don't want to be like him."

"Like . . . ?" I asked.

He ignored me. "Lately, though, ever since all this started, I can't bench-press it gone. And when that nighttime shift comes, man, Emily, it's amazing. I can let it all out. Let it all go."

Falling silent, he picked up his backpack from where he'd set it in front of his feet, opened it up, and pulled out an apple. He took a bite and went back to staring out over the baseball field.

"Well," I said after a moment, "I'm glad it helps you. Our crazy shenanigans and everything." I swallowed, not sure if I should admit what I was about to say. But if it would help him . . . "I can't lie, I kind of like it too. How I have no worries when I'm her."

I grabbed his chin, made him meet my eyes. "But Dalton, you have to start letting your daytime self seep in. You have got to keep yourself in check." The command was as much for him as it was to remind myself.

Dalton took another bite of apple. "I know," he said with a full mouth. "I will."

"Okay," I said, letting him go. "Good."

"And there's you too," he went on. "I don't know what it is, but when I'm around you during the day, I get all calm. Not even being around Nikki is like that. Not anymore."

"Oh," I said. "Dalton, I'm pretty sure that's just—"

"Pheromones, I know," he finished for me. "You told me that already. That's why you're always leaning on Spencer, isn't it? He makes your brain stop running like you do mine?"

I didn't answer right away. I somehow felt *embarrassed*. Because even then I was wishing Spencer was there to transport me away from my incredibly awkward morning.

"Yeah," I finally said. "I like Spencer. He's a nice guy. He makes me laugh."

The first bell rang then, echoing over the schoolyard and mercifully cutting short the conversation. Any kids still straggling outside began to head inside. I grabbed my bag and stood up. Dalton did the same.

"Hey! Guys! Wait up!"

Dalton and I both turned to see Spencer racing up the walkway toward us, his hair mussed and a giant grin on his face. He stopped in front of us, panting as though he'd run the whole way here.

"I found her," he said between gulping breaths. "I know who our mysterious werewolf girl is. You'll never believe it."

"Who?" I said. He wagged his eyebrows at me, so I grabbed his shoulders and playfully shook him. "No holding out! Who is it? Is it Mai?"

Spencer leaned in and looked between both of us.

"Nope, it's not Mai. It's none other than Carver High's very own super-uptight class president, Miss Tracie Townsend."

13

JUST LEAVE ME ALONE

Tracie Townsend. Perfect, prim, and perfectly, primly perky Tracie Townsend. She of the honor roll, the top of every class, the head of half the academic after-school clubs, the junior class president. Unfazed by the kids who made fun of her for being so . . . Tracie. Always hyper focused on being the best she could be.

And I'd seen her, the night before, chained to her own bed, in agony.

The girl had been going through everything I had. Not a crack in her summery armor during the school days. Well, not that I'd seen anyway.

"Whoa," Dalton said. "I never would have guessed it was her."

"Do you know for sure?" I asked Spencer. "Before we start calling her a werewolf, are you sure?"

Spencer nodded vigorously. "Oh yeah, I'm sure. Her smell was all over the place. I'm guessing all the perfume she wears at school gets washed down the drain when she showers. I saw her walk out of the exact house you told me."

"Does she have any sisters it could be?" I asked.

"Nope, only child," Dalton said. He stood tall, hands on his hips, staring at the front of the school. "Tracie . . ." A smile appeared on his lips. "Guess she's not so perfect after all, huh?"

Biting my lip, I met his eyes. "Well, we both know that no one here at school really knows the real us. Why wouldn't it be the same for her?"

He nodded slowly. "Yeah. Yeah . . ."

Spencer, scratching his arm, looked between the two of us. "I think I must have gotten left out of some conversation you guys had."

"It's nothing, Spencer," I said. I shifted my backpack on my shoulders, then smiled at him. "Dalton was just asking me some questions about the changes."

"Oh," he said. "All righty."

I locked onto Spencer's face. The shaggy hair spilling over his forehead, his wide smile. I felt myself drawn to him, an insect to an electric lamp. The confrontation with

Megan had left me on edge, and I didn't know what to think about Dalton's behavior. And now I kept seeing the wolf-girl in her bed, picturing her as Tracie, perfect Tracie scared and chaining herself up to keep at bay a change she didn't understand.

I could lean in close and let Spencer dull me down. But something inside me felt revolted by the idea.

Don't do it, Nighttime commanded. *Keep your senses. You don't need to rely on him.*

Swallowing, I tilted my head toward the school doors. "Well, the second bell is going to ring any time now. We should get to class."

The three of us walked together, though I made sure to position Dalton between me and Spencer as subtly as I could. Why would Nighttime be so adamant that I not take my one relief of the day? I mean, I'd been considering the effects of the pheromones for days; of course I knew that this attraction might not have been real at all.

And that was it, then. If it was something hard-coded into me by BioZenith, why trust it? Already the killer had tried to lure me to him using the scent. And if my brain was all mellowed, would I still have the drive to discover all there was to know about why I was made a werewolf? Could this have been their way of placating us into compliance for whatever they wanted to do to us now that we'd changed?

But if it wasn't for these insane wolf smells clinging to our minds, I never would have found Spencer or Dalton, they never would have found Tracie. We'd all still be alone, thinking that our brains had snapped, that we were slowly going insane. Instead, we were slowly forming a pack.

Like everything else about my life, I couldn't figure out the good from the bad anymore.

We entered the mostly empty front hallway, me taking a lot of short, shallow breaths, forcing myself not to get too close to Spencer. I couldn't avoid him forever. I didn't *want* to, I mean, who would? But right then I felt I needed some space to just be *me* and try to figure some things out.

"Erm, Emily, is it?"

I stopped, and Dalton and Spencer did the same. We all turned to see a small, slender man peeking out of the front office. His suit—tweed that day—was at least a size too large for him, and no matter how he combed his hair, nothing could hide the growing bald spot. He peered at me through wire-frame glasses.

"Uh, hi," I said. "Mr. Savage, right?"

I'd met him on Monday morning, very briefly. I didn't really know who he was except that he knew I'd been one of the people who "found" Dr. Elliot's body in Spencer's backyard. A counselor brought in to talk me through my feelings or whatever.

"That's right," he said. "You never came to see me after school on Monday. To talk about what you've been through."

I jacked a thumb over my shoulder. "Well, I have class now, so . . ."

Mr. Savage waved a hand. "No worries. I can write a note for your teachers. Though your friends should probably get on their way."

"Yeah," Spencer said. To me, he whispered, "I had to talk to him too. Don't worry, he's not so bad." And then he and Dalton walked off down the hall, their sneakers echoing on the linoleum.

"So . . ." I said, turning back to Mr. Savage. "Do we talk out here or . . . ?"

His smile was strangely unnerving. "No, come on in. Have a seat."

I followed him into the front office. We walked past the secretaries at their desks, filing paperwork and tapping at computers. Then I was ushered into a small office with room enough for a desk, one chair on his side, and one on mine. We both took a seat.

"Don't worry, you're not in trouble," he said, still smiling at me. I realized my face must have looked incredibly guilty. Because I *felt* incredibly guilty. With all that had happened the last few nights, the visions of dead Dr. Elliott when

I closed my eyes had been replaced with worries more immediate. But they were still there. I would never forget that night.

Suddenly I wished I hadn't abstained from partaking of Spencer's pheromones.

"Sorry," I said. "I've never been in the office before. It's where the bad kids are marched off to, so I always imagined, like, torture equipment and jail cells or something."

Mr. Savage laughed, then took off his glasses and wiped them with a cloth from his pocket. I watched and waited as he put the glasses back on.

"First I must ask how you're coping with what you saw Monday morning," he said. "I can imagine seeing the aftermath of an animal attack wasn't, ah, pleasant."

A torn-open neck. Too pale skin. A crow, bobbing its head into the wounds. Glassy, unfocused eyes. The stench of too much blood.

I shuddered and closed my eyes. I took in a steeling breath, forcing myself to think of puppies and unicorns frolicking through sugar-cookie flowers and candy grass.

"No," I said. "Not exactly pleasant."

"Do you want to talk about how it felt?"

I opened my eyes and saw him leaning forward on the desk, studying me intently. I didn't, in fact, want to tell him anything. I didn't know him. It felt too personal.

"I can't really put it into words," I said. "But I only saw him, the body I mean, for a few seconds. We went to call the police as soon as we realized what it was."

"Do you remember hearing anything during the night?" he asked me. "The wounds suggest he was attacked by rather large dogs or wolves. I would imagine that would be a bit noisy, what with all the commotion."

I shrugged. "I didn't hear anything."

"Interesting." He picked up a pen and jotted a few notes down on a piece of paper. I tried to see what he was writing, but the words would have been illegible even if they weren't upside down. Someone didn't ace penmanship.

Without looking up, he continued, "Your new friend out there, the tall one with the red hair. He's Dalton McKinney, yes? The boy who was shot by the man who also killed Emily Cooke?"

"Yes," I said. "That's him."

"I was led to believe you were only friends with one other girl here." He looked up at me. "Have you been friendly with Dalton long?"

Now, I'd never been to a counselor before, but this was definitely starting to feel more like an interrogation than any sort of touchy-feely-cry-about-your-problems session. Either he was really bad at his job, or something was up here. My first thought was, *The police are on to me*, and I could feel the panic rising in my chest. I gripped the armrest of my chair, forcing myself to stay calm.

"Dalton and I just have a class project together," I lied. "We're not really friends."

"Ah." Back to the paper he went, his thin hands dashing out loops and lines that I was almost positive had to be in some made-up alphabet. Seriously, could he even read that?

His notes written down, he smiled back up at me. "I think that's all I need for now, Emily. You can get a pass from one of the secretaries. And remember, if you do decide you want to talk about any of this, I'm here."

"All right," I said. "Thanks."

Flinging my backpack over my shoulder, I fled the small office. The panic I'd managed to keep down started to rise as I went to the nearest secretary, who started to fill out a form for me. My leg shook, my breath began to get ragged. Was this guy not a counselor at all? Was he with the police? Did they now suspect it wasn't dogs at all, but people?

How could they? The attack was clearly animal in origin. Jared, the police deputy I'd called to tell about the dead man in Spencer's backyard, had confirmed that. He'd been there with an officer on Monday afternoon to ask some questions that lasted all of ten minutes. All that horrible business was done with now, except for in my dreams. There was no way anyone suspected me and Spencer were killers. No way. I needed to relax.

Maybe I could find Spencer. Lean into him, let him envelope me, take away this new layer of stress.

No.

I took the pass from the secretary, offering a smile I didn't feel, then headed into the hall. *Deep breaths*, I told myself. *Chill out. This is not an issue. You're the alpha, remember? There are more important things to focus on: Shadowmen. BioZenith. Spencer. Dalton. And—*

I rounded the corner of the office and almost collided with someone about to walk in. She took a step back, as startled as I was.

"Whoa, there! Almost had us a fender bender."

The speaker was Tracie. Dressed in a blue blouse and tan slacks. Yes, *slacks.* As I gawked at her, she raised her eyebrows and pursed her lips.

"I don't mean to sound rude, but could you please move out of the doorway?" she asked me. "I have to drop these off." She held up a stack of papers, sign-up sheets for some club.

I couldn't move. I looked her up and down. There wasn't a wrinkle on her clothes, a crease of worry on her brow. Whatever werewolf musk she had, I couldn't smell it for some reason. I could, however, distinctly smell some sort of flowery perfume.

She blinked at me. "Well?"

I stepped to the side, unable to figure out what to say. She gave me an obligatory smile, then brushed past me.

I spun around. "Tracie, wait."

With a sigh, she turned back toward me. "Yes?"

I swallowed. I really hoped Tracie was the last werewolf, because this part—the accusation of being a mythical beast—was kind of awkward.

Figuring it was best to just rip off the Band-Aid, I leaned in close to her and whispered, "Tracie, I know what you are."

Her entire body went stiff. Paper crunched as her fingers tightened. Her eyes went wide. Through clenched teeth, she asked, "Know what now?"

Raising my hands, I stepped closer to her. "Don't worry," I whispered. "It's okay. I'm one too. So are Spencer Holt and Dalton McKinney. We've been looking for you all week." I met her eyes, and I couldn't keep myself from grinning. *Find your fellows*, some voice inside had told me. *Gather them.* And here she was, one more member of my pack. Of my family. I didn't know her at all, had never spoken to her before that moment in the hallway, but looking into her brown eyes I felt like I was seeing myself, another side of me that I never knew had been missing until just this moment. My chest ached.

She apparently wasn't having the same experience.

"What, exactly, do you think I am?" she asked.

I grabbed her gently by the arm and pulled her away from the office door and prying ears. I did not take my eyes off hers.

When we were far enough away that I could be sure that no one, especially Mr. Savage, was listening in, I took a breath. And I said the word, my voice hushed. "Werewolf."

The word seemed to echo down the empty corridor. For a moment, Tracie stood rigid, stone faced. And then her lip began to tremble.

"This isn't happening," she said, her eyes darting away from mine. "No, this is certainly not happening to me right now."

She tried to walk past me, but I stepped in front of her and held up my hands to stop her. "No, Tracie, listen to me. This is real. You haven't been going crazy. I've been exactly where you are right now. But you don't have to go through this alone. Me and Spencer and Dalton, we're figuring out why all this is happening."

Shaking her head, Tracie backed away from me. "Leave me alone, please," she said. "Just leave me alone." With that, she spun on her heel and walked straight out the front door of the school, still clenching the papers in her hand.

I raced after her, shoving through the glass door, my backpack smacking against my shoulders as I raced to catch up. Tracie sped down the walkway, her eyes straight ahead.

"Where are you going?" I asked as I came to walk next to her.

She didn't look at me. "Home."

"What about your stuff?" I asked, keeping pace with her. "Your bag, your backpack, your coat?"

Stopping, she finally turned to face me. "I asked you to leave me alone."

I shook my head at her. "I can't, Tracie. You're one of us. Emily Cooke was, too. She died because there are people out there who want to hurt us. I can't just leave you alone."

Tracie closed her eyes and took in a calming breath. "Emily, is it?" she said as she opened her eyes. "I am fairly certain that I am very, very sick, and that this right here is another hallucination. If not, I don't know how you found out that I'm not well, but I absolutely do not appreciate you mocking me like this."

I grabbed her forearm. "I'm not, I promise." She yanked her arm away but didn't move to walk any farther. "Listen, it all started with changes at night. You started to have some crazy personality shift, right? Then you turned into a full-on wolf? And sometimes you see shadows that move like men?"

"The bogey," she whispered.

"It's not a bogeyman, Tracie, not exactly," I continued. "But I promise you that this is all real. I just . . . I get so overwhelmed sometimes, and that's even with two people to talk to. I know it has to be harder for you."

Her eyes went distant. She crossed her arms, pursed her lips. For a moment, we stood there in silence, the wind whipping at our clothes.

"I need to go back to class," she finally said.

"All right," I said. "But Tracie, please come to the party at Dalton's house tonight, okay? Talk with us. We're going to be following up on some information we found out about what's going on."

She didn't answer. In the back of my head, another voice piped up. Nighttime, telling me what to say to convince her to come. *Tell her it wouldn't look good if the class president bailed on the welcome home celebration of one of the school's football stars.*

"Plus, it wouldn't look good if the class president bailed on the welcome home celebration of one of the school's football stars."

Her eyes sparked at that, shot to meet mine. Then, she

turned and walked back toward the school. I watched her go, hoping I'd managed to convince her.

All I could do now was let Spencer and Dalton know I'd spoken to her, and hope that it was enough to lead another member of my pack home.

14

YOU'RE SO BRAZEN THESE DAYS

The last time I'd been to a party, I hadn't quite been me.

It was the week before, right after I started changing into Nighttime. And she'd dressed to the nines, flirted with boys, and got awkwardly drunk.

So yeah, this time? I intended to keep a low profile.

I kept it simple: jeans, the freshly rewashed black turtleneck, hair down. I kept the glasses on, of course. Nighttime's full hi-def plasma-screen vision still hadn't yet seeped over to the day.

I wasn't exactly the picture of a girl ready to party. But I had a mission.

Spencer picked me up in the early evening, and by six we were in front of Dalton's house. Earlier than usual for a party, but apparently the cheerleaders intended the celebration to start in the afternoon and last all night. By the time we got there the streets were lined with cars, the driveway packed with smaller vehicles awkwardly sitting way too close side by side. I was guessing those people weren't planning to leave for a while.

There was no sign of Dalton's parents' cars. That was a relief.

Kids streamed over the lawn and hung out on the porch, laughing and shouting and generally having a good time. A stark contrast to the last party, which had been a wake for Emily Cooke. It was actually a relief to see. I'm not sure with all that I was trying to focus on at once that I could deal with another super-somber soiree.

Spencer parallel parked his minivan while I leaned back in my seat, scanning the yard for any sign of Tracie or Dalton. I didn't see either—but I did see Megan, all spindly limbs and white-blond hair, leaning against the front wall of the house, scowling at the mirth around her.

"She actually came," I said. My pulse began to race, and I realized I was worried about running into her. My best friend, of all people. I guess with the way I'd been acting around her, I couldn't blame her. But after the intensity that was our car ride to school, I wasn't sure I could face her. I still couldn't give her the answers she so desperately wanted from me. Who knew if I ever could.

"Who?" Spencer asked me. His head darted between various rearview mirrors, and his tongue stuck out between his teeth as he edged his mom's car into a way-too-narrow spot between two other cars.

"Megan," I told him. "We had a fight this morning because she knows I'm keeping a secret, and I can't exactly blurt out that I'm a werewolf." I huffed out a sigh and stared up at the roof of the car. "Is it just me, or has the past week been totally stressful?"

"Not just you."

And then I felt the warmth of his body nearing me, his arm wrapping around my torso. I opened my mouth to protest, but I couldn't keep his pheromones from digging into me, scrubbing my brain of fear and worry and urgency. I couldn't keep away any longer—I leaned into him and hugged him back.

"I think we're gonna get somewhere tonight," he said, his voice muffled by my hair. "Dalton's dad definitely knows something."

"Mm," I mumbled, my eyes closed. It seemed like forever since I'd felt so *calm*, and I didn't want to let go. Screw breaking into offices and werewolves and shadowmen. I just wanted to stay in that car forever, never let go of Spencer, never go back to the real world.

No, a distant voice in my head said. *Do not give in. Get to work. Focus.*

"I don't want to," I said aloud.

Spencer pulled away from me, brow furrowed. "Don't want to what?"

His scent lingered, but with him not so close, my brain began to re-form the thoughts I'd had only moments before. Right. We had a mission.

"Sorry," I said, leaning back into my seat. "Nothing. I guess we should head in."

"Yup," he said. Then he popped up in his seat, beaming. "Actually, don't move, wait right there."

Before I could protest, he unclicked his seat belt, shoved open his door, and raced around the front of the minivan. Reaching the passenger side, he opened my door and waved his free hand toward the sidewalk with a flourish. "M'lady?"

Laughing, I hopped down to the street and let him close the door for me. "Wow, what was that?"

He shrugged, still grinning goofily. "I just always wanted to do that. Seemed the gentlemanly thing to do."

I gently shoved his shoulder and said, "Well, thank you. Sometimes I do desire a big strong man to open my door for me. My tiny girl arms can barely manage."

His grin faltered, and he looked at his feet. "Oh, I'm none of those things. Just thought it would be nice."

I stepped in close to him and met his eyes as he looked back at me. Again the musks and aromas swirled, our hyperactive teenage chemistry boiling just beneath the surface of our skin. I hated seeing him look so hurt. I didn't want to do that to him. "I was just joking," I said, my voice hushed. "It was very gentlemanly of you. Thank you."

That brought his smile back, and then, as my mind began to fuzz over once again, all I could see were his big brown eyes. My heart thudded, and suddenly all I wanted was for him to lean forward, close his eyes, and—

Focus, Emily.

I took a step back and let out the breath I hadn't known I'd been holding. Our eyes flicked away and then back to each other at the same time. We both laughed.

"Um, we should go find Dalton," Spencer said. "Before too many people get here."

I looked past the minivan to see more and more cars slowly driving down the street, teens peering out their windows to find a place to park. I could see some groups of kids hiking down the sidewalk from the roads up the street, as though they'd given up on finding close parking and decided to just walk a couple of blocks.

"Yeah," I said. "Let's go."

The two of us strode across the grass toward the front

porch, some kids waving at Spencer and he waving back. No one seemed to notice me.

Except, near the front door, Megan. I tried to keep my head down, darting glances to see where her current position was. And I knew the exact moment she caught sight of me, because she shoved herself off the wall, uncrossed her arms, and ever so briefly, smiled.

Ignoring her would have been a realm beyond bitchy, even if I did sort of have a good reason to keep her in the dark.

I forced a smile back and raised a hand as I grew close to her. She walked across the grass and came to stand before me and Spencer. We were near the open front door to the house, and I could hear random thumps of a drum, the whining of guitar strings being tuned. Mostly I just heard lots and lots of voices.

"Hey, Reedy," I said.

"Hey."

Spencer looked between us both. I didn't know about my face, but Megan's was unreadable. For a moment, neither of us said anything.

"Uh, hey, Megan," Spencer finally said. To me, "Hey, Em Dub, I'm going to go find Dalton. See you inside."

"All right."

Megan watched him disappear into the crowd milling about the front porch, then turned back to me. "So—" she started.

"I—"

I smiled nervously. She just looked vaguely annoyed.

"Go ahead," I said.

"So," she began again. "I just wanted to say . . . I'm sorry, I guess. This morning was sort of . . ."

"Awkward?" I finished for her.

"That's a word that fits, yes." Crossing her arms, Megan looked at the crowd of kids. "So this is one of those famed high school parties, huh? Are they anything like the movies?"

I shrugged. "Not sure. The first and only one I went to turned out to be a wake. But Megan, are we . . . are we okay? I know I've been distant since school started, and there are things I can't say, but—"

She held up a hand, stopping me. "I don't really want to talk about it, okay? We're both here tonight. Maybe we can just hang out like we always used to. Even if it is surrounded by a bunch of Neanderthals and twits."

I bit my lip and looked over Megan's shoulder. Dalton and Spencer were inside, waiting for me. We had only a few hours to scope out Mr. McKinney's office before the nighttime changes came over us, and we had to do it tonight while we had the party as the perfect distraction.

But Megan was looking at me so expectantly. I remembered her in the car that morning, her eyes watering with tears she refused to let fall. She never got emotional, ever. Not since junior high, when she learned that showing emotions around a bunch of scornful girls was like an open invitation to full-on harassment. I knew she held a lot inside. I thought of her the past week, alone without me. . . . The same rush of emotion that had come over me when I thought of Tracie going through the werewolf change hit me then.

I could take some time out to be with her, at least for a little while. Mr. McKinney's office wasn't going anywhere. And I hated being the horrible friend I knew I'd been toward her.

"Sure," I said with a smile. "Of course! I am not letting you take on your first high school party without me."

Her face broke into an honest, happy grin. She stepped beside me and hooked her arm through mine, elbow in elbow. "Well let's go live it up, or whatever these guys do."

We walked that way, a pair of clear misfits, heads held high as we climbed the porch steps. All it took was a pointed glare from Megan and the kids by the door parted for us.

The inside wasn't as crowded as I'd expected it to be, but then again, Dalton's house was of the unimaginably huge variety, with plenty of nooks and crannies for teens to disappear into. Hanging from the ceiling in the foyer was a hand-painted sign that read WELCOME HOME, DALTON! Beyond it, there were kids lounging on the carpeted steps that led to the second floor. Others spread out on the plush couches in the den—a few girls had crowded around Max, the yellow Lab, on a love seat, giving him all the cooing attention a dog could ever want—and a bunch crowded around the dining room table, playing some game. In the back corner of the den, near a massive fireplace, a drum set had been set up, with two familiar figures standing by.

"Hey, the Bubonic Teutonics," I said to Megan, raising my voice to be heard over the din of chatter. "You got them to come."

"It wasn't hard," Megan told me. "Dalton gave their info to the cheerleaders, and they convinced his dad to actually pay a couple hundred to have them come play."

I shot Megan a look. "The cheerleaders did that? Why?"

Megan rolled her eyes. "They Googled a picture of Jared."

I looked back across the room and saw him there, behind the drums: Deputy Jared, police officer by day, drummer for a garage band by night. And I didn't blame the cheerleaders—he was basically model gorgeous, with a lean yet toned body, tan skin, and short honey-blond hair that curled at the ends. He caught sight of me and smiled, revealing perfect white teeth. He waved us over.

Megan sighed. "What does he want?"

"He actually did a lot for me," I whispered. She gave me a look, so I said, "I mean, when I was going through some stuff last week, he helped me out."

"Uh, okay," Megan said. "You mean at the club when . . . you know?"

"Yeah." I tugged on her arm. "Let's go say hi. I mean, look around, all the girls here will totally be jealous."

"You're so brazen these days," Megan said. "It's weird."

There were more than a few teen girls huddled together by the stairs and on the couches, cups in hand and giggling behind their palms. Their eyes were clearly on the percussion half of the Bubonic Teutonics duo.

Megan grinned, seeing the lascivious looks. "Actually, that sounds like fun."

Still arm in arm, Megan and I crossed into the den and made our way toward the drum set. Megan's brother, Lucas, was there too, just as tall and spindly and pale as Megan. His white-blond hair was gelled out into spikes, the tips dyed Kool-Aid blue. He fidgeted with his guitar and bent over a speaker, not noticing us.

"Hey there, Emily Webb," Jared said from his seat behind the drums as we came close. He held his drumsticks high in both hands and tapped out a light beat, waiting for his partner to finish tuning his instrument.

"Hey," I said.

"Oh, this is perfect," Megan whispered to me as she glanced over her shoulder at the girls in the room. "They definitely want to be me right now. Awesome."

"How've you been?" Jared asked me. "You were pretty shaken up on Monday."

"On Monday?" Megan interrupted, no longer concerned with the other kids at the party. "What happened on Monday?"

Jared raised his eyebrows and met my eyes. "I don't have to say anything, Emily. I just assumed you would have told Megan. It's all confidential."

Yanking her arm from mine, Megan rounded on me. "What is?" she asked. "If my brother's friend knows . . ."

I placed a hand on her shoulder, swallowing. "It's okay," I said. "It's just . . . it was me and Spencer who found the body of the guy who shot Emily Cooke. In Spencer's backyard. I called Jared when we found him because I didn't know what else to do."

A look of understanding came over Megan's face. "So is that what this whole week has been about? All that hanging out with Spencer and Dalton? I mean, Em, that's pretty dark. I would have understood if you were upset about seeing a dead guy."

"Yeah," I lied. "Yeah it was mostly that. I'm sorry I couldn't tell you earlier. It just felt . . . weird."

I remembered, then, Mr. Savage. The counselor who was supposed to talk me through my feelings about dead Dr. Elliott but who asked unusual questions instead. I turned to Jared.

"Hey, do you know a Mr. Savage?" I asked.

He drummed a quick beat, then shook his head no. "Who's that?"

"No one," I said. "Some counselor at school. I thought maybe he was with the police."

Jared shrugged his delightfully broad shoulders. "No one by that name works with us."

"Oh. Okay."

"Yeah, all right, nice chat, Jared," Megan said, stepping between us. "Shouldn't you two be playing something?"

"Yes, we should." Lucas finally turned from his speaker and sighed at us. "If Jared ever stops flirting with every underage girl here."

Jared laughed. "I make it a point not to flirt with the jailbait," he said. "I can't help it if the groupies swarm to me." He winked at me. "See you later, Emily."

The duo began to play a quiet song to start their set, and Megan and I stepped back. The room started to get a bit crowded as kids streamed in from other areas of the house to listen. Megan listened for half a second before dragging me through the laughing people in the dining room and into the kitchen, where bowls of chips and other snacks were sitting all over the counters.

Megan leaned against the counter near the refrigerator and popped a pretzel into her mouth. The Bubonic Teutonics were getting louder now, and I heard some people cheering. I'm not much of a music person, but I thought they sounded pretty good.

Shaking her head, Megan was back to smiling. "Wow, a dead body," she said. "That's intense, Em! I am officially sorry for not just letting you deal. I mean, if you found the body with Spencer, of course you'd want to talk with him about it."

I forced a smile back. "Yeah. He totally understands what it's like. It's been easier to talk to him than that counselor the school gave me, that's for sure."

Megan snatched another pretzel but didn't put it in her mouth. She stared thoughtfully at the linoleum.

I looked above her, at a clock on the wall. Six thirty. I'd already been at the party for half an hour, and time was running short.

"So what did it, like, look like?" Megan finally asked me. "I know it's morbid, but was it like in horror movies?"

I shuddered, suddenly feeling a chill even though the

body heat from all the kids in the house had warmed the rooms up considerably. I didn't know what to say, really. *No, Megan, real dead bodies don't look like rubber mannequins with red corn syrup poured all over them.*

I was spared from answering as soon as I saw Megan's face turn into her usual default expression: unreadable but probably annoyed. His smell came first, then the warmth of his body. The visions of dead Dr. Elliott flushed clear from my mind.

I turned to find Spencer standing there. He had a handful of cheddar popcorn in his hand. "Hey Em Dub, there you are," he said. He popped the remaining handful of popcorn into his mouth and swallowed it down. Half muffled, he said to Megan, "And hey again." Swallowing again, he continued, "Can I steal Emily for a little bit? We were supposed to, uh, do a project. Right?"

"Yeah, right," I said. "We left some notes here the other day."

Megan sighed and bit off a piece of her pretzel. Her eyes lit up at the sight of something behind us, in the living room that was past the other end of the kitchen.

"Sure, fine," she said. "But wait here one sec."

Tossing the remainder of her pretzel back in the bowl, she darted past us and into the living room. It was dark except for the glow of the massive flat-screen TV a bunch of guys were playing some video game on. I shrugged at Spencer.

A moment later, Megan returned, dragging a boy behind her. A very familiar boy: tall, brooding Patrick Kelly.

Megan hooked her arm through Patrick's just as she had done back in the library. "Em, I just wanted to officially introduce you to Patrick since I didn't at the library. He's from London. We've been hanging out lately."

He nodded at me. He had a strange look on his face, like he was seeing something that I couldn't. "Emily and I met last weekend, actually," he muttered. "At a corner store."

I could feel myself blushing. "You remember that, huh?"

"Hard to forget."

"Hey, man," Spencer greeted. To Megan, "Yeah, we met already too, he's my new neighbor."

"Oh," Megan said. "Neat. Anyway, I just wanted you to meet my new friend. He and I can hang out while you do . . . whatever."

"Cool," I said. "I'll catch up with you later, Megan."

She made a show of pretending she didn't care I was being dragged off, leading Patrick past us toward the dining room. "Sure, Em," she said over her shoulder. "Take your time."

I let out a deep breath when Megan finally left the room. Okay, well, that hadn't been entirely as horrifically awkward as I'd expected. But it wasn't exactly a comfortable reunion of old besties either. Progress, I guess. Even if I'd inadvertently lied to her about why I'd been sort of avoiding her all week.

"So," I said to Spencer as he devoured another handful of popcorn. "Did you find Dalton anywhere?"

"I did. He's busy trying to get away from Nikki." He wagged his eyebrows at me and held up a keycard, like what they use for hotel doors. "But I got us our way into his dad's office."

15

DO NOT ENTER ♥

No one noticed as Spencer and I passed through the boys whooping over the video games and disappeared down the hall with the clearly marked DO NOT ENTER ♥ signs that I was guessing were put up by the cheerleaders. Impressively, no one had, and the hall to Mr. McKinney's office was dark and empty. Distantly, the thumping music of the Bubonic Teutonics echoed. It almost felt like we weren't in the same house as them and the rest of the party at all.

We reached the door to the office. I tried the handle. Locked, of course. For the first time I noticed a card reader next to the door. I looked around the hallway as Spencer swiped the keycard. None of the other doors were similarly equipped. Mr. McKinney had gone all fancy just for this specific room.

The card reader beeped, and a blue light lit up on its side. There came a thunk inside the door as the lock unlocked. This time when I pressed down the steel handle, the door opened.

"Awesome," Spencer whispered as we tiptoed into the room. "I feel like I'm in a spy movie or something. I'm all Tom Cruise in *Mission Impossible* right now."

"Pre-couch-jumping Tom, I assume," I whispered back as I gently shut the door behind us.

He laughed. "Yeah. I'm old-school Cruise, for sure."

Through soft gray lighting that barely lit up the room, it looked as though Mr. McKinney's office was exactly the same as we'd last seen it. The glass-and-steel desk with its computer, the strange overdesigned balance-chairs he'd had us sit on, the sparse bookshelves lining the walls. I hadn't paid much attention to it earlier, but behind the desk was a modern painting in a black frame—gray boxes of various sizes and shades, arranged like a pixelated version of cells you'd see under a microscope.

"So," I said, scoping out the room. "Where do we start?"

"Probably the computer," Spencer said, already rounding the desk. He plopped into the leather chair and it reclined back, startling him. He laughed at his own shock, then spun the chair back and forth, bouncing off the tip of his toes.

I went to the shelves nearest me. There were only a few books on each shelf, each impenetrable science tome and scientific journal propped up by little marble bookends. There were also photos of him, his wife, and Dalton, plus other people I didn't know but who were probably extended family members.

Muffled voices came from the other side of the door, one loud and masculine, the other higher pitched. I stiffened, and Spencer stopped spinning in the chair. For a moment I was sure it was Dalton's parents arguing just outside the office.

A fist banged against the door. "Guys, it's me. Open the door."

Dalton.

I let out a breath, then ran to the door. It opened with another loud thunk as I pushed down the handle—revealing Dalton on the other side, gripping Tracie Townsend by the wrist.

"Let me go!" Tracie shouted. With a yank, she pulled herself free from Dalton's grasp. Furious, she put her hands on her hips and glared at me. "And *you*. Of course it's you, too. I never should have come here. I told you this morning and I'm telling you now"—she pointed a finger between me and Dalton—"the *both* of you: Leave. Me. Alone." With a curt sigh, she brushed her purple skirt smooth, then adjusted her matching headband. "I'm going to make my rounds here, put in the face time that's expected of me. And then I'm going home. I want nothing to do with this."

Without waiting for a response, she turned and stormed off down the dark hallway.

I looked up at Dalton. "What was *that*?"

He shrugged and looked down at his shoes, sheepish. "Sorry. You said you talked to her. I thought she'd be— She'd want to work with us."

I sighed. "She'll come around. I hope. Come in, though, before someone sees us."

Dalton brushed past me, and I quietly shut the door once more. I turned to find him looking aimlessly about the dimly lit room while Spencer absentmindedly spun in the office chair.

I rounded the desk, crouched on my knees next to Spencer, and leaned onto the desk. "So, start with the computer, right?"

"Yes!" Spencer said, stopping his spinning. He scooted the chair closer to the desk and waved the wireless mouse. The computer monitor, previously blank, clicked on, casting our faces in a glow of blue. The computer's desktop background was plain black and sparse of icons, the task bars a steely gray. Mr. McKinney definitely had a specific aesthetic.

Dalton came to the other side of Spencer, and the two of us watched as Spencer clicked open folders and files, looking for anything that had anything to do with BioZenith. There were tax documents, letters to family members, a schedule much like the one I'd seen on Dalton's computer. No matter what he clicked, though, it proved to be completely . . . normal. The same boring stuff anyone's dad would keep on his computer. The most recent program opened was solitaire.

"So there's nothing, then?" I said after many minutes of this, exasperated. "Dalton stole his dad's keycard and we snuck in here for nothing?"

Dalton stood up, peering around the room. "He comes in here to work all the time, though. He says he does, anyway. He has to have work files here."

"Unless he has them on an external drive," Spencer said, still clicking through the files. "That's what I'd do if—" He stopped midsentence, breaking into laughter.

"What is it?" I said, leaning forward to look at the screen.

"Man, I totally found your dad's porn file!" Spencer said. "Oh wow, he must really like his alone time if he put a keycard lock on his door just for that." The mouse icon hovered over a video file, as though Spencer intended to double-click.

Blushing, I leaned forward and pressed the power button on the monitor. "Um, no. We're not here for that."

Spencer laughed again. "Can you imagine Mr. McKinney all—"

"Dude!" Dalton said.

Ducking his head, Spencer said, "Sorry."

I refused to believe that steely Mr. McKinney spent all his free time locked in his office, playing solitaire and . . . well, *playing solitaire*. Of course he wouldn't leave super-top-secret files about his shady company lying on the desktop of his password-less computer, labeled, "Werewolf mysteries solved! Click here!" Either he had those hidden somewhere deep in his regular PC, or we were looking in the wrong place. Or maybe everything was on an external drive, but wouldn't we see some of those files in his recent history, even if they obviously couldn't be opened?

I stood up and began to pace behind Spencer and the desk chair. I scanned the shelves again, then the top of Mr. McKinney's desk, wondering if maybe he had books with hidden compartments like something out of an "old lady solving mysteries with her cat, Snookums Smith-Plasse" type book.

And as I paced again and again behind the chair, I heard a faint buzzing. At first I thought it was one of the pale fluorescents, but there was no light next to me. I stopped and looked at the wall—or, more specifically, at the abstract painting in front of me.

I couldn't help but smile. "Oh, I hope this is what I think it is."

Spencer spun the chair to face me, and Dalton leaned back against the desk.

"What is it?" Dalton asked.

I studied the edges of the black frame, looking for some sort of button to press. I didn't see or feel anything, so instead I grabbed the frame by either end and gently pulled forward.

With a hiss, the painting pulled free from the wall. I let go and, of its own accord, it lowered itself to rest against the wall below, opening like some futuristic panel from the deck of the *Enterprise*. Behind it, embedded in the wall, was a glass screen.

"No way," Spencer said.

"I can't believe that worked," I said, shaking my head. "We really are trapped inside a movie right now, aren't we?"

"I wonder if we can get those realistic-looking masks Tom Cruise wore, too?" Spencer asked me.

Dalton didn't say anything. He leaned in close to the blank screen, then raised a finger and touched the corner.

And the screen buzzed to life.

It was like a giant version of Mr. McKinney's desktop

background—plain black, with giant steel-colored icons hovering in the center of the screen. One appeared to be for companywide communications, another for collected information on Mr. McKinney's current project at work, one for archives, and others that weren't labeled at all.

We all gaped for a moment before Spencer got to his feet and tried to tap an icon. Immediately everything on-screen faded, as though a shadow had been cast in front of it. A password box appeared, followed by letter and number keys beneath it.

"Oh, this is sweet," Spencer said. "It's like a giant iPad. I have got to get me one of these."

"A password," I said. "Okay, so this is getting somewhere." I turned to Dalton. "You, uh, wouldn't happen to know your dad's password, would you?"

Dalton scratched his head, right next to the bandage. He shrugged, then tapped the screen, typing in some letters. He hit enter, and the screen beeped at us. The password field went blank.

"Nope, that's not it."

"What did you put in?" Spencer asked.

"I tried 'password.'"

Spencer laughed at that, then began digging in the pockets of his jacket, first the right and then the left, as though he couldn't remember where he'd put whatever he was searching for. "That actually isn't a bad guess. You'd be surprised how many people actually do put that as their password. They're the ones who get their identities stolen." He unzipped his jacket and reached into a pocket inside. "Here we go."

Producing a thumb drive, he bent forward and studied the wall just beneath the screen. I could see faint lines that would have been hidden by the painting. Spencer pressed against the wall and a little panel clicked open, revealing a bunch of computer ports.

"Exactly where I would have put 'em," he said, mostly to himself. He scanned the various ports, then found the little rectangle USB one. He stuck his thumb drive in.

"What's that going to do?" Dalton asked. "Don't destroy my father's computer, man. He can't know we were in here."

"No worries at all, my friend," Spencer said. "This is just a little program I like to use when there's a password in the way. Watch."

He pressed a button on the top of the thumb drive. It flashed a light—and the giant screen went blank. A prompt blinked in the top corner, and then plain computery white text started to scroll on the screen, just like when you boot up a PC. I had absolutely no idea what was going on, just that the words flashed by so fast I couldn't read them.

Then, the main screen appeared once more, icons and all. We didn't have to touch the screen this time for the password prompt to appear. Without typing a single thing, it populated itself with a string of fifteen little asterisks, then disappeared.

I reached forward and touched the nearest icon—the interoffice mailbox—and dragged it with my finger to the bottom of the screen. I let go and it flew back into its original position. We were in.

I could help but smile at Spencer. "You really are a programmer, aren't you?"

Dalton was shaking his head, similarly grinning. "I had no idea you were into all this stuff, man."

Spencer didn't look at either of us. He pressed on the far right icon, opening up what looked to be a contact list of employees. Nothing much to see there, so he closed it.

"Yeah, it's been my hobby forever," he said. "When I can focus myself, anyway. I usually have a bunch of different programs I'm working on at once that I jump between. I—"

He reached out and grabbed another icon, this one about Mr. McKinney's current project. It opened up a new screen with more icons. Spencer began to touch them, his eyes flicking back and forth over the screen.

"I . . . what?" I asked him.

He blinked, then looked at me. "Oh, I was just going

205

to say I didn't make my password breaker until last week, when I changed at night. It was pretty sweet having so much focus. Too bad it leads to being a werewolf and I have to make myself sleep."

"I'm better at night, too," Dalton said, peering close to the screen and reading the heavily science-talk captions of each icon. "That's what I told Emily and why I said not to take sleeping pills."

"What?" Spencer said. He looked between me and Dalton, then back to me. "What does he mean, Emily? Have you guys not been taking the sleeping pills?"

"I, uh . . ." I stammered.

Dalton stiffened. "Oh. Oops. Sorry, Emily."

"Man, I knew it," Spencer said. He plopped back down in the leather chair and crossed his arms. "I could just *tell* you guys had some secret. What, did you change and go clubbing or something?"

"There was a drag race," Dalton muttered.

I sighed. "No, last night we went to look at BioZenith. It wasn't planned, it just happened. I meant to tell you, but . . ."

"So I was making myself go to bed at eight p.m. like a five-year-old, and you guys went to find out more without me," Spencer grumbled. "Yeah, that's fair."

"I didn't want you to get hurt," I said.

Grimacing, Spencer looked up at me. "You didn't want me to get hurt? You do know I have the same superpowers you do, right? Why do you get to decide what's too dangerous for me, and not dangerous to you or jock boy here?"

Because I'm your alpha, a voice inside me snarled. Whether the voice was nighttime or werewolf me, I couldn't be sure.

Obviously I couldn't say that. I'm not sure how they'd take me telling them I was, indeed, their boss. Or at least that's what my wolf side told me.

I kneeled down beside the chair and placed my hands on Spencer's arms. "You're right," I said. "I should have told you. It's just, we didn't really get much done, and I didn't want you to be . . ."

He arched an eyebrow. "Jealous? You didn't want me to be jealous, huh?" And though he tried to hide it, his lips cracked into a tiny smile.

Dalton groaned. "So fine, neither of you take sleeping pills. I'm not. Let's go back to BioZenith again or something. If Spence can hack this computer, he probably can do it there, too."

"BioZenith or not, I'm not taking the sleeping pills again, Em Dub," Spencer said. "I don't like waking up all woozy from those pills, and I don't like not being the nighttime version of me. If you guys get to run around and do crazy stuff, I . . . Well, I want to, too."

I stood up. "Fine," I said. "Fine, none of us is taking sleeping pills today. But only because we're going to go to BioZenith and finally get inside." I met Dalton's eyes. "No detours."

"Fine with me," Dalton said.

Spencer popped back up to his feet. "Sweet." Producing another thumb drive from his pocket, this one on a lanyard, he went back to stand before the screen. "I'm going to start transferring stuff onto this," he said as he plugged it into another USB port. "Then we can go over it tomorrow."

"Sounds good," I said.

I took Spencer's place in the leather chair, semi-watching as he went about moving the files. But I wasn't entirely focused on our little break-in anymore. This was nothing compared to BioZenith, with its armed guards and who knew what else. I thought about Megan at the party, the shadowmen looming around every corner, my uncertainty about how all my changes worked. I shoved those thoughts down, though, focusing: This was it. No more playing around. I wanted to find out all there was to know about BioZenith and about why I was created. Only then could any of this begin to make sense.

I watched the clock tick in the corner of the giant screen, ever closer to eight o'clock. Just as Spencer finished the file transfer and removed both his thumb drives, a shudder rushed through me and I closed my eyes.

When I opened them again, I was back. I took off my glasses and shoved them in my pocket, because I didn't need them anymore. And I turned to Spencer and Dalton and said, "Let's go get some answers, boys."

Details of Video Footage Recorded Oct. 31, 2010,
Part 4

21:10:29 PST—Detention Block, Sublevel Sector D

Vesper 1(B) and Vesper 2.1(A), having manually
unlocked the access doors to the lower level of
Sector D (perhaps better password protocol is
necessary?), Agreed. Bring it up next meeting.—MH have
made their way to the detention block. Previously,
Vesper 1(B) was held here, along with the other
captured Deviants. All but Branch B's Vesper 4 had
been moved by this time stamp.

Vesper 2.1(A) stands in front of the door to
Detention Cell 7 and raises a single hand, and the
door buckles inward and opens.

21:11:24 PST—Detention Cell 7

One subject is in the room, identified as:

—Tracie Townsend, Branch B's Vesper 4 (designated "Deviant")
Black female, 16 years old

Vesper 4(B) wears a gray jumpsuit and sits at a table in the center of the room. Printer paper is stacked neatly and straight next to her, and she is drawing on one sheet with a crayon. She does not seem to realize that the door has opened and that she has visitors.

VESPER 1(B): Tracie! We're here to rescue you.

Vesper 4(B) sets down the crayon and, blinking, looks up at the two other girls.

VESPER 4(B): Oh. It's you.

Vesper 1(B) goes to Vesper 4(B)'s side, crouches beside her chair, and places a hand on the girl's arm. Unlike Vesper 1(B), Vesper 4(B) has not been chained to her table.

VESPER 1(B): We're breaking out of here, Tracie. All of us. We found you, but we also need to find—
VESPER 4(B): Evan?
VESPER 2.1(A): We know where Evan is. And there's no way we're going there, at least not tonight.
VESPER 4(B): Ah. Then I do know where we need to go.

Vesper 4(B) stands up and straightens her already straightened stack of papers, then places the crayon she was using back in its plastic tub. That done, she and the other two Deviants exit Detention Cell 7.

Part 4 of Relevant Video Footage Concluded

16

JUST A SLIGHT DISAGREEMENT BETWEEN GIRLS

I oversaw Dalton and Spencer as they made sure everything was back in place. Dalton was the same as he'd been both nights out: jittery and constantly bobbing as though moving to a beat only he could hear. Spencer's change, however, was brand-new to me. He darted about quickly, like a lizard, efficiently closing the port panel, logging out of the screen computer with a fly of his fingers, and then putting the painting back in place with another mechanical hiss. And then he was sitting up perfectly straight at the desk, clicking nonstop, making sure not a single thing was out of place on the computer's desktop. His eyes flicked back and forth, laser focused.

"You got everything, Dalton?" I asked. "We need to

move. I'm tired of this place."

He was busy staring at a picture on one of the shelves, his hand against his thigh, constantly slapping out a rhythm. "Yeah, I'm good. I'm ready."

Spencer's hand flew up in the air even as the other continued to dart the mouse around, still clicking. Between his fingers was the keycard. Not looking up, he said, "Not done yet, man. Take this."

Dalton snatched the keycard from Spencer's fingers, then came to my side. With a few more clicks, Spencer jumped to his feet and put the desk chair back in the exact position we'd found it.

"You cover all our tracks, Tom Cruise?" I asked him.

He rolled his eyes. "Of course. Here." He came forward and strung the thumb drive with the lanyard around my neck. "You keep this one. I'll keep the other. My program automatically logs all system checks and passwords when it runs, so if something happens to one of us, we either have a way to get at the information again or you'll already have it all."

"Smart guy," I said, shoving the drive down the front of my shirt. "But nothing is going to happen to us."

"Hell no, of course nothing will," Dalton said. He put his arms over my shoulders and leaned on me, grinning down at Spencer. "She took some guy out in a chokehold last night. It was badass, man."

Spencer sighed. "I know what she can do, Dalton, I was there when we took down Dr. Elliott." To me, he said, "We should leave now. The wolf change generally happens two hours, thirty-seven minutes, and fourteen seconds after the initial phase."

"Well, that's specific," I said, pulling myself out from underneath Dalton.

Spencer shrugged. "I calculated the averages based on the nights I fully changed."

"That's good to know. Follow me."

We exited the office and let the door close with another thunk of its lock behind us. I led the way, head high, shoulders back, down the hallway, with my two soldiers behind me. Soldiers! Ha. I felt like the leader of some sort of hyper-trained SWAT team.

The nearer we came to the end of the hallway, the louder the partyers became. I could still hear the Bubonic Teutonics playing their generic alt-rock music in the den, punctuated by the occasional excited bark from Max and a cheer from the adoring crowd. Much closer were the video gamers, shouting about kill shots.

Just before we could turn the corner and make our way to the front door, four girls appeared, silhouetted by the lights behind them. It took me a moment, but then I realized it was Nikki Tate in the lead with the Delgado triplets backing her up as usual. Nikki and Amy both had their arms crossed. Brittany, the sister with the most makeup on and the hoochiest outfit, examined her nails. Beside her, Casey Delgado held her arms behind her back, her face unreadable.

Oh, but Nikki's and Amy's feelings were written on every pore. I was officially getting tired of these girls showing up to scowl at me all the time. I mean, seriously.

"Dalton," Nikki said coolly. "I have been looking for you all night. This is supposed to be *your* party and we had *your* cake delivered and we've been waiting for *you* to show up to serve it and actually appreciate all these people who came out to celebrate with you."

Dalton grunted behind me.

I stepped forward, crossing my arms to match Nikki's stance. "Hi, Nik." She was looking past me at Dalton, clearly pissed. I snapped my fingers, and, taken aback, she finally looked at me. "Yeah, hi. Dalton, Spencer, and I are busy. With . . . projects. And it sounds like everyone here is having a grand old time without their guest of honor. So if you'll just let us through."

I made to pass Nikki, but Amy stepped up next to her, blocking my way. "What is with your attitude, skank?" she spat at me.

"Seriously," Brittany muttered, now checking out the nails on her other hand.

Nikki's face had gone red at this point. She dropped her hands to her side, balling them into fists. Her lower lip trembled. I'd never seen her so mad.

"I do not get you, Emily Webb," she said. "You don't talk to anyone for years, and then you decide you suddenly want to start talking to boys, and for some reason you just have to start with my boyfriend? Why are you always around sneaking off with *my boyfriend*?"

So the girl was upset. *Uh, understandably,* Daytime said in the back of my head. But really, if anything it was Dalton who had been all over *me* the past few days. And I was so damn tired of this basic high school drama.

So I leaned forward and said, "Maybe if you were a better girlfriend, he wouldn't have to escape from you with me, now would he?"

Nikki gasped. And in a flash, her hand shot through the air, palm aimed to slap me on the cheek.

My own hand darted up, instinctively catching her by the wrist, just before she made contact. She tried to yank her hand back, but I held on tight, glaring into her eyes, demanding her with a look to just *back off*.

"You did not!" Amy shouted. She made to lunge at me.

And then somewhere in the house, a girl began to

scream and voices rose. Amy stopped moving, and she and her sisters turned toward the sound of the commotion.

Spencer grabbed my sleeve. "It's Tracie," he said.

I let go of Nikki's hand and gestured for Dalton and Spencer. They dutifully followed as I moved past a stunned Nikki on her left. Casey stepped aside casually, letting us pass.

We forced our way through the crowd in the living room, most of its inhabitants not paying attention to the sounds of a girl clearly in distress. Great guys. But I could hear Tracie clearly, shouting demands and screaming, sounding on the verge of tears.

Behind me, I heard one of the triplets shout, "You are not getting away that easy!"

I ignored her.

We shoved our way through the kitchen and dining room and finally back into the den. The Bubonic Teutonics had stopped playing, and Jared was now near the front door, trying to grab onto the flailing girl that was Tracie Townsend. She backed away from him, her eyes wide and frightened. She heaved gasping, sobbing breaths and clawed at her hair. Her headband was all askew.

"Hey, what is it?" Jared was asking her. "It's all right, it's all right. Did you take something? I'm a police officer."

"No," Tracie sobbed. "No! Leave me alone! I have to

get out. I have to get out!" She shoved Jared in the chest, and he careened backward, barely maintaining his balance.

I leaped forward and grabbed Jared by the delightfully large bicep. "I've got this," I said. "She's a friend. She's . . . claustrophobic. We just need to get her outside."

Without my having to say anything, Dalton and Spencer went to either side of Tracie and grabbed her by the arms. Spencer was whispering something in soft, lulling tones, and Tracie seemed to stop freaking out as much. She gulped, and tears were streaming down her cheeks, but she was no longer thrashing.

Everyone in the living room was staring at the girl as Dalton and Spencer began to guide her outside. Behind me, I heard a few girls gossiping and giggling.

"Oh my God, do you think she's on meth or something? Like that's how she gets all As?"

"Oh, totally. 'I'm so excited! I'm so excited! I'm so . . . *scared!*'"

"I don't get it."

"Ohmigod, I am so showing you that on YouTube later."

I rolled my eyes.

Jared tried to rush past me to follow the guys leading Tracie out, but I placed a hand on his chest. "I've got it, really," I said. "We're going to take her home."

"You sure?" he asked me.

I stepped back and crossed my chest. "Hope to die. Well, not literally. You've got your groupies waiting."

He nodded at me. "Call me if you need help."

Jared Miller. What a Boy Scout.

I left the giggling crowd behind and went through the front door. There wasn't anyone out here now; all the kids were somewhere inside. The lawn was dark, barely lit up by the lights from inside and the few streetlamps. I saw Spencer and Dalton walking Tracie toward Spencer's minivan.

Pumping my arms, I jogged across the yard and came to stand in front of Tracie. She was no longer crying, but I could still make out the shiny tracks down her cheeks. She was breathing steadily, but her limbs were trembling. Spencer still whispered in her ear.

She was so upset, Tracie Townsend. I felt the other sides of me both rise up then—Daytime and werewolf. Both hurt for her. I couldn't stop from feeling it.

"Hey," I said, coming in close. "Tracie, it's all right. I told you this morning, we're like you. We know what you're going through. You're safe."

Swallowing, she looked up at me. "No," she whispered. "I'm sick. I'm very sick. For the past week and half, night comes and my brain breaks. Everything around me goes out of order, and nothing makes sense."

"But you're not sick," Dalton said.

She ignored him. "Everything I look at is *wrong*. I don't understand what's happening to me. I think I'm schizophrenic. I think I'm imagining all of this."

I thought about our changes. About what they unlocked. For me, all the wild inhibitions I kept hidden deep down. For Dalton, his anger. For Spencer, the laser focus he couldn't harness during the day.

And Tracie, who was Spencer's opposite in that way. Who by day had every aspect of her life completely under control. I couldn't imagine what the shift did to her. Couldn't imagine what it felt like to lose all sense of order.

"I am very sick," Tracie said again, looking at the ground now. "No one can know. No one."

"But you're not sick!" Dalton said, letting her arm drop and stepping back. His brow tightened. "We're superheroes now, Tracie. We can do anything. I don't know how you can't understand that!"

"There are no superheroes," she said. "Or maybe there are here. I don't know!" She looked between me and Spencer, tears forming once again.

"Shh, it's all right," Spencer said to her. He wrapped his arm around her shoulder, and for a moment I felt a twinge of jealousy. Stupid. He was just helping one of my pack. As he should.

"Hey!"

The shout echoed across the yard and into the street. I stepped past Tracie, leaving her with Spencer to continue whispering whatever it was he was whispering to her. Shadowed on the front porch were Amy with Nikki and Brittany behind her. Casey was nowhere to be seen.

Amy stomped toward me, arms swinging at her side. "I told you we weren't finished," she said. As she grew near, she aimed her hand at my chest like she was about to push me.

I marched toward her, smirking. "Well, too bad, because I'm finished with—"

But instead of hitting me, Amy raised her arm. And I rose with it. I gasped, shocked as the ground disappeared and nothing was beneath my feet but chill night air. Everyone below—Dalton, Tracie, Spencer, Nikki, Brittany—stared at me hovering fifteen feet in the air.

"Whoa, what are you doing?" Dalton asked. "You can fly?"

"I'm not doing this!" I shouted, my voice shrill.

It was Amy's turn to smirk up at me. She flicked her hand, and I dropped. The ground hurtled toward me, but I landed easily in a crouch and then was back on my feet.

"Amy!" Brittany hissed, coming up behind her sister. "You know we're not supposed to do that."

"Let her," Nikki commanded. She came to Amy's

side, glaring daggers at me. "I am done acting nice to this boyfriend-stealing bitch."

"Whoa," Dalton said, looking between his girlfriend and Amy.

"What is happening?" Spencer asked.

"None of this can be real, right?" Tracie murmured. "None of it."

But it was. And I remembered then all the little, seemingly innocuous things I'd seen Amy do. That day at the hospital I felt someone shove me, only to turn around and see Amy at the other end of the hall, her hand raised. In Dalton's dining room two days ago, a flick of her wrist making the back of my head prickle.

The bitch was telekinetic.

Balling my fists, I tightened my jaw and looked Amy square in the eye. "Oh, it's real all right. Looks like we're not the only ones in town with superpowers. Which means there's no need to hold back."

I leaped forward, tensing back my arm, my fist aimed at Amy's jaw. She blinked in surprise, not expecting my speed.

And it was Nikki's turn to raise a hand. It felt like someone tackled me in my chest as I fell backward, sliding across the grass, the wind knocked out of me.

"Leave her alone!" someone shouted.

Megan.

I looked up from where I lay on the ground and saw her racing toward the tussle. Some other kids were streaming out the front door, too, hearing the noise of our impromptu smackdown. I could make out Megan's new friend Patrick, hanging back, watching her leap into the fray.

Megan slammed into Nikki, sending her flying sideways, though the girl kept her balance. Megan made to jump her again, her hands arched like claws, her nails ready to scratch Nikki's eyes out.

"Megan, don't!" I shouted. I jumped to my feet and ran to get between her and a raging Nikki.

"What do you mean *don't?*" she said, exasperated. "These bimbos were shoving you, and everyone is just standing around watching! I saw it!"

"You don't know what you saw."

Out of the corner of my eye, I caught a glimpse of Amy's hand rising, her palm aimed toward Megan. My arm shot out and caught her by the wrist. With a twist of my forearm, I forced her hand down. "Don't you touch her," I snarled.

Amy smirked once more. "I wasn't planning to."

"What's going on out here?" another voice shouted from the front door. This time it was Deputy Jared, and more and more kids were spilling onto the lawn, cups and snacks in hand, taking in the show. Some boys were chanting,

224

"Catfight, catfight, catfight!"

Amy yanked herself free from my grip and stepped back, hands raised in the air. "Nothing, Officer Miller," she said sweetly. "Just a slight disagreement between girls."

I glared at her. "Yeah, Jared. I'm fine."

He came between us and looked at us both. To Nikki, Amy, and Brittany he said, "Why don't you girls go back inside?" Then, to me, "Aren't you taking your friend home?"

"Yeah," I said, finally tearing my gaze from my new archrivals to meet his blue eyes. "We were before we got distracted."

"Okay, well, get on it then, Emily," he whispered to me as the cheerleaders headed back toward the house. "No one here's supposed to know this, but Mr. McKinney hired me to keep an eye on the place as well as play with the band, so I can't have people going nuts."

"Aye, aye, Officer."

He smiled and patted me on the shoulder, then went back toward the front door himself. I remembered a week ago how attracted I'd been to him. But with Spencer by my side, he felt more like a big, protective brother. A super-hot big brother, but still.

Megan immediately ran to my side, grabbing my hands, inspecting my face.

"Are you okay?" she asked me. "Those whores didn't hurt you, did they? Where are your glasses? Did they break your glasses?"

"I'm fine," I said, yanking myself free of her. "I promise you. And I don't want you trying to get revenge or whatever, either."

"Excuse me for trying to defend my best friend!"

I couldn't deal with this right then. My gut began to boil over with anger. I had *plans*. I had a *mission*. We were supposed to be at BioZenith already, discovering why we were werewolves, looking for any information we could find about the shadowmen. I did not have time for the addition of high-strung, psychically powered cheerleaders. I did not have time for an overly needy best friend who just couldn't get the hint when I needed to be away from her for a little bit.

"Yes, excuse you!" I shouted back. "Look, Reedy, I've got a lot to do tonight. I don't have time for any more high school nonsense. So go back to the party or go home, I don't care, but I can't be here right now. I'll talk to you when I talk to you."

She gaped at me, her lip quivering. I spun on my heels and marched toward Spencer's mom's minivan, motioning for the rest of my pack to follow me.

"What just happened?" Dalton asked me as he and Spencer guided Tracie into the backseat.

"Your girlfriend has been keeping some really big secrets from you, too," I said. "Sit next to Tracie."

"Yes, ma'am!"

I got into the passenger seat and Spencer started up the car, not saying anything but constantly looking in the rearview mirror to make sure the newest member of our pack was through the worst of her mental breakdown.

He pulled us out into the street, driving us at last to BioZenith. As we passed Dalton's house, I looked out the window.

Megan still stood there in the yard, alone. Watching as I drove off, leaving her behind.

17

BREAKING AND ENTERING
IS A CRIME

It was almost nine p.m. when we finally pulled onto the dark, empty street in the industrial district where BioZenith was based. As usual at this time of night, the buildings and parking lots were empty, save for a few cars here and there. Night janitors or someone working extra late in their office, probably.

But there wasn't a single car beyond the fence surrounding BioZenith.

We drove down the street once, just to scope out the place. Seeing it as dark and empty as the night before, I had Spencer park in the lot of a building a little ways down the block. He shut off the engine, and we all leaned toward each other, except Tracie.

"Man, this is so awesome," Dalton was saying. "I can't wait to bust some heads."

"Keep yourself in check, Dalton, understand?" I said. "I am so not in the mood for you getting all out of control again."

"Again?" Spencer asked. "What are you talking about?"

"It's nothing, man," Dalton said. "I'm cool."

"If you say so." Spencer turned to me. "What's the plan?"

He was too close. His pheromones were coming after me again, invading my synapses. I recoiled—that sort of thing was reserved for Daytime. I wanted my head clear.

Spencer narrowed his eyes at me. "What is it?"

"We're going in the way Dalton and I did yesterday," I said, ignoring his question. "We tore open a hole in the fence behind one of the buildings. If it's been sealed up, we'll make a new one."

"Breaking and entering is a crime," Tracie said absently. She was slouched in her seat, her clothes ruffled, her headband still askew. She stared out the window at the empty parking lot. "Probably a felony of some sort." Her brow furrowed. "Right? Perhaps the rules are different here in my head."

"Well, if all this is in your head, Tracie, you can't get in trouble, right?"

She sat up straight at that, glaring at me. "Are you mocking me? You expect me to run to you and beg for your help with my insanity, and you make fun of me?"

"Of course not, Tracie," Spencer said, reaching back and grabbing her hand. "Don't mind Emily. Or Dalton, for that matter. None of us can really control how we act at night any more than you can."

Dalton unhooked his seat belt and opened his door. "Come on, let's go already," he said, jumping out to the pavement.

"You need to come with us, Tracie," I said. "Someone could spot you in the car."

"And inside is where we'll find what's making us all sick," Spencer added. "Okay?"

Tracie nodded slowly, considering. But I knew she'd accept Spencer's words. As far as I knew, he hadn't spoken to Tracie much before today, and yet he seemed to know the exact way to break past her defenses, hack into her code, and get her to do what we needed her to do.

That could come in handy.

Finally, Tracie sighed. "Fine, I'll go in. But I am in no way dressed for this. I don't think, anyway. Dresses aren't preferable for espionage, right?"

"Not unless you're at some upscale ball and need to seduce a trade prince," I said.

Something thudded against the side of the car. I turned to see Dalton, who had apparently just punched Spencer's mom's minivan.

"Let's go already," he said again.

Dalton and I leading, the four of us ran behind the fence surrounding BioZenith. The hole in the fence was actually still there, surprisingly. Considering all the checkpoints and the armed guards, apparently the place had never had to deal with actual intruders before.

Lucky for us.

We went through the fence one by one, then leaped to the ladder to climb atop the roof. Tracie needed some goading, insisting someone might look up and see her unmentionables, but we finally got her to join us.

This time, there were no guards. Dalton smashed the palm reader and the door opened easily, revealing a stairwell.

Much like in Dalton's dad's office, there were dim fluorescents lighting up the stairwell. I took the lead, Dalton behind me, Tracie behind him, and Spencer in the rear. He let the steel door click as quietly as possible. I turned to them, a finger to my lips, and crept down the steps.

I reached a door that read BUILDING A, LEVEL 2. Much like the door above, this had another panel to read fingerprints.

"I'll smash it too," Dalton said, trying to shove past me.

"No," I commanded. "The one on the roof was noisy

enough. Let me try something."

I grabbed the handle. It was cool to the touch. Wiggling it just to be sure, I confirmed it was, of course, locked. Gripping the handle tightly, I shoved down as hard as I could.

The lock broke, and the door swung inward with a loud squeak that echoed through the stairwell.

We all froze, tense, listening. My pulse was pounding deliciously fast. I loved it, the thrill of it all, of actually getting in here. Daytime Emily certainly hadn't approved of my—our—original attempts at getting the adrenaline rushing, but this? Yeah, this was something we could both get behind.

There were no footsteps, no alarms. I wondered if perhaps BioZenith could afford only the two guards we'd taken down the night before, one of whom was probably so not up for work that night. Strange, for a place that seemed so determined to give off the vibe of a prison. But I wasn't going to question it.

I led our little group into the hallway outside the door. We found ourselves in a maze of cubicles separated by glass partitions. Each one had a desk much like the one back in Mr. McKinney's office, and all came equipped with computers and flat-screen monitors. The monitors showed a blue haze that filled the room. Beyond the cubicles were hallways leading to back offices and meeting rooms and bathrooms.

I looked around, taking it all in. Each monitor had its own screen saver, and many of the desks were stocked with personal photos, stuffed animals, potted plants, even little candy machines and the occasional action figure or two. It was a strange bit of total humanness that I didn't really expect from the place that had turned me into a monster and had sent a man to murder us.

Quietly, we each went to a computer and began to click through the files and folders. All except for Tracie, who clung to Spencer as if he was the only thing anchoring her to the world. She sat at the edge of a chair in the cubicle he worked at, hands over her eyes, completely still.

I clicked at a couple of computers myself, but there was nothing here. Whatever this part of the building was, it must have been administrative or something equally boring. Guess even mad scientists need an HR department.

"Ugh, screw this," Dalton said. He shoved back from the desk he'd been typing at, the chair slamming into the wall of the cubicle. Some framed photos fell over, but he didn't bother to put them back in place.

"Agreed," Spencer said. "More useless junk. This is a waste of our time."

My eye caught a framed piece of paper on the wall next

to the door we'd come in. I got up from my chair and went to it. It turned out to be a map of the facility, showing fire exits and escape routes.

I grabbed the frame and tore it from the wall. It came free in a cloud of white dust, a piece of plaster ripped off with it. I found where we were, then looked over the rest of the map. It seemed that beneath us would be the main lobby of the building, which was probably similarly useless. Back behind the cubicles were some fancier offices, which could be handy but which could also be just as dull. Tracing with my finger, I found an exit here on the second floor that went across the glass walkway I'd seen outside and into Building B. There, on the top level, were a bunch of rooms labeled "laboratories."

The first floor of Building B apparently and strangely had no exits. It also had no rooms, at least none that were marked. That seemed highly suspicious. My curiosity was officially piqued.

By this time, Dalton, Spencer, and Tracie were all heading back toward me. I dropped the map to the carpet at my feet, not wanting to carry it around anymore, then looked to them.

"Okay, new plan: no more messing around with desktop PCs. Come on."

We ran through the center of the floor, between the

cubicles, toward the glass-paneled door that led to the walkway. There was another fingerprint pad, another handle I easily broke with my hand. This time, the glass on the door cracked from the force of the blow.

"Oops."

"Well, it's not like we care about leaving a trail," Spencer said. "Though it occurs to me we should have brought gloves."

Gloves. Huh. Well, it was too late now, and I didn't want to admit I hadn't thought of it. I shushed Spencer, then motioned for the four of us to crouch down. Leaning forward, I looked through the glass windows of the walkway.

No one outside. Perfect.

Still crouching, we more or less ran the length of the walkway. One more door. Handle twisted. Lock broken. Glass crunching from the force. The door pulled open toward me, and with it came a blast of cool air that smelled weirdly antiseptic, like a hospital.

I stepped through the door, taking a look at my surroundings. "Now this is what I'm talking about," I said as the others crowded around me.

We were in a hallway, on either side of which were glass walls and glass doors—everything was glass here in BioZenith, as if whoever was in charge wanted to make sure no one would have any privacy, could never hide from the eyes of their bosses. The hallways extended back deeper into the building, row upon row of glass rooms in which to do experiments.

To the immediate left and right of me were labs filled with plants: a small apple tree, a stalk of corn, various other root vegetables, exotic flowers. There were long tables covered with beakers and magnifying glasses and petri dishes, computers and scrawled notes. Whiteboards with formulas written on them.

"Huh," I said. "I didn't actually expect they'd be working on plants. I thought it was just a cover story."

"Not much of a cover story if they can't back it up," Spencer said, peering into the dimly lit lab opposite the one I was looking at.

I turned to find Tracie staring into the same lab, her face pressed against the glass. Her breath steamed the glass, fogging it up.

"Look at it," she said, her voice whimsical. "It's alive, isn't it? I can see it moving."

"Alive, maybe," I said. "But I doubt they can move very far."

Spencer tilted his head musingly. "What if they're wereplants? Human by day, plants by night?"

I barked a laugh. "Let's not go there just yet."

"Yo!" Dalton shouted, and we all turned to find him

farther down the main hallway. He leaned against a white concrete wall next to a gray steel door, with yet one more level of security via a keypad and palm reader combo. "Come on!" he yelled, his leg shaking, his lips in a tight line. "I don't care about plants."

Motioning with my head, I went to Dalton, Spencer and Tracie behind me. Dalton had already grabbed the handle of the door, and when he twisted it, it broke completely free from the metal frame, leaving a gaping, jagged hole.

Dalton laughed. "I guess I don't know my own strength," he said in an affected, high-pitched voice, then laughed again as if it was the wittiest bon mot that had ever been bon motted.

Blinking rapidly, Tracie grabbed my arm. "I—"

"What?" I asked her. "What is it?"

She just shook her head. "I lost it. It'll come back to me."

Dalton raised a leg and kicked open the door. It flew back and slammed loudly, sending the glass walls back in the main hall shuddering. He stalked through the doorway, and the three of us followed.

And found what we'd been looking for.

There were more labs here on either side of us, with the same white workbenches, the same polished steel equipment.

Only the samples in here were not of the flora variety. It was fauna all the way.

In the lab to my left, on a multilevel shelf built into the walls, were jar upon glass jar of preserved organs. Hearts with weird, ropy black growths encasing them. A brain with one hemisphere larger than the other. The pickled remnants of some sort of fetal creature that was definitely not human, or if it ever was, it had mutated into something unrecognizable.

It was here, in all its gory glory. Absolute proof that BioZenith was doing some sort of tests on what looked to be human and animal body parts. For some reason, it was all hush-hush. And I guessed that reason was because no one could know they'd succeeded at some point long ago. Had done something to the DNA of five human fetuses that would eventually cause them to mutate into fearsome beasts.

"Oh wow," Spencer whispered. "Gross."

I turned and looked into the opposite lab. My hands immediately clenched into fists. There weren't jars in this room, no. There were two big glass tubes going floor to ceiling, filled with some sort of green gel.

And inside that gel were the bodies of two small children. No more than five or six. Only they were hardly human now. One's face had split in two, half its head bulging, much like the brain in the opposite room. A small appendage that could have been the start of a tail was at the base of its back.

Its hands were claws that were much too big for its body, gnarled talons like a vulture's.

The other child's head was flattened, like a ball of dough crushed by a giant hand, though the skin wasn't broken; no broken bones showed through. Almost as if she'd been born that way—and I was certain it was a she. Its chest was caved in, the flesh growing into it, forming a cavern of skin. And peeking through that skin was an impression of a heart much too big, one that would have crushed the surrounding organs.

Test subjects. Failed test subjects. Two children meant to transform into who knows what, but who died instead, and were now floating here. Cadavers in the lair of someone who couldn't just leave nature alone.

Tracie's hands went to her lips, and tears formed in her eyes. "Oh, what beautiful children," she whispered.

I wasn't paying attention to her. I was busy suppressing Daytime Emily, who was screaming in the back of my head, thrashing, trying to unsee the monstrosities right in front of me. I didn't have time for emotions right then. I had to think. What were these things? Why did they exist? Did they predate me and Spencer and Dalton and Tracie and Emily C.? That seemed absurd, for these people to still be studying failed experiments well after they had obviously fixed the problem.

"What are you talking about?" Dalton spat. "Those things are monsters!"

So if these two children occurred after us, what did that mean? That they'd lost the formula? That they were trying to make more kids like us but didn't know how? How was that possible? And I could clearly see belly buttons, so that meant these two had been birthed by someone. What mother, or father for that matter, would offer up their own child like this?

Tracie went to the glass, peering through it once more, just like she had with the plants. "How can you call them monsters? Look at his beautiful smile. Her beautiful eyes. They're so peaceful."

"Tracie," Spencer whispered, pulling her back. "You don't see the boy's face split open?"

She rounded on him. "Don't you try to mess with my head, too, Spencer!" she shouted. "I see no such thing. And—" She paused and cocked her head, ear aimed toward the ceiling. "Oh, there it is again. What I forgot earlier. Do you hear that?"

"Hear what?" I asked.

There came a hissing and whooshing as above us, ceiling panels rushed open. Four metallic orbs, the size of basketballs, dropped through and began to hover in the air over our heads. Red lights on their fronts darted back and forth throughout the dark hallway, like some obnoxious kid with a laser pointer. All at once, each orb cast a light on one of us.

A panel beneath the light opened. A tiny black metal barrel protruded.

Tracie pointed a finger up at the orbs. Flatly, she said, "That."

And the orbs began to fire.

18

THEY CAN'T HELP IT IF THEY'RE MURDEROUS ROBOTS

The sound of gunfire cracked through the air, and blasts of orange flame lit up the hall. The four of us ducked in unison, and I felt a rush of air as bullets flew over my head. Glass crunched behind me as they tore clean through the walls in front of the labs.

Bullets. These things weren't messing around.

"I knew this was too easy!" Spencer shouted over the bursts of gunfire. The robots or whatever they were fired their spray of bullets over our heads, their sensor lights apparently not picking up that we were no longer in the line of fire.

"So they want to play, huh?" I shouted back. "Well, I'm here to play, too."

Dalton laughed and whooped. "Now that's what I'm talking about!"

"You two are insane!" Tracie screamed, cowering beneath her arms.

The gunfire ended abruptly, and the mini red search lights blinked back on. They scoured beyond where we'd once stood, aimed toward the ground now, apparently looking for bodies.

I picked myself up in a crouch, then tumbled forward, behind the searchlights. The others crawled after me.

"Dalton, turn into a pommel horse," I hissed.

He nodded, then got on his hands and knees so that he was more or less a platform. I got to my feet and spun to face the robots. They still searched where we no longer were. Apparently when the AI was programmed for these suckers, the technology hadn't been all that advanced.

I wondered, briefly, if the things worked off sound and vision alike. I figured I'd try 'em both.

I bunched my legs, then shoved off. As Spencer and Tracie watched, I jumped onto Dalton's back, then sprung myself up into the air toward the nearest robot orb. It slammed into my gut, and I gripped it with arms and legs both. My weight brought us back halfway toward the floor, the thing spinning as though to shake me off.

"Gotcha!" I shouted as loud as I could.

The nearest orb whipped around in the air at the sound of my voice, its little red dot appearing on my shoulder. Before it could fire, I heaved my entire body, forcing the orb I held to spin me away. The red dot now glowed on the robot's metallic surface.

And the other orb fired.

Bullets penetrated the robot's hull in a flurry. Sparks flew and smoke belched from the rapidly growing wound. The force of the blasts and an electric shock shot me free of the orb, and I fell to my back on the floor.

A moment later, the orb I'd grabbed fell to the ground in front of me, flames licking its useless interior hull. The robot above ceased firing.

"One down," I said.

Letting out a weird sound almost like a screech, Tracie got up and began to race down the hall, toward the door that would lead down to the floor below. At the same time, Dalton leaped to his feet, jumped over me, and ran in the same direction. While Tracie fussed with the door handle to break it, Dalton leaped up higher than even I had jumped. He grabbed another of the robots in both beefy arms, and the massive weight of the muscly boy brought it slamming down to the tile floor. Face red and veins bulging on his neck, he shouted and raised a foot—then stomped on the machine. It crumpled beneath his sneakers as though he'd just smashed an aluminum can.

The other two robots, meanwhile, had found a target. Two pinpoints of blood-red light appeared on the side of Tracie's off-center headband as she put both hands on the door handle. Her face went steely cold, focused, and she shoved down.

"Tracie, get down, now!" Spencer shouted.

The door lock broke with an echoing thunk.

Tracie whipped open the door toward her.

And the machines fired.

The sound of the gunfire was like thunder, the bullets hitting metal like fist-size hail pounding against windows during a winter storm. Tracie had darted through the doorway just in time—though she left it wide open, the door resting against the end of the hall.

Much faster than I'd thought they could move, the remaining two orbs rushed forward, propelled by whatever invisible force let them hover like UFOs. Their AI must have recalibrated or something, because there was no confusion as to where their target had gone. They were following Tracie.

Dalton was too busy stomping on his orb over and over to notice what was happening. Bits of robot shrapnel flew out from the force of his shoes. I got to my feet, as did Spencer, and side by side we ran down the hall toward the stairwell door. The glass walls on either side of us were pockmarked with bullet holes, cracks snaking out to the corners.

We weren't going to be able to make it before the robots darted into the stairwell. I cursed Tracie silently. Why had she been so stupid? She shouldn't have made any move unless I'd said it. I was her alpha! Me! She was going to get killed just like Emily Cooke, another of my pack dead, and I couldn't bear it, I—

Right before the orbs reached the open doorway, a hand lashed out from the darkness and grabbed the broken door handle. Tracie swung the steel door closed, and the two orbs hovered in front of it, their little laser eyes scanning the blank door, confused as to what had just happened.

The door slammed back open, catching the two robot orbs with it and smashing them against the wall. Tracie burst out of the stairwell, then stood parallel to the door and clenched her fists.

She leaped into the air, kicking the door with both legs at once, crushing the robots with the force of her strength and the heavy steel door. She fell on her back, skirt askew, and the sounds of hissing wires and falling metal filled the air. Spencer and I both stopped running, gaping at her as she got back to her feet.

For a moment, no one said a thing.

"That was *awesome*!" Dalton bellowed. He whooped a

laugh and ran forward, putting both hands on my shoulders and jumping up in pure glee. "Oh man, did you see that? We killed those bastards! They shot at us and we took 'em down like they were nothing!"

I couldn't help but grin, even as I pulled myself away from bouncy Dalton's grip. I stepped forward and grabbed Tracie's arm.

"Tracie, what possessed you to do that?" I asked. "I mean, it was sick and all, but . . ."

She shook her head. "I'm not sure. I shouldn't have done that, right? The correct response would have been to stay low and out of sight. But I . . . saw it differently, I think. I just knew that if I did the irrational, I could confuse the machinery and trap it. Does that make sense?" She put her hand on her head. "Does any of this make sense?"

"I think it's starting to," I said.

"Hey, Em Dub, we aren't out of the woods yet," Spencer said, interrupting me and Tracie. "Obviously there's an automated security system. We need to get on these computers and find what we need."

"No," I said. "We're going down below. These labs can't be all there is. There's something down there."

"Then let's go!" Dalton said, running through the open door. "Maybe more of those robots are down there!"

Tracie crossed her arms, looking at the two robots

Dalton and I had taken down. "Poor things," she said with a *tsk*. "They were just doing as they were programmed to do. They can't help it if they're murderous robots."

I narrowed my eyes at Tracie. I wasn't exactly sure yet what her shtick was as Nighttime, but something about the words resonated in the back of my brain. Daytime seemed to understand. Maybe even Wolftime.

I didn't want to think about it. I deeply disliked the idea of being programmed to act a certain way.

I waved Tracie and Spencer along. "Let's go. One last place to scope out."

The trip down the stairwell to the story below was completely uneventful. As was breaking the lock. Whoever had designed this place hadn't counted on it being infiltrated by teenagers with superstrength, apparently.

I didn't know what, exactly, to expect as I opened that last door. A storage bay, maybe? Some sort of robot ninja training center? A thousand more tubes filled with deformed children trapped in lime Jell-O?

What I got was pure, total blackness. A complete absence of light, save for what dim glow from the stairwell's fluorescents shone past us into the room. It was cool down here, and even without the map and without light I got the sense that beyond lay one massive, open room.

I patted the walls on either side of the door, but aside from a keypad panel, there was nothing, no sort of light switch. With a shrug to the others, I took a few steps in, my shadow disappearing into the darkness before me.

After three steps, I heard a click, then the whirring sounds of several machines powering up. Electric buzzes sounded high above me, and then row after row of achingly bright fluorescent lights turned on, revealing at last the strange cavernous room that had one single entrance.

It was almost like being on the set of the *Enterprise*. The new one, not old-school or Next Gen. We're talking full Apple-store style, J. J. Abrams–directed, solar-flare-at-the-lens *Enterprise* deck here.

There were four large computer bays in the shape of a quarter circle in each corner of the room. The whirring sounds were the computer monitors and systems powering on. Above each bay, large flat-screen monitors half the size of a movie screen hung from the ceiling. They blinked on, revealing the BioZenith company logo.

But that wasn't what immediately caught our attention. No, that would have been the round platform that took up the majority of the center of the room. Specifically, what was on top of it: Several fifteen-foot, gleaming silver rings that rotated slowly, like some sort of 3D representation of the solar system's orbit or something. They oscillated around one another, outlining an empty, spherical area. I didn't know why, but somehow I could just feel that the rings were in fact circling *something*. What that something was, I had no clue.

Between the bays and near the rings were various extraneous machinery, yellow-and-black-striped platforms that could lift someone up to the ceiling, a crane or two. But really, nothing compared to the spectacle of those rings, moving almost like liquid mercury, hovering of their own accord.

"I feel like I'm in the future," Spencer said, awe filling his voice. "I don't even know where to begin."

"How about the computers?" I asked. "I think out of any in this building, these are bound to have at least something."

Cracking his knuckles, Spencer was already heading to the closest bay. "Don't have to ask me twice." He sat in one of the swiveling chairs and immediately began tapping at the screen, scrolling through menus and cycling through subroutines, or whatever. He took his password-cracking thumb drive out of his pocket, found a port, and plugged it in.

"Is it just me, or is there something very strange about those rings?" Tracie mused beside me. She had become considerably calmer ever since we'd started our trek through the facility. And here she was, finally getting involved, asking questions. About time.

"It's not just you," I said. "There's something there. I can feel it."

"Hey, Em Dub, I need your thumb drive." Not looking up from his screen, Spencer lifted one hand and waved me over.

I trotted over to him, pulling the lanyard over my head. I handed it to him, then looked up, back at those strange rings. My eyes settled on Dalton next. He was in front of the bay where Spencer sat, pacing back and forth, muttering to himself. One hand was balled into a fist that continually punched his thigh. The other kept scratching at his stubbly red hair.

"You doing all right over there, Sparky?" I shouted.

Dalton nodded, much too rapidly. "Man, I just wish they'd come already. Those guards or robots. I can't deal with this waiting anymore."

"Don't worry, we'll be done soon," Spencer called. He flicked at various icons as though he'd been using the proprietary BioZenith software his entire life. "Their processors are major fast, I can barely keep up with all the info they want to give me. Okay, here, I think that's all of it." He pulled my thumb drive out and handed it back to me. I looped it back over my neck.

"You finished?" I asked him. "See anything interesting?"

"Not yet," he said. "I think I found something Dr. Elliott created, or accessed, anyway. The files have been scrubbed clean of any identifying name, but all the rest list who worked on them. And the program was last successfully accessed on September seventh." He shot me a look. "The night we started to change."

Tracie wandered over to us and rested her chin on the top of the bay. Dalton still kept pacing, still kept smacking himself.

"September seventh was the Tuesday before last, right?" she asked. Without waiting for an answer, she continued. "That was the night I first got sick. I remember because the next morning was when we found out Emily Cooke died."

"How many times do we have to tell you that you aren't sick?" Dalton said. "Come on! You just killed two robots! Enjoy it!"

Tracie let out a huff, but didn't say anything more.

"Hey, I got it," Spencer said, grinning widely up at me as though looking for approval. It was all I could do to not pat his head like a puppy.

"What did you get?" I asked instead, leaning over him.

He pointed at the screen. "Something called 'Havoc.' He accessed it that day and started some sort of timer, then put in some encryptions so no one would see what he'd done."

My face tightened. "After which he grabbed a gun and killed Emily Cooke."

One of my pack, werewolf me seethed.

"Looks like it."

Tracie leaned farther over the bay, her eyes darting over the timer's scrolling numbers. She chewed her lip but didn't say anything.

Spencer went back to the monitor and began tapping. "Maybe this is one last access code to hack through," he said. "If I can figure out . . ." His voice petered out, brow furrowing. A few more taps and the constantly rotating numbers stopped.

00:00:00 flashed in bright green numbers like a digital clock.

Something *clicked* inside me, and I gasped. In the chair, Spencer doubled over, clutching his stomach. Tracie backed away from the bay, shaking her head back and forth, her fear coming back all at once.

And Dalton reared back his head and howled into the rafters, then laughed and laughed, wouldn't stop laughing.

My vision snapped gray, and I was hybrid Emily again. Only I wasn't three distinct girls anymore, I was one massively confused one. I wheeled around, clutching for anything to grab on to. This wasn't like any of the previous transformations. Those had grown increasingly smooth.

Now, somehow this was coming too soon. I felt it deep inside that this was *not supposed to happen*, and I started to hyperventilate.

As the world swirled around me, I looked back at those endlessly orbiting rings floating above the massive platform. Only with the gray wolf vision, the space between the rings was no longer empty. The air was torn, ripped to shreds at the edges, and through the gap I could see tall, black skyscrapers, or towers, or castles—*something*—crumbling to pieces. I could see creatures with wings, or planes, or both zipping through the sky, leaving behind a trail of dark clouds. I saw shadowy figures run past, not noticing the hole next to them, just running in droves, carrying long sticks or bats or guns, I couldn't tell.

A shudder ran through me, and I closed my eyes, gasping. I was transforming into the werewolf. I wasn't ready. My body wasn't ready, hadn't had enough time to transition between Daytime and Nighttime and Wolftime. I tried to focus, because we were deep in the bowels of some terrifying and strange laboratory filled with preserved monstrosities and machines that couldn't exist and holes in the wind.

"Take off anything that won't stretch with you," I gasped. "We can't leave behind our clothes! Take them off and force the wolf to carry—argh!"

I fell to the floor, my fingers fumbling for my belt. I couldn't see what anyone else was doing, could just hear their agony. Finally I got my pants free, my underwear, not caring that anyone could see. I shoved them down to my ankles, realized my shoes were still on. I kicked them off, tore at my socks.

My spine cracked, sending a shudder up to my shoulders. Pins prickled all over my body as the wolf fur began to sprout, bursting up from my skin. I could feel my jaw crunching, elongating.

I focused on my clothes—my shirt would stretch, the thumb drive on the lanyard would hang on. I knotted my shoelaces together even as my fingers started to stretch, even as my nails blackened and dug free of my cuticles.

Another shudder ran through me and I doubled over, feeling as though I was going to vomit. My insides were shifting, squishing inside my gut, my chest cavity, and oh God I could hear it! It hadn't been like this last time, not even the first time I remembered changing. I wanted to scream, but nothing would come out.

"It's the program," I heard Spencer shout, his voice deepening, his words starting to slur. "The computer. He activated it, that's why we changed. I must have— uuugggggrrrrl." His words disappeared as his vocal cords stiffened in places, loosened in others. I knew because it was happening to me too. Desperately I balled my pants and underwear together, then strung the tied-together shoes around my neck.

My spine continued to tug, crunching as it formed a tail at the base of my back. The numbing effect of the change hadn't spread there and I howled, feeling as though someone was tearing a piece of my flesh off with their bare hands.

And then, it was done. I lay there, a wolf-girl in a stretched-out turtleneck, with shoes around my neck and jeans clutched in my claws. I'm sure I looked fairly ridiculous, but I didn't care. Shivers of pain quaked through my body, aftershocks of an earthquake I hadn't really felt. I have no idea how long I was incapacitated. I just knew my limbs weren't working yet.

A roar echoed through the vast room.

I looked up. Dalton was there in front of me. In front of the computer bay. He had shed all his clothes and sniffed at the monitor that Spencer had been working on. Like me, Spencer lay on the ground, clothes clenched in his half-human, half-wolf hands, shoes tied around his neck.

I tilted my head back and saw Tracie on all fours, shivering like a dog left out in the cold. The headband was still on her head. Her purple dress hung in tatters from her shoulders. Her shoes, now scraps. Deep in the back of my head, daytime me observed that Tracie now looked like someone's teacup Chihuahua all dressed up like a little princess, and if I'd had the capacity to find things funny at that moment, I'd have laughed until I was hoarse.

Dalton let loose another roar. Of the four of us, he appeared to be the only one fully recovered. I looked back at him just in time to see him leap onto the computer bay he'd been sniffing at. He punched down with one clawed fist, tearing into the machinery. He stomped with his powerful leg, smashing the monitor that had the countdown timer. Glass flew through the air. There were sparks, and the stench of burning plastic that was deeply unpleasant to my wolf nose.

And a loud, screeching alarm blared throughout the room.

Still standing atop the destroyed computer bay, he spread his arms, arched his back, and howled along with the horrible din of the alarm. I could sense it in the echoes of his booming voice: This was what werewolf Dalton wanted. Not answers. Not research.

Alarms meant robots. Or guards.

Something to fight.

He leaped down from the computer bay. Several of the swivel chairs fell as he passed. He bounded past all of us to the door leading to the upper level.

I jumped to my feet, growling at Spencer and Tracie

until they did the same. I gestured with my snout toward the door. *Follow.* They understood.

Still clutching my human self's clothes, I ran around the computer bay and found Dalton's jeans, shirt, jacket, and shoes. I scooped them all up, even as the werewolf side of me protested, then I turned to follow Spencer and Tracie.

The alarms were going to draw attention. Lots of it.

And the daytime version of myself was there, for just a moment, speaking to wolf me: *I need to keep Dalton from doing something he would regret for the rest of his life.*

19

YOU'VE DONE ENOUGH

I lumbered up the stairwell into the laboratory. All my wolf instincts told me to drop the bundle of cloth in my arms and run on all fours. It would be faster, and I needed to be fast.

Daytime and Nighttime both asserted themselves. *Do not let them go,* they told wolf me. *Do not leave more evidence of who you are than you already have.*

I whined deep in my throat. But I listened.

Dodging broken glass and jagged robot parts, I bounded toward the door to the walkway. Tracie and Spencer were already there, Tracie still looking like something out of a nightmarish Berenstain Bears book in her prim dress.

Managing to catch up to them, I let out a sharp bark. *Keep moving.* They knew what it meant, darted into the walkway. And stopped when we found Dalton.

He stood in the center of the walkway, looking through the plate-glass window at the parking lot. It was no longer empty. A gray van had pulled through the front gate, and two men, dressed like the guards from the night before, jumped out. They both had rifles. They were followed by two brown-and-black dogs, all narrow and sleek with pointed jaws and sharp ears. Dobermans.

Growling, Dalton rammed his shoulder into the window. It cracked. He rammed again and again, the crack growing wider and wider.

I barked again at Spencer and Tracie. *Don't stop. Go to the roof. Escape from here. I'll get Dalton.*

A lot of sentiments for one bark to convey. But somehow we knew even without words what our wolf selves meant. It was some combination of inflection, of scents I naturally emitted, of the flick of my ears, the narrowing of my eyes.

They obeyed, running past Dalton, Tracie on all fours and Spencer on two. They disappeared into the first building we'd come into.

I ran up to Dalton as he rammed one more time into the window. It was now a crystalline web, a windshield after a high-speed crash. I growled and nipped at his side. He growled louder, lunged at me, snapped at my snout.

One more barrel into the window. And it shattered.

Shards of glass rained to the asphalt below. The noise alerted the guards, and the two dogs started barking wildly. The driver of the van, another guard, leaped out of the vehicle and ran to join his companions.

Before I could do anything, Dalton leaped through the open window. He landed with a heavy thud against the asphalt. His eyes were on the guards.

"What is that?" the driver of the van shouted. "What the hell is *that*?"

The other two didn't react, though they made no move forward, just watched wide-eyed as Dalton took one step toward them, then another. He stepped into the glare of the van's headlights, and he was fully illuminated to the three men. His ears were flat against his skull. His teeth were bared.

Dalton looked between the three men one by one. Then, as in the lower level of the labs, he arched his back and howled up into the sky. The sound echoed throughout the night.

The driver of the van turned and ran.

The howl had been defiant. Murderous. Werewolf Dalton lusted for blood and he needed it, would defy his alpha to obtain it.

I had to stop him.

I leaped through the window as well, narrowly missing

the pile of shattered glass as I landed in the parking lot. I dropped Dalton's clothes and my pants to the ground, then stalked forward, growling.

Dalton's ears twitched. I knew he could hear me, could hear the warning I was so clearly giving. But he did not back down.

The driver leaped into the van and slammed the door shut. I heard the engine turn over.

One of the guards looked back over his shoulder. "Don't you leave us, man! Don't you go nowhere!" At his feet, his dog was backing away, its tail tucked between its legs.

I stalked ever closer to Dalton. Growls burst from my jaws, louder and louder. *Back down*, I was commanding. *Come with me. Now.*

Everything happened at once.

The only guard who hadn't spoken leveled his gun, aiming it at Dalton's torso.

That guard's Doberman darted toward Dalton, yapping and barking, stupidly baring its teeth.

And I howled one last plea for Dalton to stop.

The guard fired, the boom of his rifle cracking between the buildings. Dalton ducked the bullet easily and lunged forward, going for the Doberman. His jaws wrapped around the Doberman's throat, and he reared back, shaking the poor creature back and forth, snapping its neck, killing it instantly.

The other Doberman yelped and fled back toward the van, followed by his guard, who made crosses over his chest as he dove into the vehicle. The remaining guard—the one who'd fired—dropped his gun, staring stupefied as Dalton wrenched the dead Doberman back and forth, back and forth.

Blood leaked from Dalton's teeth, dripped down his chin. The dog hung from his jaws, lifeless. Dalton's eyes narrowed on the man who'd tried to shoot him. With one last wrench of his head, he tore free the Doberman's throat and tossed its body at the guard.

The man leaped back, narrowly missing being hit square in the chest. He let out a devastated sound somewhere between a moan and a scream.

Dalton bunched his legs, preparing to leap at the man, to kill him just as he'd done the dog.

I leaped first.

I landed on Dalton's back with both feet, flattening him to the ground. He roared in protest. Straddling him, I roared right back.

The lone remaining guard stood there watching us, every limb shaking. Behind him, the van's wheels screeched as its driver forced it to turn much too fast, to get them away from the devil wolf creatures they probably weren't warned were the source of the alarm.

I met the man's eyes, growling. I flicked my jaw toward the van. He got the hint and turned and ran, screaming for the men in the van to wait for him.

Dalton growled beneath me and snapped at my heels. *Get off me!*

I swatted his face with my clawed hand. *Stop. You've done enough.*

He bucked beneath me, struggling to force me off as he barked his protests, his eyes manic and wild. *Let me go, you bitch! Let me feed!*

No.

He carried on like that, for how long I didn't know. But he couldn't buck me free. I stayed focused, wouldn't let him best me. Wouldn't let him hurt anyone else.

As I did, I tried not to look at the dead dog. Tried not to smell its blood, its meat. Forced myself to bury the urges that made me want to bite into its flesh and—

No. I would never.

Eventually, Dalton's adrenaline died down. He lay mostly still beneath my bulk, his chest heaving. Blood still dripped from his jaws and coated his fur, but his eyes had calmed. He was still angry at me, I was sure of it. But he was calm.

I climbed off him slowly. Growled once more. *Come.*

He made no noise of response. Did not flick his ears. Did not gesture with his eyes or snout. I stood and watched as he walked slowly back the way we'd come, to the pile of clothes on the ground. Stopping just before them, he looked back over his shoulder at his kill. I barked. He bent over and collected our clothing.

Exhaustion flooded my furry limbs. I walked behind him, forcing him through the tear in the fence and toward the trees. The night had been long. Eventful. Much too eventful. I wasn't sure if I even had the energy to run home, but the smell of the woods soothed me. There was earth here instead of asphalt. The scent of pine needles instead of the stench of melted plastic.

We were almost to the trees when a chill rushed through me, shoulders to tail.

The shadowmen.

My whole body stiffened. I watched them appear, one by one, the shadowy man-shaped figures that had been stalking me the entire week. Just like the night of the drag race, there were dozens of them. One second nothing, then one would appear. In front of me, blocking the woods. Behind me, guarding the way we'd come.

Any semblance of Dalton's rage faded then. He howled, not loud and defiant, but plaintive, frightened. Much like the Doberman that had escaped its confrontation with a werewolf, Dalton tucked his tail between his legs and came to stand close to me.

The shadows stood in their staggered pattern, some very close to me, some deeper in the trees. Not a single one moved. They just watched. Always watching.

Werewolf me could not move. Could not take another step. These things, whatever they were, had some sort of DNA memory with the wolf side of me that I could not escape. Fear flooded over me, drowning me. I whimpered.

And in the absence of the wolf's instincts to guide me, Nighttime took control. Commanded with a bark for me and Dalton. *Run!*

I did just that, barreling forward past the nearest shadowmen. Dalton's claws clacked against the asphalt as he followed. *These guys are incorporeal*, Nighttime reasoned. *What can they do? Nothing! Not a thing!*

To prove herself right, Nighttime guided werewolf me to bound through a shadowman directly between me and the trees. If that night in my room was any indication, I'd bound through it none the worse for wear. Perhaps with a slight chill.

Nighttime laughed defiantly in the back of my mind. I lowered my head and made to leap through the shadowman.

I thudded against a solid, icy body. Stunned, I fell back, and Dalton skidded to a stop in the dirt next to me.

The shadowman I'd tried to tackle wasn't incorporeal at all. It was very much physically there. Which was impossible, because it was just a wispy, smoky figure! I could see right through it! My hand had gone *through* it when I was human!

Tilting its head, the shadowman raised a hand toward my face, as though to stroke my jaw.

Nighttime Emily was no longer in control. The wolf took over. I howled at the sky in absolute terror, then I ran, my shoes slapping against my chest. I darted around the shadows as they reached out to touch me with their frozen fingers, wolf me not caring if Dalton was following me or not.

I made for the woods, hearing Dalton galloping at my heels. I ran, the world becoming a haze around me until I got to my backyard, where I collapsed in the grass next to the shed. Dalton was there too, sapped of energy, unable to get back to his own house.

Distantly, I sensed someone there, watching us. Another shadowman, probably. Always shadowmen. I whimpered and curled up into a fetal position.

Somehow, I fell asleep.

20

YOU ARE NOT A KILLER

I have vague memories of becoming human again in the middle of the night. Of ushering Dalton into the shed and both of us groggily putting our clothes back on. It felt like a dream at the time, but considering we both woke up the next morning dressed in wrinkled, slobbered-on clothes and hidden behind the shed's doors, it must have happened something like that.

The first thing I clearly remember after the night in BioZenith, though, was waking up to gray morning light and crisp, damp air on my skin. My eyes fluttered open, taking in the plywood walls around me, the tools hanging from nails above me, and I thought, *Wow, déjà vu.*

Only this time, I wasn't naked with splinters in my back.

And this time, I wasn't alone.

Realizing that, I sat up with a start. The blurry figure of Dalton sat across from me, knees to chest, back against the wall. He was rocking back and forth, shivering from the chill. I pulled my glasses out of my pocket and placed them on my face, seeing him clearly. There were rips in his pants and his jacket, but they were still wearable.

His chin was coated with rust-red blood.

He blinked at me as I sat up, his stare haunted. He opened his mouth to say something, but only a dry croak came out.

"Sit still," I whispered. "It's okay. Just sit still."

Groaning, I got to my feet. My whole body ached, from sleeping on the hard, dusty floor all night, or the untimely forced change into a werewolf, or the fight with the cheerleaders. Or all three. New information threatened to overwhelm me—*Robots! Psychics! Solid shadowmen! Creatures in jars!*—but I made myself focus on one thing, and that was Dalton.

The shed's door groaned as I opened it. I squinted, the light burning my eyes. There was no one around. It felt really early—there was that damp feeling of early morning, and the silence of no cars, no kids awake, and no TVs blaring. It was day, but no one was up yet.

My shoes were still in the shed, so my bare feet squelched

in the grass as I went to the side of the building. I uncoiled the hose there, cranked on the faucet. Cool water gurgled from the hose's end.

I brought the hose to the front of the shed and told Dalton to drink. He grabbed it from me and gulped down the water, and even though it was cold outside, he held the hose over his head and let the water cascade down his forehead. He pulled the hose away quickly, shaking his head to free the excess water.

The blood on his chin had not yet washed away.

"Here," I said softly. I crouched next to him and took over the water. I made him jut his chin out toward me. But water wasn't enough. I stuck the end of my shirt over my hand and used it as a rag, scrubbing at his face until the only red on it was from the cloth rubbing his skin raw.

I put the hose away. When I came back, Dalton had retreated inside the shed and was back to sitting, rocking back and forth. I crawled inside myself and pulled the shed door closed.

For a moment, we both sat there in silence, not really looking at each other.

"I killed that dog," Dalton said flatly.

I swallowed. "I know."

His eyes still weren't focused on me. "I wanted to kill those men, too. I wanted it so bad, Emily. Just to go at them and slice them open and watch them bleed at my feet."

"Dalton . . ."

His hazel eyes snapped to mine. "I don't understand," he said. "All I can see now is that poor dog just lying there. And I did that to it; its blood was all over my face. I would never do that. I love dogs. What if it had been Max I did that to instead? What if I—"

I leaned forward on my knees and grabbed both his hands in mine. I whispered "Shhh" and let him rock there. All I could think about as I watched him there was the night Spencer and I killed Dr. Elliott. How after I lost the high of Spencer's calming pheromones, after being interrogated by the police about what we saw, all I could do was sit in my room and clutch Ein and stare at the wall. Seeing Dr. Elliott's face. Seeing his horrible wound. Smelling the coppery scent of his blood.

Knowing that as the wolf I'd wanted nothing so bad as to rip the man apart.

Knowing I was a monster.

Dalton grabbed my hands back, gripping them hard. "I told you before, I get angry a lot. I never really told anyone but you. I always kept it down, just shoved it way deep down, because I'm not allowed to be that guy. I'm Big D. I'm the superhero." He licked his chapped lips and took in a shaky breath. "It felt really good letting it all burst out the

271

past few nights. But I killed that little dog. I wanted to—"

"Hey," I said, placing a hand on his cheek. "Look at me." He did. "You are not a killer. There is that wolf side in all of us now, and it's dangerous, and it's deadly, and that's why we've got to learn to keep it in check. You're only as much of a monster as you choose to be."

And as I said the words, I knew they weren't just for Dalton. It was something I'd needed to tell myself for a while now.

"Emily, what if I can never control it?" Dalton whispered. "I keep trying, or telling myself to try, but each time I change, the nighttime side of me cares less and less about what I want."

"But you did, though," I said. "You got through to the wolf at least. You followed me when I asked."

Shaking his head, Dalton pulled my hand away from his cheek. "I was planning to attack you when we reached the woods. I was going to bite you and kill you because of how you stopped me in front of the prey—the guards, I mean. If it wasn't for the shadowmen showing up, I would have."

I didn't know what to say to that. I dropped my hands and rocked backward to sit on my butt.

"You hate me now," Dalton said.

"No," I said quickly, much too quickly. I'm sure I

sounded shrill too. Way to lie, Emily. "No," I said again, calmer this time. "I'm just scared for you. For all of us. All that's happened, it's a lot to take in."

Running his hand through his short hair, Dalton looked back up at me. "Hey, yeah, isn't Nikki some sort of psychic? Wow, when did that happen?"

I laughed. Couldn't help myself. It was all pretty absurd. "I have no idea."

Dalton and I both put our shoes on and gathered our things. We stepped out of the shed, and I made sure the door was shut tight.

"I'm gonna go home now," Dalton said, staring past my house to the street. He leaned in close to me, suddenly, gathering me into a hug. I stood there, arms unsure what to do. I awkwardly patted his back, and I heard him sniff in, loudly.

And I realized: He was smelling me. Calming himself. Like I always did with Spencer.

Oh yeah, Spencer. And Tracie. I'd need to get inside, get in touch. . . . There was so much to deal with still.

Dalton's body went slack, and when he let go of me, his eyes were glassy, his smile vacant. "Okay, now I'm going home."

I grabbed his wrist, stopping him from going. "Dalton, tonight you need to take some sleeping pills before you change, okay? Until we find out what those files say about us, at least. Just to be safe. Okay?"

He nodded solemnly. "I will. I promise I will. I don't want to keep hurting people."

He wandered off then, to the sidewalk and down the street in the general direction of his house. It occurred to me that if any neighbor saw some random boy leaving my backyard, it would seem sort of strange. But I figured, with how early it was on a Saturday? I could probably relax.

My keys were in my pocket, thankfully, somehow not having fallen out during the trek home. I let myself in through the back door, tiptoeing my way to the stairs and up to my room. I held my breath the entire time, certain that this would be the morning someone would catch me, that the jig would finally be up.

I made it to my room and quietly shut the door. Good thing my entire family are late sleepers.

I collapsed onto my bed, arms spread wide. I kicked off my shoes, then grabbed my comforter on either side of me and pulled it to envelop me, wrap me in a cloth cocoon.

So. Where to start, brain? I asked myself.

I cycled through everything: The suddenly corporeal shadowmen. The human experiments in BioZenith. The strange city visible through the spinning rings. Hovering robots. Telekinetic cheerleaders who loathed me. My new pack. The super-high-tech flat-screen computers everywhere full of . . . files!

My hand shot to my throat, and then beneath my shirt. It was still there, the thumb drive on the lanyard. I sighed in relief.

I leaned over my bed and found my phone, charging on the bedside table. I unplugged it, then lay flat on my back once more. Holding it above my face, I flicked through the contact list to the one person I needed to see most.

Spencer.

A quick back-and-forth text convo revealed that Spencer had gotten Tracie home before he'd managed to sneak into his own bedroom safely. Like me, he was groggy and disturbed, but he agreed to come over.

Though first he'd have to take a taxi to pick up his mom's minivan where we'd left it the night before.

I set my phone aside, flush with relief. I'd been endlessly debating internally whether I should let myself go with this whole pheromone high, but honestly? I was ready for it.

While I waited for him to arrive, I stuck the thumb drive in my USB port and began clicking through the files. Most were labeled with serial numbers in no particular order that I could see. I clicked aimlessly, opening spreadsheet after document full of long, impenetrable phrases I didn't have the first clue how to parse.

Then, with a few more clicks, I stumbled into the folder labeled HAVOC.

Biting my lip, my finger hovered over the button atop my mouse. Something about the name, as though whatever it contained was meant to cause trouble, made me hesitate. But we'd come so far. Gone through so much to get at least this little bit of info.

I double-clicked. A bunch of documents populated the screen. One of the first read "Biological Imperatives."

I'm not sure why, but my eye was drawn to that one. I opened it, scanned the first few useless paragraphs—and then things got interesting.

One decision was to utilize the technology to place an inherent fail-safe in each Vesper, it read.

Utilizing natural pheromones from within the wolves used as our base, we created a certain sensory pattern that would force the Vespers to focus on nothing except locating one another, once active. It is our hope this makes our subjects more likely to bond in the necessary pack mentality for our goals. Using our base wolf subjects, our tests in adjusting the pheromones proved successful in achieving these goals.

My lips were tight as I read. I breathed in heavily through my nose, in and out, faster and faster.

One advantage of adjusting the pheromone levels is

that, when the Vespers come of age and are activated, we can easily placate each subject if the need arises. It is still uncertain how the human and animal DNA will ultimately react, though the Akhakhu research we have been privy to shows that in most cases, using their particular bindings, hybrid combinations more often than not . . .

The screen went blurry there. I stopped reading. I didn't know what the rest of the report was saying, really, but I'd gotten the gist of it from just those two paragraphs.

The pheromones? The ones that calmed me down, set me to "find my fellows," that made me rush with excitement at the sight of Spencer, that had let a killer draw me into a trap?

It was planned. Just like everything else, my life's course had been decided for me. Become a werewolf. Lust after a particular boy. Be placated when *they* wanted me to be. Be used for whatever *they* wanted, if they ever found us. To kill and dissect? To use for some other purpose? I didn't know. I didn't care.

I sat there, unmoving, questioning everything. Again. Like I always did lately. I mean, you have to remember my life before this. I was utterly average. Boring. I had my one friend, my nice little family, school, books, movies. No matter how much headway I made into becoming Little Miss Confident, the alpha, there always seemed to be some horrible thing lurking around the corner to send me running with my tail between my legs.

A knock at my door. I jumped. Blinking rapidly, I spun in my desk chair.

"Yeah?" I said, my voice a squeak. I coughed to clear my voice. "Yeah?" I said again.

"Hey, you have a visitor." Dawn, her voice tired and muffled. "He said you had some sort of project."

I spun back toward my desk. My hand flew to the mouse, moving the pointer to close the open document, then select it in the folder. I hit the delete button.

I didn't want Spencer to see this. Not right away. I'd fish it out of the trash bin and read it again later.

"Yeah," I said one more time. "It's cool, I'm dressed. He can come in."

My door creaked open to reveal Dawn standing there in sweat pants and a T-shirt, her hair pulled back. Naturally she still looked gorgeous. With a yawn, she waved her hand forward and Spencer appeared around the corner. He offered me a shy wave and a grin as he walked in.

"Have fun, you two," Dawn said as she turned to head back downstairs. In a singsongy voice, she finished, "But not tooooo much fun!"

"It's just a project!" I called after her. But she was downstairs by then.

I motioned for Spencer to shut the door. He did so, then

plopped onto my bed, his eyes scanning my room.

"Wow, lots of movies," he said, patting his thighs nervously. "You're not very frilly, huh?"

I hugged myself, feeling awkward. I'd never had a boy in my room before. I hadn't exactly gussied it up for visitors. "Not really," I said.

I shoved my desk chair back, sitting as far away from him as I could. Even with that effort, his stupidly alluring musk began to overtake my room. I jumped up and opened my window, then took in a big gulp of the fresh, chill air that gushed in.

I couldn't let myself fall back into the pattern of sniffing and pawing at Spencer. Not now. Not after what I knew for certain.

"So, hey," Spencer said behind me. "I wanted to say . . . I'm sorry about last night. I mean, I got stupidly jealous and made us change. I just didn't like the idea of you and Dalton going out without me."

I sat back down in my desk chair. "It's okay," I said. "We got into BioZenith and found some info, at least. So it was worth it."

Swallowing, Spencer leaned forward on his knees. "No, I mean, I was *really* jealous. I didn't really realize it until then, but, uh . . ." He laughed, nervous. "I really like you, Emily."

I blinked, staring at him wide eyed. I didn't know what to say. How to break it to him that whatever we felt was all a lie.

He jumped to his feet and began to pace. "It's not just because you saved me, either," he said. "I've just really liked hanging out with you lately. You're the chillest girl I've ever met, and you're really smart and funny, like, real funny."

"Spencer," I whispered.

He didn't seem to hear me. Like always, he was off in his own world. "And it's weird, because when Tracie showed up last night, she had this *smell*, you know? It wasn't like a perfume, not really, it was sort of animalistic. I'd sort of smelled it on you, but with her it was overwhelming. And I kept thinking, 'She's my mate. Tracie is my mate.' Uh, not that I wanted to, like, have sex with her. But my brain kept saying that over and over. And I kept telling it to shut up, because I don't care about what some smell tells me." He stopped pacing and met my eyes. "I, uh, care about you."

Well. That was unexpected.

This was supposed to be my big moment. The end of the movie where the guy comes with the boom box to profess his love, either because it's the legit Cameron Crowe film or one of the zillions of parody scenes that came out years later. There was supposed to be fanfare. Me swooning. The two of us leaping into each other's arms, swirling in the air, kissing, credits.

But I didn't know what to say or do. Spencer avoided his "biological imperative." I hadn't. Whatever he felt could be real. Maybe not me.

This was not what I needed. There were more important things, right? Crazy, insane things? I couldn't start getting wrapped up in emotional foibles for the first time ever. I didn't know if I was strong enough to handle this on top of everything else.

I didn't realize it, but I'd been silent for ages by that point. Spencer picked at his jeans and ducked his head. "Uh, just wanted to let you know that," he said. "So, do with that information whatever you want."

Forcing a smile, I met his eyes. They were too damned sad, and he had that whole puppy vibe again. I cringed, feeling all Cruella de Vil.

"Thanks," I said softly. "I really . . . Thanks, Spencer. I like you too."

He grinned at me. Sticking his hands in his pockets, he rocked back and forth on his feet. "So, yeah. I guess you asked me to come over for a reason. Can I take a look?"

"Of course," I said, vacating the desk chair. "You're our resident computer guy, after all."

He took my place and hunched over the keyboard, his hand on the mouse sending the corresponding pointer flying over the screen as he scanned all the files in the HAVOC folder.

I resisted the urge to lean over him and watch the screen. I couldn't get too close, not yet. Not until we had some breathing room to focus on whatever we'd found out at BioZenith. Instead, I collapsed back onto my bed.

A buzzing and clattering from my end table. Narrowing my eyes, I peered over at my phone. It buzzed again.

"Hey, you got a text," Spencer said, his eyes still on the screen as he looked through various files.

"Yeah, I know." I reached for the phone. "But you're the only one who ever texts me."

He shrugged. "Maybe Dalton or Tracie?"

I peered at the screen. It read REEDY. It also read 7:36 AM, which was not a time Megan would ever choose to be awake if she had a choice. She's not in the least a morning person.

I flicked open the phone and read the text.

> 7:36 AM PST: I saw you and Dalton change this morning. I know what you are.

The Vesper Company
"Envisioning the brightest stars, to lead our way."
- Internal Document, Do Not Reproduce -

Details of Video Footage Recorded Oct. 31, 2010,
Part 5

21:30:07 PST—Hall 3, Sublevel Sector E

Vesper 1(B), Vesper 2.1(A), and Vesper 4(B) enter
the hall. Per protocol, this hallway is guarded by
Vesper Co. brand Sentinels, the orb-shaped, machine-
gun-equipped hovering robots that are especially
popular with our international arms customers.

Three Sentinels swoop down from above, aim, and let
free a flurry of bullets. Vesper 2.1(A) waves a hand,
and the bullets stop in place. Vesper 1(B) runs
forward, jumps to one wall, uses it as a platform
to jump across to another, and then leaps once more
to tackle all three Sentinels from behind. They are
so focused on Vesper 2.1(A) that they do not turn to
fire.

Vesper 1(B) and the Sentinels crash to the floor.
She cries out, raises her fists, and smashes two

of the machines, damaging their power cores. The third rolls toward Vesper 4(B), its laser targeting system flashing throughout the hall, unable to find a target. Vesper 4(B) steps on the Sentinel, destroying it. At the same time, Vesper 2.1(A) lowers her hands, and the bullets she stopped in midair rain to the ground.

I have been reprimanded for inserting personal opinions into these documents, so let me make this clear: The following are observations only and do not necessarily reflect the opinion of the transcriber.

Had the Deviants been unsuccessful in fending off the Sentinels, they would all have been shot multiple times and died in this hallway. As we desire to keep most of the Deviant subtypes of the Vespers alive, perhaps a tranquilizer upgrade for the Sentinels is required.

It was remarkably easy for three teenage girls to disrupt and destroy what should be military-ready robotic machinery. Granted, the girls are imbued with telekinesis and superstrength, respectively, but perhaps take this into account with the next redesign.

Perhaps it is best if we not tell our clients of these particular weaknesses.

21:34:42 PST—Hall 23, Sublevel Sector E

The Deviants turn down Hall 23, which is unguarded.
They walk toward their destination.

VESPER 4(B): So, Amy, where are your sisters? And
Nikki?

Vesper 2.1(A) is visibly distressed by this question.
Vesper 1(B) chooses to answer for her.

VESPER 1(B): We'll have to tell you later, Tracie.
We're here.

They have reached the intersection of Hall 23 and
Hall 7, at the end of which is Super Holding Cell
E1. Per protocol, the door is guarded by both human
officers and robot Sentinels. The Deviants peer
around the corner, taking stock of the situation.
They then whisper unintelligibly among themselves,
presumably planning their next move.

Part 5 of Relevant Video Footage Concluded

21

I KNOW WHAT YOU ARE

I froze, staring at the words on my phone, reading them over and over and over again.

I know what you are.

This was heavier even than the abstract notions of scientists and shadowmen. I had no idea what all Megan had seen, but she'd been so specific—she'd seen me and Dalton *change*. Unless she caught us putting on our clothes in the shed, she could only mean the werewolf.

God, how I wished she only meant changing clothes.

Panic rose in my chest. I had no idea what she would do now. Where she would go, who she would tell. It felt like so long since the reality of real-life werewolves was foreign to me that I almost couldn't imagine the shock and horror of seeing our bodies mutate and shift right before her eyes.

What if she thought I was a monster? What if she was scared of me now?

Spencer saw me shaking. He stood from the desk and placed a hand on my shoulder. "Hey, Em Dub, are you all right?"

I shook my head, couldn't form words. I just handed him the phone, and Spencer read the text himself.

"Oh," he said. "Okay. I don't think this is a good thing."

"No," I finally managed to say. I jumped up from the bed, grabbing my shoes and looking around for my keys. "We have to go find her. I have to explain everything to her before she tells anyone." I froze. "I have absolutely no idea what I'm going to say to her. It's one thing talking about it with you and Dalton and Tracie, but she's not like us! How is she ever going to understand?"

Spencer stood and put his arm around my shoulder. I almost recoiled, but stopped myself, not wanting to hurt his feelings. His pheromones wafted through the air, and I held my breath, still refusing to let the people at BioZenith mess with my head more than they already had.

"She's your best friend, right?" Spencer asked.

I nodded.

"Then she'll probably understand. At the very least, she'll finally know the real reason you've been hanging out with me so much. You don't have to pretend we're dating anymore."

He looked hurt as he said it. I wanted to comfort him. Smile at him and hug him and let him kiss me, my very first kiss. Hold each other and forget about this latest bit of trouble that I had to deal with.

But I stepped away from him, bending over to pull my shoes on. "Can you drive me to her house, please?"

"Sure," he said, sitting back down on the desk chair. "Of course."

Shoes and coats on, we busted down the stairs. My dad, stepmom, and Dawn sat around the dining room table, eating our usual Saturday morning breakfast: eggs Benedict, cantaloupe slices, blueberry pancakes, coffee, orange juice. My dad's specialty. My stomach ached at the smells.

"You guys heading out?" Dawn asked me, a piece of cantaloupe speared on her fork.

"Yeah," I said, mind racing for an excuse. "We're supposed to, uh, observe flora in the woods throughout the day and see how it changes. Science class stuff."

Katherine stood up, smiling politely between me and Spencer. "Do you two have time for breakfast? We have far too much food. You're welcome to join us, Spencer."

Eyes wide and almost salivating, Spencer began to nod and head for a chair. I yanked his arm.

"We really have to get out there before it's too late," I answered, forcing a disappointed expression.

My dad, engrossed in his unwieldy newspaper, held up a free hand, which I squeezed. "Have fun."

"Oh, we will."

Then, mercifully, we were out the door, in Spencer's mom's minivan, on the road. He made small talk about how nice my family seemed, but I couldn't do more than grunt in response. All I could think about was Megan.

We pulled into her driveway. Her car wasn't there. I left Spencer in the car and raced to the door, then rang the doorbell once, twice. A groggy Lucas answered, but he basically told me to shove off after confirming Megan wasn't there.

Back to the car. Back on the road. We drove all over the neighborhood, by the library, the school. I didn't see her car anywhere, and it was so early it wasn't like she could actually *do* anything.

The entire time I kept dialing her phone and texting her. Leaving frantic messages. "Call me, Megan, we really need to talk. Please." Each message sounded more desperate than the last.

After an hour of nothing, I finally sagged into my seat and asked Spencer to take me home. I was starving, and Megan had disappeared.

* * *

I opened the front door and slogged into the foyer/computer room, my eyes not focused on anything. My stomach gurgled and I clutched it.

"Hey Leelee, back so soon?"

I tore off my jacket and tossed it over a dining room chair. I shrugged at my dad at his desk, trying not to let my anxiety show. I pulled my phone from my pocket and checked it again. No calls. No texts.

Breakfast had been cleared, but the bowl at the center of the table had been filled with fresh apples. I grabbed one and bit into it.

Dad swiveled in his desk chair and looked at me, concerned. "You all right?"

No, I thought. *Nothing is ever all right.*

With the back of my palm, I wiped sweet apple juice from my lips. "Yeah, I'm fine. Thanks, Dad."

He sighed, then shook his head. "Well, Megan's here, I should let you know. She asked to wait in your room, so I—"

I stiffened, set the apple on the table, then spun to face my father. "She's here? How long has she been here?"

He shrugged. "Not too long, maybe half an hour. It's okay I let her in your room, right?"

"Yes, definitely," I said. I darted over to him and kissed

him on his bald spot. "Thanks, Dad. I mean it."

He laughed. "Sometimes lately you can be inscrutable, Leelee. Guess it's a teenage girl thing."

I was already halfway to the stairs. "Guess so!" I called over my shoulder.

I bounded up the steps two at a time, then burst into my room. Megan was indeed there, sitting at the edge of my bed, flipping through one of my books. She jumped, startled by my sudden entrance. And then her entire body went still, her eyes darting, studying me.

"I parked in the alley down the street," she said, her voice flat. "I didn't want you to know I was here and avoid me again. Are you really still Emily?"

I held up my hands, approaching her slowly as though she was some small woodland creature that would dash away if I wasn't careful. "It's all right," I said. "It's still me."

"Even with what I think I saw?" she asked, still not moving.

"Yes," I said.

"So I saw what I think I saw, then," she said. "I wasn't imagining it. It was real."

Lowering my hands, I nodded.

"It wasn't costumes or anything, was it?" she asked. "It was dark, but it didn't seem like costumes."

I swallowed, then pulled out my desk chair and sat

down, facing her. "No costumes," I whispered. "I wish it was just makeup. But it's not. I . . . wasn't exactly hu—"

"All right!" Megan said, her voice loud, shrill. Calmer, she continued, "I get it. I think I do. This is the real reason you were avoiding me, right? Because you're . . . different now. You did change after all. And Dalton is like you, too."

I tried to swallow again, but the nervous ball in my throat refused to be shoved down. I was no longer hungry. "I spent all morning driving everywhere looking for you. I kept calling and texting. You didn't . . . go somewhere or tell anyone, did you?"

She laughed, running her fingers from her temples back through her long hair.

"No, Emily, I didn't tell anyone, because I didn't even know if what I saw was real. You don't have to worry, your secret is safe with me." She scowled. "Which it would have been even if you'd told me when this all started."

"I tried," I said weakly. "I told you I thought I was sick. You didn't believe me."

She threw her hands up in the air. "Well, you know what, Emily, how was I to know that a symptom of being . . . *you know* . . . involved drugging me and stealing my car?"

"I'm still sorry about that," I said. "About everything. I'm not me at night, not entirely."

"So that wasn't you yesterday who abandoned me at the

party after I tried to defend you? It wasn't you during the days all week ignoring me, doing your best to avoid talking to me?"

"I've been under a bit of stress, okay? I'm sorry that I can't worry about hurting your feelings when I have to spend all day and all night, every single day, wondering if someone is going to try and kill me *again*."

Megan sat there silent, clutching my messy comforter. She blinked at me, at a loss for what to say.

Finally, she said, "Again?"

"Yes," I said, looking down at my lap. "Again. The killer shot Emily Cooke because she was like me. Same with Dalton. He came after me, too, that night I went to the club. And the night before—the night before his body was found."

Her whole body went stiff again. Quietly, she asked, "You did that to him? You stopped the killer?"

"Yes."

Silence again. I looked past Megan at my computer, with the files still sitting on the screen, waiting to be delved into. Waiting to divulge more secrets that would erase even more of what I thought had been real about myself my entire life.

"You don't know a fraction of what I've been through lately," I said softly. "About all the crazy stuff that's out there."

"I would have if you'd confided in me."

"I didn't want you to get involved and get hurt."

Jumping to her feet, Megan began to pace across the carpet. "I don't care about getting hurt, Emily. Not when it comes to you. I'd do anything for you, don't you know that?"

I nodded. "I know. That's why I had to keep this from you."

Again she tossed her arms in the air, sighing in exasperation. "Why do you get to decide for me, huh? I can't choose if I want to stand by the side of my best friend?" I started to speak, but she held up a finger, silencing me. "Don't, Em. I don't know anything you've gone through, it's true. All I know is that the past week I've been lonelier than I ever thought I could be. I know I act like I don't need anyone, but it's not true, because I need you, Em, I really need you, okay? Dammit!" Tears flooded her eyes, spilled over her lids, trailed down her cheeks. She didn't bother to wipe them away. "No one else gets me like you do, and I can't stand going through each day not talking to you and hanging out with you. I thought I could, I tried, but I just *can't*."

I met her eyes. "What about Patrick Kelly?" I asked. "You said you were friends."

She barked an angry laugh. "He's my lab partner, Emily.

He barely even talks. He lets me talk to him, but I doubt he cares about a thing I say. I just didn't want to feel like an idiot while you kept wandering off with your new boy toys."

I didn't know what to say. I knew Megan cared for me, of course she did, we'd been each other's worlds for so long. Except now I had a new world that was warped and twisted, like the movies Megan and I watched made real. I didn't know how to bring her into it. I didn't *want* to, which I hated to admit to myself. Spencer and Dalton and Tracie, who I'd only known for a week at most, they felt like my family now. I looked at Megan and I loved her, but I didn't see how she could fit in my bizarre new existence.

She sat on the edge of my bed again, elbows resting on her knees, her head resting in her palms. She stared at the floor, sniffling, still crying.

I ached inside. It hurt worse than all the physical pain I'd gone through recently combined. Tears were forming in my eyes too, blurring my vision. All of this was horrible. All the death. All the lies. All the changes I was having to make, changes parts of me longed for while other parts of me screamed and thrashed inside, wanting to go back to the simple, boring life I'd once had.

Not looking up, Megan spoke, so softly I couldn't make out what she'd said.

"What?" I asked her.

She looked up, her long hair hanging in front of her face. She wiped her cheeks with the back of her fist.

"Bite me," she said.

I gaped at her. "I . . . what? Why?"

"That's how it works, doesn't it?" she said. "A bite or a scratch and the curse is mine, too."

I almost laughed, it was so melodramatic. But if there was any time for melodrama, it was now.

"I'll be a werewolf like you then," she continued. "Then you don't have to worry about me getting hurt. I can be like you and Dalton, I can be part of your new group."

Stammering, I fought for the words. "But it— Reedy, no, it doesn't work like that. None of us were bit. We were made like this by some scientists who messed with our DNA before we were even born. This isn't like movies or books."

"How do you know?" It was both a question and a demand. "Just because you started in a lab, how do you know you can't pass it on to others?"

"Because it doesn't work like that!"

She dove off the bed, landing on her knees in front of me. She grabbed my thigh and held her bare arm up toward my face. "Just try it," she said. "Just bite me and see what happens."

I recoiled, twisting my head away from her pale arm. "Megan, no. I'm telling you, it—"

Her fingernails dug into my leg. "Just *try*!"

We sat there for a moment, me as far back in my computer chair as I could be, her gripping my leg, her arm wavering as it hung in the air. Her lip trembled as she watched me, and her temple began to twitch.

She jumped up to her feet. "Fine, Emily. Fine. If you won't even try, I don't need you."

She spun away from me and snatched her coat off of my bed. Not looking back, she tore open my bedroom door and stormed into the hall, down the stairs, out the front door.

I sat there, breathing shakily. I had to go after her. I needed to solve this somehow, smooth things over with her and convince her to keep it all a secret. But I couldn't move. I couldn't face her again. Before the changes, we never fought like this. *Never.* All my memories of the two of us were of laughing at sleepovers, curling up on the couch and watching DVDs, creating milkshake concoctions, talking on the phone or online well into the night about anything and everything.

Now whenever I thought of Megan, I just thought of the horrible anxiety I felt every time I was near her.

Her last words echoed in my head. *I don't need you.*

She could have meant she didn't need me as a friend anymore. But in a flash, I realized—she hadn't just seen me change from werewolf to human. She'd seen Dalton, too.

She didn't need me to bite her because she thought she had another werewolf who could infect her with lycanthropy.

And if she reached Dalton as he shifted into Nighttime...

"Oh no," I gasped. I lunged for my phone and clicked over to Spencer in the contact list. I typed: MEET ME AT DALTON'S HOUSE. EMERGENCY!!

I ran to my bedroom window and looked out, but of course Megan was long gone, had made it to her car a block away and was driving to Dalton's.

I couldn't wait for a ride. I hustled down the stairs and burst out my front door, whooshing past my bewildered father.

And I ran.

22

BITE ME

The houses, the sidewalks, cars, children, pets, trees, flower beds, jungle gyms, stop signs—all blurs of messy, smeared color as I forced myself to run faster than I'd ever run as my normal, average self.

Sweat poured down my forehead, dripped into my eyes, soaked my hair. My muscles began to ache, but I kept going, forcing myself to run as fast as non-superhero-humanly possible. My evenings as Nighttime had tightened up my calves, my thighs. She'd improved my stamina by pure force of energy. But it was still a strain on my body without whatever receptors appeared in my brain by night, shifting me into a state between human and werewolf.

I wound around pedestrians having leisurely walks. I

barreled across streets without bothering to stop and look for traffic. I was panting now, but I refused to let myself stop.

And finally, finally, I reached Dalton's neighborhood. I saw his giant house, his vast, heavily gardened lawn. Red and blue plastic cups littered the ground, and there were muddy footsteps all over the driveway. Remnants of the party that seemed as if it happened ages and ages ago.

Megan's car was parked in the driveway. At an awkward angle, as though she'd pulled in fast and didn't bother to straighten out.

I stood on the corner of the street, hands on my knees, gulping at the crisp fall air. I was here. I only had to move a little bit more. It wasn't anywhere near eight p.m. I could find Megan and convince her to leave Dalton alone.

Body aching, I hobbled across the street, onto the lawn. The front door was right there, so close. Just had to go to it, ring the bell.

From the corner of the house I heard a crunching of plastic and rustling of a bag. I blinked and turned toward the sound to see Casey Delgado standing there, paused between picking up one of the cups and throwing it into the garbage bag.

She looked me up and down. "Did you come to help clean up?"

That was the last thing I'd expected one of Nikki's lackeys, Amy's sister no less, to say.

"Uh, no," I said, wiping my forehead on my sleeve. I'm sure my hair was a mess. "I'm looking for my friend Megan. Her car's in the driveway."

"Who?" Casey asked.

"Tall, skinny girl?" I said, raising my hand to indicate her height. "Really long blond hair? She jumped in last night when, y'know. When your sister and I got into a fight."

"Oh, yes, her." She shook her head. "No, I haven't seen her."

I heard footsteps and voices from around the corner of the house. I suppressed a groan, knowing exactly who it would be.

"Casey, who are you talking to?"

Amy rounded the corner and stopped in her tracks at the sight of me. Nikki and Brittany came next.

Amy dropped the garbage bag she'd been holding. It crumpled to the ground, party debris spilling over the lawn. Hands on her hips, she walked over the mess and marched toward me.

"You are seriously asking for it, girl," she said. "Do you need another demonstration of what we can do before you get the hint and back off?"

I didn't mean to, but I rolled my eyes. "I am not here to

steal Dalton, and I am not here to fight with you. My friend is going to get herself in trouble and I need to find her, okay? Then I'll leave you alone forever."

"Oh, please," Amy said. "Look, Emily Webb, I know exactly what you are—"

I scrunched my forehead. "Wait, what? You do?"

"—and I don't care. I know I can take you on, woman to woman, any day. I'm not letting you hurt anybody, let alone steal my friend's man."

"Mm-mm, no you aren't," Brittany said.

Nikki remained silent and glaring.

I let out an exasperated sigh. "I really, really don't have time for this. You guys have no idea what is happening. Just get out of my way." I resumed my path to the front door, hoping Megan was inside, sitting safe and sound in a plush armchair, petting Max and chatting with Dalton.

A pair of ghostly hands gripped me beneath my armpits and lifted me into the sky. I screamed, my feet dangling above the matted grass. I struggled but couldn't free myself from the invisible harness that had hoisted me into the air.

Amy laughed, and I glared down at her. "Put me down! Please. I need to go!"

"If you say so," Amy said.

She flicked her hand and I flew toward the side of the house. I raised my arms in front of my face, bracing for the blow, and I smacked hard against the siding. I collapsed to the grass, the wind knocked out of me.

And something shifted inside of me.

My vision went gray. Energy and strength surged through my limbs. All three sides of me were there, a co-op in my brain. I was the hybrid version of me, the all-in-one shop for any flavor of Emily Webb you could want.

And maybe it was what had happened in the lab when Spencer set off the timer, or maybe I'd just grown to understand this during my shifts over the previous days, but I finally knew what I was in this state—more specifically, what I could do. And that was to choose to be all three at once, each with her own abilities that came to the forefront, and each with her own weaknesses bolstered by the strengths of another.

Or I could choose exactly which Emily I felt like being.

Though it was the middle of the day, I chose to go Nighttime.

Color returned to my vision. I yanked off my glasses and shoved them in the pocket of my hoodie. I snapped my head toward Amy, pretty and feisty little Amy Delgado, who thought just because she had psychic powers she could bully me.

And something I'd realized a lot over the past few weeks: I absolutely despised being bullied.

The cheerleader raised her palms again, attempting to toss me once more. I crouched low and launched myself toward her. I raised my arms and grasped her wrists, yanked to spin her toward the house, and forced her back until she slammed against the same wall she'd tossed me into. I pinned her there, her arms raised above her head, useless.

"Ow!" she screeched.

"Get off her!" Nikki shouted. She was raising her hand, preparing to use her own powers on me.

I spun Amy around and flung her easily at Nikki. The two girls collided, landing in a heap on the grass.

Brittany started to move her hand toward me as well. I let the werewolf personality surge forward, for just a moment. I spun on her, snarling. Startled, she backed away.

Then, I shifted back into the hybrid, where I chose—*I chose*—to go back to Daytime Emily. I pulled my glasses from my pocket and returned them to my face.

"I told you, I don't want to fight you. I'm just looking for my friend."

Amy struggled with Nikki, the two girls shoving at each other as they tried to get up. "You think we care?" Amy asked. "Really?"

I was exhausted. I probably should have stayed Nighttime. But she would have wanted to keep fighting. I opened my mouth to respond, trying to think of some witty retort and failing miserably.

Angry shouting and loud barks echoed around us.

"What was that?" Casey asked, looking around.

"I think it came from the backyard," Brittany said.

Another shout, louder. Enraged. More barks, angry, defensive.

It was Megan, and Dalton's dog, Max.

I forgot all about the cheerleaders. I leaped over their fallen garbage bags, wound past Nikki and Amy still struggling to stand. I turned the corner of the house and pushed myself full force to the backyard.

Only then did I realize that if I could transform to Nighttime in midday, or even the werewolf if I wanted—Dalton probably could too.

I pumped my arms faster.

I saw her in the backyard, standing next to the McKinneys' empty swimming pool. Dalton was there too, staring at the slender girl, bewildered. Max hopped behind Dalton, snarling and barking at Megan, though the Lab made no move to jump at her.

Megan slapped Dalton across the face.

"Bite me!" she screamed. "Just do it! You're probably the one who made her like this, aren't you? You took her away from me!" She pounded a fist against his chest. "Bite me!"

Dalton stood rigid as a statue, gritting his teeth. His hands were clenched at his side, all his muscles tensed and his skin flushing red as though struggling to keep something at bay.

Struggling to keep the werewolf side down.

Max barked. Wouldn't stop barking.

Frustrated tears appeared in Dalton's eyes. "Stop it!" he bellowed. "Please! I don't know what you're talking about. It doesn't work like that!"

I forced myself to run faster, but the house was so big, the backyard and pool so far away. I took in a breath, trying to force myself back into the hybrid state so I could become Nighttime again. It didn't work.

Megan took a step forward, shoving Dalton so hard that he almost fell over the edge, into the empty pool. He grimaced, clutching at his stomach. "Stop," he wheezed.

Megan stepped back, eyes darting, watching as Dalton gasped and doubled over again. "Are you doing it? Are you changing?"

"Get away from him, Megan!" I screamed between breaths. They didn't seem to be getting closer. Why was Dalton's house and yard so damn big?

Defiant, Megan ignored me. She crossed her arms and looked down her nose at Dalton. Her eyes were clearly frightened, but she refused to move.

And Dalton began to transform.

It happened quickly, with a crunch of bone and suction of flesh pulling from muscle. Dalton fell to his knees, his mouth open in a silent scream as his jaw lengthened, his teeth sharpened into points, and his ears climbed his head. His already taut arms bulged with stronger, tighter muscles as his fingers lengthened, sprouted into claws. His pants and shirt ripped as his body bulged larger and grew a coating of brown-and-black fur, and his clothes fell to tatters around him.

Max yelped, tucked his tail between his legs, and raced away behind the house.

Megan didn't have the sense to do the same.

"Megan!" I wheezed one more time, desperation making my voice a screech.

Her whole body trembled, her eyes were wide. But she didn't move.

And Dalton stood to his full, massive height, spread his arms wide, looked up into the sky, and let out a roar that echoed all around us.

Behind me, I vaguely heard the cheerleaders giving chase. Vaguely heard their startled cries at the sight of the monstrous creature standing at the edge of the pool in the mansion's backyard.

I was almost there. Almost close enough to barrel into

Megan, shove her away from danger. To command Dalton to control himself.

"Bite me," Megan said flatly.

Dalton looked down at her, his dark wolf eyes narrowed. His black lips pulled back into a snarl, revealing spotted gums and dripping fangs.

He lunged forward and clamped his jaws around Megan's shoulder. He bit down, and she screamed, loud, shrill. Blood oozed from between Dalton's teeth, stained Megan's shirt, dripped at her feet.

"Dalton!" I shouted, gasping for breath as I ran. I was almost to them now. "Dalton, let her go, now! You can control this! You are not a killer!"

His eyes shot to me, narrowing further. Hating me. Though pheromones identified me to him as his "mate" by day, clearly his wolf self rejected the idea. Getting down on all fours, he began to run deeper into the backyard, toward a line of trees. He did not let go of Megan. He bit down harder, dragging her through the grass as he ran.

She wasn't screaming anymore. She was gasping for air, grabbing futilely at blades of grass. Her skin was paler than normal, and she looked back at me with terrified eyes.

Then, they disappeared into the woods.

I stopped, fell to my knees, struggling so hard for air that I almost began to gag. I wasn't going to reach her in time. I wasn't going to make it.

No. Nighttime in the back of my head. *No*, the wolf, refusing to give up. *No!* Daytime me, angry at my mistakes. This wasn't going to happen. I wasn't going to lose Megan. I wasn't going to lose Dalton, either.

My body trembling, I forced myself to my feet. Behind me I could still hear the cheerleaders, tepidly following now, no longer running. Screw them. If it wasn't for them, I'd have caught up to Megan in time.

I'd deal with them later.

I stalked forward, commanding myself to go hybrid.

Nothing happened.

I kicked off my shoes so that I was barefoot. Grass squelched between my toes. I unbuttoned my jeans, kicked them off, slung them over my arm. Walked in the middle of the day in nothing but my underwear and a hoodie.

"What the hell is she doing?" I heard one of the girls shout behind me.

Go hybrid, I demanded. I concentrated on nothing but making that change. On finding out how to make it happen when I needed it.

I was at the tree line now. Ahead, I could hear the crunching of grass, the snapping of twigs. I yanked off the hoodie, stuck my glasses in its pocket. I pulled off my T-shirt and draped it and the hoodie over my arm with my jeans. I awkwardly unhooked my bra, added it to the pile.

I was almost entirely naked. My skin bristled with bumps. My feet crunched over hard pine cones and rocks. I didn't care.

Sounds met my ears. Megan's muffled whimpers. Dalton's deep, guttural growls.

Go by— I started to think.

I didn't need to finish.

Strength surged into my limbs. My vision went crystal clear, gray, aware of every small movement around me. Megan was still alive. Dalton wasn't a murderer.

Yet.

WHAT DID YOU DO?

Energy and adrenaline flooded my veins. I burst into a run, darting beneath branches and leaping over bushes. I shoved through leaves and found myself in a clearing. I stopped, dropped to my knees, and took in the scene.

Megan lay there, to my left, at the edge of the trees. Tears poured down her cheeks and she let out gulping sobs, her hands grasping at her shoulder. Blood gushed from the jagged wound and began to pool beneath her.

And with my wolf vision, I saw something strange above her. An oval distortion in the air, not unlike the one I'd seen back in the BioZenith lab. Only this one wasn't *open*, I suppose is the word. I saw nothing through it. It was like an endlessly rippling pool turned on its side. It was such a bizarre, abnormal thing to see that my mind immediately tried to reconcile it as CGI, just some movie illusion. But of course it couldn't be. This was real, right in front of me. Not even the best James Cameron tech could produce that.

Before I could completely make sense of what I was seeing, Dalton appeared as if from nowhere to my right. He surged forward, snarling once more. He bit into Megan's side and she gasped, then screamed, so shrilly it hurt my ears.

He began to yank her side to side, struggling to rip her apart.

"Dalton!" I commanded. "No!"

I dropped my clothes to my feet. Stood to my full height. Dalton let go of Megan's side and rounded on me, his teeth stained bright red.

"No," I said again.

Dalton roared. And he lunged at me.

I jumped to the side, just in time, and the wolf-boy barreled past me into the woods.

Well, if that was how he was going to play it.

I focused on the hybrid. Chose who I wanted to be: Werewolf.

The change came over me, even quicker than Dalton. I stood like a linebacker, facing the trees and waiting for him. As I did, fur bristled over my body. My muscles twisted into steel. Claws and teeth appeared. My face stretched into a snout. And my tail burst from my spine, tearing free my underwear.

Can't say you can be all that modest when you're a werewolf.

Dalton leaped from the trees and aimed toward my chest. His claws met my midsection and he gripped me, intending to tackle me to the ground.

But I'd been ready.

Using his own momentum, I grabbed his arms, spun, and tossed him into the clearing with a roar of my own. He rolled across the grass before smacking into the trunk of an evergreen.

I raced forward, one hand clawing into the earth, sending up clumps of dirt as I propelled myself forward. I jumped on top of Dalton where he'd fallen, and straddled him like I had in the BioZenith parking lot. I growled down at him. *Stop. Change back.*

He trembled beneath me, his bloody teeth bared, always bared. His eyes darting, angry, manic.

"Help," Megan gurgled behind me. "Help me. . . ."

I let my guard down, for just a moment. Dared to glance at Megan, still lying prone beneath the strange distortion. More blood seeped from the new wound on her side. I could smell it, warm and enticing.

Enticing.

My stomach roiled as the human sides of me became nauseous.

Dalton kicked up with his powerful legs, shoved with his strong arms. In an instant I was spun over and slammed onto my spine against the dirt. Dalton was on top of me now, growling as he stared deep into my eyes.

Then, before I could make a countermove, one of his hands slashed at my side. Long, deadly claws sliced into my gut, and I howled in pain. Still staring into my eyes, he dug his fingers deeper, deeper, before finally pulling them free from my midsection with a sick squelch.

I was wounded. Badly. I knew that. Dalton knew that. His snarl didn't seem so much deadly anymore as it seemed like a sick laugh.

Blood gushed from my side, rushing through the tears in my flesh like flaming lava. It was agony. There was only one way to stop it before I bled out. Only one way to heal myself so that I could save Megan.

Except then I'd be even less strong than I was now.

No choice.

I closed my eyes. Slowed my breathing. Told myself to slip back into the hybrid.

The change happened quickly, easily. It was easier every time now. My muscles, my fur, my sharp points faded and receded. The wound in my side sealed itself shut, and I lay there beneath the fearsome beast that was Dalton, tiny and pink and naked, shivering in the cold.

I chose to go back to myself then. Back to my normal, daytime self.

I opened my eyes.

Dalton was still above me, watching me, eyes on my face. They were still manic and dark. But I could remember him from that morning, when his eyes were hazel and sad and afraid. I'd killed a person, or at least had helped to. I couldn't let that happen to him, too. Not when the idea that he had that in him had terrified him so.

Reaching up, I petted the short, sleek fur of his snout. He almost jumped back, startled, then chose not to move. I looked into his eyes and smiled at him as reassuringly as I could.

"You are not a killer, Dalton," I said. Our mantra.

He growled.

I grabbed both sides of his snout and forced him to lean in closer to my face. He sniffed at my neck, and his body relaxed.

"This is not what you are," I whispered. "I know that inside there are things that you want to let go, even though they're deadly. But sometimes, we need to keep them in place. We need to keep our humanity. It's harder for you than me, Dalton, I know that. But if I can control this, you can, too. You *can*."

Dalton's eyes went glassy and then shut. He breathed out through his mouth, and hot, stinky air washed over my face. I didn't move. The fur beneath my palms gave way to warm skin. The heavy, monstrous body above me shrank back into a naked and frightened boy.

Dalton lay on top of me, my hands still cupping his face. His eyes were hazel again. They were thankful.

"You did it," I whispered. "You took control. I knew you could."

"I did," Dalton said, smiling down at me. "You showed me how, Emily, you—"

"Em . . ." Megan gasped behind us.

"Oh no," I said, letting go of Dalton. "Oh God."

Dalton rolled off me into the grass, then shuffled back, knees to chest. I jumped up and ran to Megan's side. She was still bleeding, still wheezing.

I hovered over her, panicking. Then, I took in a breath. I could keep it together. I could. I had to. I was the alpha, right? I could handle this.

"Hold on, Megan," I pleaded. "Please hold on."

I darted back to the bushes where I'd dropped my clothes. I quickly pulled on my T-shirt and jeans, then ran back to Megan's side. I pressed my hoodie against her bleeding side and shoulder, holding it in place as tight as I could.

"I did that to her," Dalton said behind me. "I . . ."

I looked back behind me to see the naked boy rocking back and forth, his eyes now distant.

"Dalton, she'll be okay," I said. "But we have to hurry. Go call for help."

"I can't believe I did that," he said.

I let out an exasperated sigh. I pulled one hand free from applying pressure to Megan's side, and she groaned. Her eyes were closed now. She was fading into unconsciousness.

I felt the pocket of my jeans. My phone wasn't there. I felt the other pocket. Not there either.

It had fallen out.

There came a crunching behind me as several people stomped through the trees. Nikki and the triplets appeared then, their eyes wide as they took in the strange scene.

"Dalton?" Nikki said. Then, running to his side, she screamed, "Dalton!"

"What did you do?" Amy Delgado demanded of me.

I ignored her. "You," I said, pointing a bloody finger at Casey. "Come hold this against her. She's bleeding really bad."

The girl nodded and came to my side. She cringed at the sight of the blood, but made no complaint as she pressed my stained hoodie against Megan's side.

Leaping to my feet, I shoved between Amy and Brittany and looked in the bushes where I'd dropped my clothes. There, by my fallen bra: the phone. I reached down and picked it up.

"This is so weird," Brittany said behind me.

"Hey." A strong hand grabbed my shoulder and spun me around, just as I flicked the phone open to dial.

Amy. In my face. As usual.

"What did you do to Dalton?" she demanded.

I yanked myself free. "I didn't do anything. You saw exactly what happened, I know you did. He turned into a werewolf and tried to kill my friend. Which I could have stopped if you hadn't gotten in my *way*!" I shoved my finger into her chest.

Hands balled into fists, Amy shook her head and came forward, ready to swing at me.

Before she could, both Nikki and Casey cried out.

"Something's happening!" Casey shouted, looking at me frantically.

"Dalton?" Nikki said. "Dalton, what's wrong? What are you doing?"

Without even thinking, I slipped back into the hybrid state. Almost as if it was instinctual. I blinked, and my vision went gray.

And I gasped.

There were shadowmen here now, several of them. Behind them, another distortion, only this one was different from the one above Megan. It was more like a rip in the air, like a torn movie screen, and the clearing was just a projection. Through the rip, there was nothing but blackness.

All three shadowmen held Dalton by his arms. They were pulling him backward toward the tear in the clearing.

And on the opposite side of the clearing, the rippling oval distortion had opened. Through it I could see that same dark, frightening city of spindly spires and flying shapes, some other world made up of darkness and fear. Another world where the shadowmen lived when they weren't stalking me here.

Something was coming through.

One dark arm, bent at the elbow, climbed through. Then another, the limbs long and jagged, a spider emerging from its lair.

Another shadowman.

As I watched, the shadowman dug one of its sharp hands into Megan's chest, and its solid-but-not-solid, smoky, hazy limb disappeared inside her. Megan's back arched up in startled pain, and she began to convulse. Foaming spittle seeped from her mouth.

The shadowmen were back. And they were no longer

content with just standing and watching. I stood, frozen, not sure what to do.

To my left, the long and slender shadow, flatter than the others I'd seen, almost seemed to ooze out of its distortion. Both of its spindly arms disappeared inside Megan's chest now. Her back arched even higher, and her jaw went slack. Casey fell back from her, and my bloodstained hoodie fell to the dirt.

To my right, Nikki was screaming and grabbing onto Dalton's legs and arms. The naked boy struggled, kicking and shouting as the three solid shadowmen dragged him faster and faster toward the rip in the universe.

I had no time to save both of them.

Blood wept from Megan's wounds.

Dalton's face was chiseled into terror, his frantic eyes on me, pleading for me to help.

Megan's shadowman was almost halfway into her body. Dalton was almost to the doorway that led to nothingness.

I leaped forward, to Megan. Shoving Casey out of the way, I grabbed Megan's arm and leg and began to drag her away from the distortion. "Use your powers," I screamed over my shoulder at the cheerleaders. "They're trying to take Dalton. Use your powers!"

I caught a single glimpse of the girls raising their hands, focusing and struggling to pull Dalton back toward them.

But my focus was on Megan, poor abandoned Megan, leaking red and being invaded by . . . whatever these things were.

I dug my heels into the ground and pulled as hard as I could. The shadowman inside her clung on tight, refusing to let go. Megan coughed, hacking horribly. I refused to let her go. I'd let things get this far with her by keeping her in the dark. She would not be hurt because of me. She would not!

"Aaargh!" I screamed. With one last tug, Megan flew up at me, slamming into my gut and knocking me into the ground. Like a rubber band pulled to its limit, the shadowman that had been digging its way through her skin popped out and was flung back through the distortion. As it did, the image of the city went black, and then the distortion swirled into those same pulsing ripples in the sky.

"No!" Nikki screamed. "Help him! Emily, help him!"

I pushed Megan's unconscious body off me as gently as I could, then jumped up and spun to face Dalton.

The shadowmen that had been clutching at his limbs had already disappeared into the blackness through the rip in the air. Dalton was almost through. He was silent, resigned. Still looked at me with sad eyes.

I took a step, thinking maybe there was still time, maybe I could save him, too.

Then he was through the hole, and in an instant it was as if nothing was there.

For a moment, the five of us who were conscious in the clearing stood there, gaping at the spot where Dalton had been only moments ago. Nikki and the triplets lowered their hands one by one, their faces disbelieving.

Nikki fell to her knees. Opened her mouth to scream, but nothing came out. She gulped in a breath, then wailed, "No!"

"Dalton," I whispered.

Another one of my pack. Gone. Taken by the shadowmen to who knows where. How? *How?* How was this possible?

"What did you do?" Amy roared at me. She stomped toward me, rage distorting her features into an ugly mask. "Where did he go?"

I was still hybrid. But daytime me was devastated, and werewolf me too busy howling inside my brain about the shadowmen.

I pushed Nighttime forward. Color filled my vision once more as I coalesced into one distinct person.

Snapping my head to face Amy, I stepped to her so that we were nose to nose. In a low voice, I said, "So you know what I am, right? And you know what Dalton is, too. Well, *sweetie*, I'm not in the mood to hear more accusations from girls like you who are clearly up to something." I shoved her shoulder, but she stood her ground. "I did nothing to Dalton. It was the shadowmen. If you don't know who they are, I suggest some research. That's what I had to do. All I know is that if you hadn't gotten in my way, I could have stopped all of this. *All of this.* Now if you'll excuse me, my friend is bleeding to death."

She didn't respond. Daytime me knew I hadn't exactly cut her down. Which meant, as I suspected, that she knew more about this than she'd let on.

The cheerleaders, including Casey, did nothing but stare at me uselessly as I collected my hoodie and pressed it against Megan's side once more. Nikki cried silently where Dalton had disappeared.

Megan's wounds wrapped as best I could, I lifted her in my arms, then walked barefoot through the woods back into Dalton's backyard. Daytime's internal numbness threatened to seep back into my consciousness, but I kept her down for now. She was a strong girl. She could deal. But later. Later.

I hiked around the side of Dalton's house, past the fallen garbage bags. Spencer was parked there, looking at his phone. Catching sight of me, his eyes went wide and he raced to my side.

"Holy crap!" he said. "What happened? Oh my God!"

I gestured toward the car with my chin. "Open the backseat. We need to get her to the hospital."

He ran ahead without any further questions. Reaching the van myself, I gingerly set Megan in the backseat, then crouched beside it. Before I could close the van door, I heard a voice shouting from across the lawn.

"Hey! What's going on? I've been getting noise complaints."

Mr. McKinney stormed across the grass, glaring, grimacing. It wasn't until he caught sight of me, wearing nothing but wrinkled jeans and a T-shirt, barefoot and bloody, my hair a tangled mess, that he stopped.

"W-what—" he stammered.

"This is what your son did," I said, staring deep into him. "This is what you made him and let him become. Secrets tend to bite you in the ass, Mr. McKinney."

"Where's Dalton?" he said. "Where's my son?"

I blinked at him. Smiled. I'm sure my white teeth were quite a contrast to the red blood that had spattered across my cheeks.

"They took him, Mr. McKinney. Those shadowmen. I don't know what they are. But I bet you do."

He lunged forward as if to jump into the van. "What do you know?" he demanded. "What are you talking about?"

I reached forward and pulled the door shut before he could get inside. Through the tinted window, I said, "I know more than you think. And I lost a lot to find it. Now it's your turn to figure things out."

Megan stirred on the seat. I gestured for Spencer to go. He gunned it, and we left a gaping Mr. McKinney in the dust.

Deep inside, daytime me felt guilty for mocking a man whose son had just been stolen. But as Nighttime? I didn't care.

If people like him were going to mess with me, try to direct how I was going to live my life, send killers after me, and keep me in the dark as I tried to handle it all?

Then they deserved everything they were going to get.

PROJECT LEAD

Spencer pulled us right up to the emergency room door. The nurses at the front desk took one look at me and Megan and ushered us in right away. While Spencer was told to wait in the lobby, Megan was placed on one of those rolling beds and was rushed to be looked at. Once I was examined and they determined I had no injuries of my own, I was allowed to wash up in a bathroom.

The bathroom was small, sparkling white. There were instructions near the toilet on how to take a pee sample to give to the nurses. I leaned over the sink, letting the water run warm, staring at myself in the mirror. I was still Nighttime at this point, with my blood-red war paint on my cheeks and nose where I'd absently rubbed myself while taking care of Megan. I splashed my face and watched the water swirl pink down the drain. I splashed again and let myself recede into the hybrid. Once more and I was normal me again.

The last splash was more for the tears that threatened to burst from my eyes than the blood.

I dried my face, then pulled my glasses from my pocket and put them on my nose so I could see clearly. I'd rescued them from my hoodie before Megan had been carted off.

I was still numb, I think. The shadowmen were more dangerous than I'd ever imagined, even when terrified out of my mind. The cheerleaders knew secrets. One of my pack had disappeared into the ether. The only really good thing I had to cling to was the ease of my transformations now.

It had started before we'd smashed the machine in BioZenith, but I guessed the hybrid became easier after that. I wasn't sure entirely how I knew, but I could control this now. Control when and how I changed. Maybe there were limits; in fact, there had to be, because I hadn't been able to slip into the hybrid state right away when I was chasing after Megan.

But at least all these sides of me were at last coming together. I could teach it to Spencer and Tracie and Dalt . . .

I closed my eyes, took in a shuddering breath. He couldn't be gone. Not forever. I'd saved Megan because she wasn't like us. Wherever Dalton had been taken, I would save him. I *would* save him.

More or less composed, I left the washroom to discover a kind nurse had left me a pair of booties to walk around in. I found Spencer in the waiting room, absently watching a TV he couldn't hear, a stack of papers on a clipboard next to him. Seeing me emerge, one of the nurses came to ask me details on what had happened, who the girl who'd been attacked was, if there were people we needed to call. I gave them Megan's parents' numbers, as well as my own.

And then, I sat next to Spencer. Curled my legs up underneath me and leaned into him. I inhaled his pheromones and felt myself relax.

"Hey," he whispered at me. "What happened back there? For real?"

I moaned, content. "I'll tell you later. For now, I just want to sit here like this. With you. Okay?"

"Okay."

I decided then, so what if these pheromones had been programmed into us? So were the changes in general. If they were there, I was going to take advantage of them.

Especially since I was quite certain in that moment that it wasn't just the musky scent that made me feel so comfortable around Spencer. As he leaned his head against mine, I took his hand in my own, linking our fingers together. I could see us together like this, even if we were never werewolves.

It wasn't long before Megan's parents and brother showed up and were ushered through to see her. And then my dad and stepmom were there, pulling me into hugs, asking me if I was okay, telling me they were so glad I was safe, expressing how lucky it was I'd been there to keep Megan from getting hurt worse than she had by those damn feral dogs plaguing the neighborhood.

An hour or two passed before Lucas came out from the emergency room and into the waiting area. He assured us that Megan was all right. She was being given blood transfusions and treated preemptively for common diseases like rabies, just in case. She had been awake long enough to say hello to her family.

"Do you think I can see her?" I asked him.

He grimaced and looked down at his shoes awkwardly. "I don't think so, Emily. She . . . she said she doesn't want to see you right now."

It was getting late. I wanted to wait longer, just to make sure she was truly, one hundred percent all right. But I knew, deep down, things were fractured between me and Megan. It would take more than a few hours to bridge the rift that had come between us.

So I said my good-byes to Lucas and Spencer, and my dad and Katherine drove us all home.

* * *

That night, I managed to go to sleep without the use of any sleeping pills. I simply told Nighttime I needed the rest. She didn't argue.

I didn't dream of dead Dr. Elliott. Those memories were faded and distant now. Instead, I saw the shadowmen. I saw their strange, spindly cities. Saw Dalton huddled and alone, surrounded by creatures he didn't understand.

Not exactly a step up. But at least these dreams weren't all bloody.

The next day, we got a call from Megan's mother. Megan was indeed all right. Not wanting visitors, but all right just the same.

I had breakfast with the family, though I was basically Debbie Downer the whole time. They didn't need to question why. The rest of my Sunday was spent up in my bedroom, staring blankly at the files we'd managed to steal from BioZenith.

BioZenith. It was strange, their lax security. A lot of this was strange. Mr. McKinney hadn't gone to the police about Dalton, not that I'd heard of anyway. Neither had any of the cheerleaders. They were keeping what happened at Dalton's house quiet.

Which meant they were all hiding something. Together, maybe?

I got an email midday from Tracie, basically telling

me once more to leave her alone. I was happy to oblige. I'd already lost Dalton. The thought of losing her, too . . .

At least Spencer still texted me. Still trusted me.

So this was what it was like to be an alpha, huh? Leader of the pack. The head honcho. All the weight of the supernatural world on your narrow shoulders. No map to guide your way. You know how some people complained Buffy was all super bitchy sometimes? Let me tell you, folks: Walk a few feet in her shoes, and you will absolutely get it.

I suppose at least I'd gained some ground. I'd uncovered a few mysteries. I'd learned more about how I worked. I forgave myself for Dr. Elliott. That's something.

It still didn't bring back Dalton.

Musing on all I'd seen, I decided I knew what those shadowmen were. Beings from another world. Not quite aliens, not really. Other-dimensional beings. What they wanted from me? Who knows. But it had to involve what I'd seen with Megan, the way the shadowman had climbed into her, invaded her body. . . .

I shuddered. I figured the best way to distract myself was to see if I could find anything in the files about the shadowmen. Maybe that portal in the BioZenith labs was some way into the shadowmen's world? If so, maybe I could use it to get to Dalton.

Clinging to that idea, I clicked through file after file,

scanning for any relevant info. I didn't get very far before someone knocked on my door.

"I'm busy!" I called.

The door creaked open anyway. I spun in my desk chair, prepared to politely tell whichever family member was currently concerned about me that I was fine.

Instead, I found Casey Delgado.

She offered me a weak smile. "Um, hi. Do you think we can talk?"

Biting my lip, I thought for a moment. These girls obviously knew something about what was going on, but they hadn't exactly been forthcoming with the info. They had attacked me. Prevented me from keeping Megan and Dalton safe.

Or at least, the others had. I remember Casey at Megan's side, holding back the flow of blood while I tried to call for help.

"Sure," I finally said. "Come in."

Straightening out my comforter, she took a seat, then smiled at me again. "So. I suppose we have a lot to talk about."

"I'd say that's just a tad of an understatement."

She laughed politely, then went serious. "My sisters don't know I'm here," she said softly. "But I think you deserve to know what's going on. Especially after what happened behind Dalton's house."

Leaning forward, I motioned for her to continue.

Her hand fluttered to her chest. "I mean, I don't want you to think we know everything, either. Just . . . Okay. The beginning. Nikki, Amy, Brittany, and I have known we have these . . . abilities since we were very young. Our parents trained us how to use them. I guess you didn't know about your own abilities?"

I shook my head. "Not a clue. I only just found out two weeks ago that I was even like this. I've been stumbling to find out why ever since."

Her eyes fell, sad. "Oh. We didn't . . . Well, okay. Recently our parents told us to look out for other kids at school, like you, who started to act strangely. They didn't tell us exactly what that meant, but I at least kind of got the hint when you started going nuts at Mikey's party."

"Yeah," I muttered. "I guess that'd do it."

Again Casey laughed politely. "Um, but we weren't sure if you were just acting that way for attention or what. Which is why my sisters have been kind of . . . mean. But anyway, all we were told was that once we knew who you were, we were supposed to keep you safe from . . . something. We didn't know entirely what that something was. I don't know why, but Amy and Nikki got it in their heads that Dalton was who we were supposed to protect, and you were what was after him. But that's not right, is it?"

Sighing, I leaned back into my chair. "Yeah, not quite. I don't know exactly what all you saw, but me and Dalton, and Spencer and Tracie for that matter, we were made into werewolves. By some company called BioZenith. You know about them?"

Casey shook her head. "No. But maybe I can ask my parents. So, but okay, you and all of them are . . . werewolves? That's what we were looking out for?"

I shrugged. "Guess so."

Crossing her legs at the ankle, Casey looked down. "Anyway, I came here because yesterday I saw a friend of mine disappear into thin air. I don't know what exactly we were supposed to protect him from, but clearly we . . . clearly we failed." She took in a sharp breath, then met my eyes. "So I guess I thought I should come talk to you, since it seemed like Spencer and Tracie were listening to you at the party. I'm guessing something bigger is going on than what our parents told us. And maybe together, all of us, we can stop it."

I met Casey's eyes. They were earnest, or at least they appeared to be. After the way her sisters had treated me, I wasn't sure if I could trust anyone.

But if she was telling the whole truth, if she'd come to me in good faith, then I couldn't say no. I may have been designated an alpha for whatever reason, but clearly I couldn't figure all of this out alone. And you know what? I didn't want to. The idea of us werewolves and a bunch of psychic cheerleaders taking on some crazy scientists . . .

Well, frankly, the idea seemed straight out of a Syfy channel original movie. But that was my life now. And I liked the notion.

I stood up and offered Casey my hand. She stood and shook it.

"You know what, Casey?" I asked. "I wouldn't mind having some help."

She smiled at me. "Well, good! Now we just have to convince my sisters and Nikki."

Sitting back down in my chair, I tilted my head at Casey, suddenly full of questions. "So your sisters and Nikki, you knew about yourselves all your lives? Your parents trained you guys how to use your abilities? How? Are they telekinetic too?"

Casey shook her head. "No. My parents and Nikki's dad were all scientists years ago, so they observed us and helped us along."

"Scientists like Dalton's dad," I said. "And Emily Cooke's."

Cocking an eyebrow at me, Casey tilted her head. "Oh? I didn't know that."

"Yeah. Sounds like a pattern. I'm learning lately that patterns usually mean something."

Biting my lip, I spun my chair toward my computer, then clicked open the files from the thumb drive Spencer had given me. Casey watched silently as I opened up the HAVOC folder and found a document called "Project Mission Statement and Personnel."

"What is that?" Casey asked as I scanned through the document.

"We got all these files from BioZenith, where Dalton's dad works," I explained as I read. "We've barely had a chance to go through any of them."

"Is there anything interesting in the file you just opened?"

I shook my head, but didn't say anything. I wasn't entirely sure what I expected to find, just that I had this nagging little idea in the back of my head telling me to start here if I really wanted answers.

I held my breath and scrolled through. The first several pages were a bunch of densely overwritten scientific explanations about the project. There was discussion about the goal—to create hybrid human and animal "vespers," whatever that meant, which would experience the world on a different level and be able to help with . . . something. It wasn't entirely clear. I kept seeing a word I didn't recognize pop up: Akhakhu. Mostly as part of the phrase "Akhakhu technology."

There were links to further documents going into greater detail about the project, code-named HAVOC, but I didn't want to read that now. Instead, I scrolled down to the names of the people who were involved in the experiments.

Several familiar last names were there. Holt. McKinney. Cooke. Townsend.

And, under the heading "Project Lead": Caroline Webb.

My mother. My mother, who I was told died when I was two, whose job was at Microsoft, not a bioengineering laboratory.

My hands went limp, and I could not look away from the screen. I'd suspected it, vaguely, but I'd hoped I wouldn't see her name there. Wouldn't see what was written beneath it.

"What is it?" Casey asked, placing a hand on my shoulder. "What does it say?"

I didn't answer. I was too busy scanning the notes under her name. Her contributions to the project. Her spearheading of the initial experiments using the "Akhakhu technology." Her volunteering to carry to term the first "vesper" they would create.

Me.

And, at the very end, there was something more than I ever expected to see.

"Emily, what is it?" Casey asked again.

I turned to her, my eyes wide. "I think I just found out who made me like this," I said.

Casey's eyes went wide. "Who?"

I could barely say the words. "My mother." I paused as I turned back to the monitor. "And this says that she went . . . *there*, Casey. To the same place where Dalton was taken."

"There?" Casey asked. "Where's there?"

I couldn't tear my eyes away from the document in front of me. "This is going to sound totally crazy," I said, my voice hushed. "But I think *there* is another world, where we saw Dalton get taken. Another dimension."

Casey blinked at me. "Another . . . dimension? You're right. That does sound crazy."

Meeting Casey's eyes, I whispered, "I know. But over there my mother and Dalton might still be alive. If we can get there, we can save Dalton, and we can get some answers from the woman behind all of this."

Leaning forward, Casey said, "You think we can go over there?" she asked. "To another world? How?"

I shook my head, my confusion fading to be replaced by a pounding anger at all the lies and deception that had apparently surrounded me my whole life.

338

"I don't know, Casey. But you, me, the werewolves, and the cheerleaders, we'll figure it out." My eyes leaped back to the monitor, rereading the words *Project Lead: Caroline Webb* over and over again. "If she can find a way over there, then her daughter will, too."

The Vesper Company
"Envisioning the brightest stars, to lead our way."
- Internal Document, Do Not Reproduce -

Details of Video Footage Recorded Oct. 31, 2010,
Part 6

21:37:23 PST—Hall 7, Sublevel Sector E

With Vesper 1(B) in the lead, Vesper 2.1(A) and
Vesper 4(B) storm the hallway, taking the guards by
surprise. They are easily crippled by a combination
of the two Branch B Deviants, while Vesper 2.1(A)
uses her telekinesis to smash the Sentinels against
a wall.

I have to recommend that these transcripts and the
related video footage not get released to anyone
who might spread this information to our clients. I
can't imagine it would be good for our reputation.

With the guards much too easily eliminated, the
Deviants bust down the door to Super Holding Cell E1.

21:45:02 PST—Super Holding Cell E1

In the corner of the padded room, contained by a
straitjacket clasped with reinforced steel buckles,
is an individual identified as:

—Dalton McKinney, Branch B's Vesper 3 (designated
"Deviant")
White male, 16 years old

Vesper 1(B) runs to the boy's side and struggles
with the locks. Vesper 3(B) watches blankly as she
works the fasteners, while the other two Deviants
watch from thenhyju7nhyju7nhyju7
nhyju7nhyj
u7nhyju7n nhyju7[;p0-
']
\/[;n
dszk468iouy tiyowtraioy*()^&
!~ijbkd/?<%$Eeilorutjih
dsakjlsadkjsadkjlsdjkladsakjldsjkluwierotczuxio
ewuro48357HDJKUIEWRERWIUOEEUWIROåquirwø
ÔÓØ¨ˆÁiyˆÄ¨ˇˇ¨&Áˇˇˇˇ¨ˆÁˆˈ©˚åßdfskhfhkdsdfjsh
0000ˆ¨øøˆ¨ˆ¨øˆ¨ø¨ˆøˆø¨ˆ¨øˈ¥ˆ¨¥ˆ¨¥ˆ¶•ª¶•ª¶•ª•¶ª•¶ª
JJJ/#
slkdj¶•ª¶•ª¶•ª•¶ª•¶ªffgfgcfgds shjEJKFKL51412
8KIJ7HIUWGø¨ˆ¨

Hi there! Emily Webb here. A few minutes ago there
was a woman here, watching movies and typing stuff.
I think her name is Limon, and apparently she's been

watching surveillance videos, transcribing them, and then sending them off for review. I caught her in the midst of this one. She seemed surprised to see me, since it's been a few days since we escaped. Currently Limon is running down a hallway, screaming obscenities at some friends of mine and clutching her forehead where I slammed her head against this keyboard. Quite a mouth on that one.

Also, you guys have some super-resilient computer equipment.

So I've been looking through these papers you guys have in here. There are lots and lots of details on me. You guys are basically obsessed. I mean, really, transcribing my every move through your facility? Stalker much?

Well, let me finish this one for you. After a long, exhausting trek through your mazelike buildings, and after knocking out your guards (those guys deserve a raise), we finally found Dalton. He hasn't been quite right in the head since . . . Well, you know. The poor boy has been through a lot.

What Ms. Limon was about to type above was probably something like this:

VesperEmily: Dalton, it's Emily. It's me. We have to get out of here, okay? We need to run.
DeviantDalton: It's too late.
VesperEmily: What is?
DeviantDalton: It's too late, Emily. They're already here. We've already lost.

Something you probably learned about me watching
these tapes: I don't like to lose. So I think
I'm done letting you read what happened to me.
Done letting you watch me from the safety of your
observation rooms.

So I'm going to hit send and let this go where
it's supposed to go. Just know, from now on, Vesper
Co.? It's you who gets to be in the dark. Let's see
how you like it.

See you soon!

Hugs and kisses,
Emily

Part 6 of Relevant Video Footage Concluded